Stranglehold

When a young girl is raped and murdered and her body left in a deserted house, it is not discovered for two days and there are few clues at the scene of the crime to incriminate her killer.

When a second murder follows, it becomes obvious that the hunt is for a serial killer, who is almost certain to kill again. Moreover, the way the bodies are laid out seems to indicate not only a warped mind but a wish to taunt the police. In the quiet country town of Oldford, a whole community is struck with terror as it waits for the nocturnal killer to strike again.

The police machine throws up several suspects, but the fact that there is no obvious motive for the killings makes the investigation more than usually complex—especially when it is suggested that the murderer may come from the ranks of the police themselves.

Superintendent John Lambert feels the strain, as do others around him, but aided by Sergeant Bert Hook and the other members of his team, he eventually brings the investigation to its thrilling and startling conclusion.

J. M. GREGSON

Stranglehold

THE CRIME CLUB
An Imprint of HarperCollins *Publishers*

First published in Great Britain in 1993
by The Crime Club, an imprint of
HarperCollins Publishers, 77–85 Fulham Palace Road,
Hammersmith, London W6 8JB

9 8 7 6 5 4 3 2 1

J. M. Gregson asserts the moral right to be identified
as the author of this work.

A catalogue record for this book is
available from the British Library

ISBN 0 00 232449 0

Photoset in Linotron Baskerville by
Rowland Phototypesetting Ltd
Bury St Edmunds, Suffolk
Printed and bound in Great Britain by
HarperCollins Book Manufacturing, Glasgow

CHAPTER 1

The light shone into the man's face, white and unrelenting. The room was hot and airless. On its stark and functional furniture, there was no room for dust to gather. But there was a faint odour of stale sweat within these bleak and narrow walls.

It was almost two in the morning, but in the airless and windowless interview room it might have been any time. Only the fatigue of the three men who fought each other with words within this place gave any clue that this might be an hour when the remainder of the world was at rest.

Lambert watched the cassette which turned almost silently beside him, recording each syllable of this so far pointless performance. He hoped the tension was building within the figure opposite him, but he suspected the man had been through these sessions too often to panic now. He resisted the feeling of hopelessness within himself; it troubled him more and more these days, whenever he approached the point of exhaustion.

'You might as well admit it, Tommy. You were in Union Street at the time. You were seen. We can document it, if we have to. You—'

'I was at home.' Tommy Clinton repeated the statement for the seventh time that night, as though he were making the response in some bizarre secular litany.

'And who says so?'

'I've told you. My mother. But she was asleep at the time you're talking about. Like a decent old lady should be.'

Lambert smiled sourly. An old lady, nodding a little with Parkinson's disease, who had lied before for her son, who would bring herself to believe her own lies by the time they had prepared a case. Whom he could never put in court for cross-examination, in any case. They both knew the score.

5

He drove himself on to what he knew he must do. He was helped by the irritation he felt that this man should best him. Tommy Clinton was a pathetic figure. His frayed shirt was grubby about the neck: it had been worn at least two days too long. His grey hair was greasy, untidy now from the four hours he had been at the station. His grey eyes were carefully blank; that came from his experience of petty crime, of hours of questioning like this.

He was only here because of his grubby past, and that held no more than minor, even comic crimes, the kind even the police laughed at when he was gone. Tommy was no threat. But here he was, outsmarting the CID.

'You're a flasher, Tommy. Tried and convicted.'

'I've given up all that, Mr Lambert. I've told you.'

He had, several times. No doubt he would go on doing so. Unless they could frighten him.

'Flashers go on to bigger things, sometimes. You know that, Tommy, and so do we.' It wasn't true, it was a rarity. But not unknown. And Tommy didn't know the statistics: for the first time, he looked a little scared.

'I haven't done nothing. I told you.' He kept his hands on the table between them, with the dirty fingernails turned towards the two men opposite him. But for the first time in twenty minutes, the hands became mobile. The fingers did not tremble, but they began to massage each other a little. All three men watched them in silence, like deaf men trying to interpret a new sign language.

Lambert saw the first stirring of apprehension and went for it, like a fencer seeing an opening in his opponent's defence. No, nothing so subtle, he thought wryly: like a boxer seeing the chance to put in a bludgeoning blow. Not a knockout, merely something that might weaken the adversary a little, score him an extra point with the non-existent judges.

'This is big, you see, Tommy. Big and nasty. The girl was killed. And before she was killed, she was sexually assaulted. That's what it will say in the papers. You and I know what that means. Clothes torn off; fist rammed in

6

her mouth; face bashed until it bled; legs forced apart; tights—'

'It's not my sort of crime, Mr Lambert.' Clinton was desperate to stop the flow of detail, and Lambert scarcely less desperate to be interrupted. Both of them breathed hard as they stared at each other. 'I've never been one for violence. I—I've had my little weaknesses with women, God knows, but I've never been charged with hitting them.'

It was probably true, but Lambert was too weary to care. He smelt the fear on the man, and he went for it. 'And when the man had finished with her, he killed her. Brutally, with his bare hands. Just to stop her talking. Or to give himself more pleasure. You tell us which, Tommy.'

The police usually kept the facts from men like Clinton, hoping to make them uneasy by keeping them in ignorance of what the investigation was about, collecting bits of information which men like him often revealed when they jumped to false conclusions.

This sudden revelation when he least expected it threw Clinton off balance. 'You're not setting me up for the Julie Salmon killing?' His voice was almost a shout, bouncing off the walls at them, shocking in its alarm after his earlier calm. They smelt his stale breath, gusting at them now across the table as he struggled to control it.

'You're in the frame, Clinton. And you're not helping yourself.' Lambert sat back, recoiling a little from that awful stench, estimating the state of his man from a few inches further away. The little man knew the name of the victim; Lambert cudgelled his tired brain to decide whether there could be any significance in that. 'We have a witness who saw you that night, not far from where the body was found. And at about the right time. There you are: I've levelled with you now. It's about time you did the same with us.'

The man was still frightened. The fingers twined and untwined rapidly, as if with a life of their own. Clinton watched them as though they were someone else's, making no attempt to stop them moving. He was scared, but after the first shock, his fear took on the unthinking sullenness

7

of a panic-ridden child. 'I didn't do it. I wouldn't do anything like that. You can't pin this on me.'

His voice carried no conviction. In his world, the creed was that the pigs could pin most things on you if they had a mind to.

Lambert, recognizing the doors being closed behind that blank, sullen face, eased his chair back a fraction. The man beside him knew the way he worked so well that no glance was needed between them to indicate what was required. Instead, there was the briefest of pauses. Then Bert Hook, who had not spoken for half an hour, took up the questioning, his voice unexpectedly restrained, even friendly, in that room which was designed to be unfriendly to men like Clinton.

'You see, Tommy, we'd like to help you. To help you to help yourself.' Hook felt unhurriedly through his pockets, watching the face opposite him, looking for the first hint of cooperation. The man had not asked for a lawyer, but that did not mean he felt he had nothing to fear. The petty fringe of the underworld in which men like Clinton lived did not deal with lawyers. Only, later on, with legal aid.

Hook found the packet and shoved it on to his edge of the table. 'Want a fag, Tommy?'

Clinton's hands moved a couple of inches towards the cigarettes, then drew back. 'No. Keep your snout.' His lips had betrayed him into the prison word before he could control them.

But it was his hands which had given away his need for nicotine, as they had earlier given away his apprehension. Hook pushed the packet across the small square table between them, then struck a match as Clinton fumbled out a cigarette from it. The smoke smelt strong in the tiny, overheated room, the more so as both the policemen were reformed smokers themselves. Both of them found themselves with their eyes on the packet; Clinton's had been only the second tube extracted from it. It was at the ends of days like this that they missed the relief of tobacco most.

Hook forced himself to something near affability as he said, 'Where were you, then, Tommy, on that night?'

Clinton, grateful for the cigarette, looked up at the man opposite him, seeing the sweat under the arms of his white shirt and the tiredness on the sergeant's face, feeling a bond between them from these signs of physical weakness as much as from the tobacco he had been given. But he looked down, resisting false friendship from men who must be his enemies by their calling. He shook his head stubbornly, then drew again upon the cigarette.

'You see, Tommy, we know you were there. When you deny it, naturally we have to think bad things about you.' Hook would not admit that their 'witness' was a prostitute who thought she had glimpsed him through the darkness: scarcely the most reliable of sightings. He saw Clinton's little start of fear at his use of 'bad things', which the man obviously considered a euphemism.

'My mum'll tell you. I was at home.'

'I don't think we'll even bother to ask her, Tommy. Old ladies like her should be left with clear consciences, I always feel.'

Clinton said sullenly, trying to disguise his fear, 'I was nowhere near that murder. I didn't see anything. I can't help you nail the man who did it.'

It was the first perceptible switch of ground, and all of them were expert enough in these exchanges to detect it. Hook, playing this nervous fish which had taken his fly, did not hurry. 'You see, Tommy, if we can just eliminate you as a suspect, we can concentrate on others. And because you were in the area that night, you will probably have seen some little thing which will be of interest to us, even though it doesn't seem significant to you.'

On the surface at least, Clinton was being treated almost as an equal; he liked the big words, the careful explanation. He was not used to being treated by many men with anything more than a routine contempt, and he did not find it easy to deal with this. He rose a little in his chair, as a cat rises a little under the knuckles which gently stroke its head. 'If I was in that area, it was much earlier in the evening.'

The brains of the men opposite him, trained over many years to dissect such vagaries, wondered automatically how much information the Press Officer had dispensed to the press about the time of the murder.

'All right, Tommy. Let's accept for the moment that you were tucked up in bed at home like a good boy when poor Julie Salmon was killed. Where were you earlier that night?'

Clinton looked hard at the hands which would not be stilled, as though watching carefully for their reaction to what he was going to say. 'I was in the *Grapes*. Having a couple of drinks.'

'And who was with you there, Tommy?'

'I—I don't remember. It's a few days ago now and—'

'Pity, that, Tommy. Puts you right back in the frame, that does. Especially now you've told us you were in the area.'

'Look, Sarge, the blokes I was with, they—'

'Rape and murder, Tommy. Crimes don't come any bigger. Or any worse. Are you telling me your mates—'

'All right. All right!' The hands which had been so mobile rose a little into the air, then fell back hopelessly on to the table and were still at last. 'I'll tell you all about what I did that night.'

'And all the times, Tommy.' They were the first words Lambert had spoken in over ten minutes. Clinton looked at him for a moment in shock; he had almost forgotten he was there.

It was at that moment that there was a sharp rap at the door which surprised them all. Detective-Inspector Rushton's face, reluctant but urgent, appeared as the door opened a few inches and said, 'Sir, I'm sorry to interrupt, but something's come in.'

Lambert thrust down his irritation, choked back the expletive that had sprung to his weary lips. He rose without a word and followed the younger man from the room, shutting the door firmly behind him. Sergeant Hook said to the microphone, 'Superintendent Lambert had to leave the room at this point. The interview was suspended,' and pressed the stop button on the recorder.

The two men remained silent for a moment opposite each other, each speculating on what could be important enough to stop them at this crucial stage, fellow sufferers now in their exhaustion, instead of the opponents they had been a moment earlier.

They did not have long to wait. Lambert came back grim-faced, scarcely looking at the man he had struggled with for half the night as he said, 'All right, Tommy, you can go and make your statement on your movements that night to DI Rushton or one of his men.'

Clinton followed Rushton obediently from the room. Lambert scarcely waited for the door to close before he said, his voice grating harsh in the airless room, 'There's been another one. Tonight. Not more than a couple of hours ago.'

CHAPTER 2

Lambert's exhaustion seemed to drop away with this new and appalling development. Hook, watching him surreptitiously as they sat together in the back of the car, wondered if he could really be as alert as he suddenly looked.

The Superintendent did not speak. And he had allowed himself for once to be driven to the scene of the crime, leaving his old Vauxhall within the walls of the CID car park. Gazing unblinkingly through the side window into the deep darkness of the moonless night, he seemed scarcely like a man who had turned fifty and been working now for eighteen hours. The strain was there, but it was strain channelled into a raw, fierce concentration.

They had no difficulty finding the place. Oldford did not have a red light area: it was too small a town for that. Most of its inhabitants would have said it was too respectable, but the police knew better than that. The white car with its police emblem on the side drove through an area which had come down in the world, where practitioners of that oldest of trades walked their streets, where men like Tommy Clinton did their drinking.

A little to Hook's surprise, they drove right through that

11

area, out to the edge of the town, where the country came rather abruptly to meet it. They had no difficulty finding the place, for the floodlights were already blazing white and garish behind the hastily erected canvas walls, which were almost complete now around the spot where the corpse had been discovered.

The long ribbons of 'incident tape' which would keep out a curious public and allow the Scene of Crime team to search the whole area minutely were already in place. At three o'clock in the morning, neither they nor the young uniformed constable who guarded the entrance seemed strictly necessary, but it was a reassurance to the man who would take charge of the investigation to see them there. Murder has its rituals, and the men charged with detection are rightly tetchy if the ones they have devised are not observed.

The police surgeon was already there: whatever the gore and violence, it was necessary to have the fact of death professionally confirmed. Lambert met Dr Donald Haworth as he came from the canvas enclosure. He was a tall man, who could have secured for himself had he wished it that adjective 'distinguished' which seems to be so highly desired by medical men. Perhaps he felt himself too young for that: he was still no more than thirty. Instead, he chose a deliberate informality; there was always a hint of untidiness about him, and the haste of a busy man in most of his actions.

He did not wait now for Lambert to ask the questions he knew were inevitable. 'She's dead, and it's murder all right, I'm afraid, John.' He asserted his civilian status by the use of the Superintendent's first name; they knew each other through a succession of professional contacts, but had scarcely met apart from these. Haworth had but recently arrived in the area; the grapevine said that there was a failed marriage behind him, but that was scarcely material for comment nowadays.

'How was she killed?'

'Strangulation, almost certainly. I haven't disturbed her more than was strictly necessary, but there are pinpoint haemorrhages in her eyes.' Haworth carried his torch in his hand still; the lights behind him made him scarcely more than a silhouette to Lambert and Hook, but the Edinburgh accent came softly to them through the darkness, the words carefully and economically chosen and delivered.

'Has she been sexually assaulted?' Lambert thought suddenly that he sounded like a journalist: that was always the first thing they wanted to know. An affirmative reply would double the size of their headlines.

'I can't tell you that. I didn't want to lose evidence. No doubt your pathologist will be able to tell you.' Some slight nuance in his tone suggested a little resentment; perhaps he had at some early stage of his career as a police surgeon gone beyond his brief, and been reprimanded for it by the forensic medical men who followed behind him.

'No, of course.' Lambert turned to Sergeant Johnson, the Scene of Crime Officer. 'Has Dr Burgess been contacted?'

'Yes, sir. He should be here within the hour, and he'll do the PM first thing in the morning.'

Haworth said, 'I'm sure the good Burgess will confirm she's been strangled. Vagal inhibition, if you prefer it. Probably by someone wearing gloves, I'm afraid.' He brushed away a shock of hair which had been allowed to grow a little too long, so that it fell over the side of his face. This time Lambert was sure he caught a note of irony, a touch of resentment as the younger man mentioned Burgess, the pathologist. It was understandable enough: the two would be chalk and cheese. Lambert thrust the thought away, angry with himself for indulging it, when it was so irrelevant to his business here.

'Any idea how long ago she died?' He saw what he thought was a professional caution descending upon the police surgeon's features, and said irritably, 'Only an opinion, Don. No one's going to hold you to it.' He was surprised to find himself using the doctor's name; he liked the air of helpful spontaneity which the man carried about him. He might be something of a loner, but they were often the most useful among those who assisted the police from outside the system.

13

Haworth grinned. 'I know that. I was only thinking how I might be as precise as possible.' He looked up at the starless sky, sniffing the night air a little as he assessed the temperature. 'I would guess between two and three hours ago. But that is a guess. The body hasn't cooled much, and the bruises around the throat look quite fresh.'

Ahead of them an unseen hand drew back the canvas a little to admit Sergeant Johnson, and the shaft of light from the canvas enclosure fell briefly across the doctor's feet. Lambert was surprised to see them encased in training shoes beneath the polythene bags which all visitors to this site would now be required to wear, looking slightly ridiculous at the end of the trousers of a formal dark suit. He grinned a little at himself and his out-of-date ideas, which expected a professional man to be wearing city shoes, even when he was called out in the middle of the night. He said, 'We won't hold you to it, but thank you for trying to be so precise.'

His gratitude was genuine. The early inquiries were often the most productive, and he could send his team now to find who had been seen around here at a precise hour. He said, to Hook and himself as much as to Haworth, 'Around midnight, then. After the pubs had shut.'

Haworth pursed his lips. 'Maybe a little later. I'd say this probably happened between twelve and one.'

Lambert was surprised but pleased to find him trying so hard to pinpoint a time for them. In his experience most medical men were too mindful of their reputation to be actively helpful; they usually sat on the fence until they had much more evidence than had been available to this man. He volunteered in response a little more of his own thoughts than he would normally have done. 'The later the better, from our point of view, in some respects. The fewer people about, the fewer suspects. Though of course that also means fewer witnesses as well. But we only need one, if it's a good one.'

Haworth nodded. 'I wish you luck, then. I hope you find the one who did it.' It was a strange wish, like a priest stating that sin is a bad thing. But the public, when confronted by evil, often produced these nervous truisms; it seemed that by asserting their own, conventional virtue, people distanced themselves from what had disturbed them. Haworth by his calling must have seen death often. But he had not been a police surgeon very long: Julie Salmon and this were his first murders, apart from the routine domestic killings which became ever more frequent.

Lambert nodded and turned towards the spot where the body lay, but Haworth's only move was to lift his right foot a little and tap the toe of his trainer against the hard summer ground. His black businessman's case with the tools of his trade swung lightly by his knee, contrasting oddly with that informal footwear. He said, 'You'll find her—odd. She's been—well, you'll see for yourself.' He smiled briefly, so that his teeth caught what little light there was, then turned on his heel and left them.

Lambert watched him as he went to his car, a sleek low Japanese coupé. He did not look back or speak again, as if he was embarrassed by his last, halting words. Perhaps he thought a man with his background should have expressed himself better, or said nothing at all. Death should be an impersonal thing, a fact of life, for medics as for policemen.

When Lambert went into the little canvas enclosure, he saw immediately what had ruffled the doctor. This corpse had been prepared for their viewing.

The girl lay on her back. She had fair hair; it was impossible to tell in that light whether it was natural or peroxided. But it was neatly ordered. Either it had not been disturbed in death, which was unlikely, or it had been tidied up after the event. The young features had a serenity which perhaps they had not had in life, and almost certainly not in the last minutes of it.

The arrangement of the limbs was as regular as if this corpse had been laid out in a coffin in a funeral parlour. The heels and knees were together, the slim calves and shins pathetic in their youth and the absence of any trace of veins. The tight skirt was pulled decently and regularly over the knees; it was easy to see why Haworth had felt that ascertaining whether there had been a sexual assault

15

might destroy important evidence. Whoever had touched that skirt and rearranged those limbs and hair might have left traces of himself upon his gruesome handiwork. Already Lambert was assuming the killer was male; statistically that was overwhelmingly probable.

It was the arrangement of the arms which shocked even policemen attuned to such bloodier deaths than this. They were carefully composed, with the hands drawn together between the small, tight breasts as if in prayer. Whoever had done this had slipped a strong elastic band around them, holding them together until they could set into the coldness of death. And already on this warm night rigor had begun to set in upon the small muscles of the victim's face.

The murdered girl looked like a marble figure upon a cathedral tomb, or a saint in a religious painting. Her killer had mocked her, and through her the men who would try to arrest him.

Lambert decided that he could not wait for the pathologist to arrive. He needed sleep more than anything else in the world, and Hook had come on duty at the same time as him. He checked the mechanics of the investigation with 'Jack' Johnson, agreeing that the SOC team should not attempt the detailed examination of the area until daylight.

'How long is it since it rained?' he asked Johnson wearily. He had tried to compute the answer himself, but found one day merging with another in his fatigue.

'Four days. And not much then.' Johnson had worked with Lambert over many years, even though he was not CID. He knew there was no need to 'Sir' him unless an audience demanded the formalities.

'Any chance of footprints?' Lambert was stiffly removing the plastic bags which all who went into the area around the corpse would put over their shoes, to eliminate the risk of a confusion of sole-marks.

'Not a lot. It wasn't much more than a shower four days ago. The ground's pretty hard, but there might be something among the long grass. The photographer's already taken a picture of one print; it had a heel and most of a sole; it looked fairly fresh to me.'

Lambert looked round. The ragged bushes looked sinister on the edge of the harsh white floodlights, as if they held more secrets than they cared to reveal. Above them, the higher branches of a beech tree were perfectly still. The big house which had once stood behind them in the darkness had been demolished. A few yards from his head, a board said, SITE FOR 16 LUXURY FLATS, with the builder's and the agent's names beneath it. They were almost into green belt land here, but there was no need for builders to breach that when they could replace one residence with sixteen.

But recession ruins the most lucrative plans: the paint was peeling on the agent's board, and the weeds around it had grown head-high, while the builder waited for the green shoots of economic recovery that were so reluctant to show themselves. 'Do many people come here?' he asked Johnson.

The Sergeant shrugged. 'The local beat man says plenty of kids mess about here. And young couples in urgent need of a bunk-up. We've already found two rubber johnnies; no doubt there'll be plenty more tomorrow.' He looked automatically towards that silent figure in its pose of mediæval piety, as if he might have committed an impropriety by his coarseness. But the dead are less easily offended than the living.

Lambert nodded, feeling his exhaustion surge swiftly back as they moved to the detail of the investigation. 'Bert Hook and I are for bed. Would you radio in to DI Rushton with any news when Dr Burgess arrives. We'll begin the door to door inquiries first thing in the morning—but Rushton will have all that in hand.'

Johnson nodded. Lambert was one of the very few Superintendents who did not run his investigation by directing his team from an office, preferring to be closer to events himself. It occasionally led to tensions in the ranks above and below him, but he had men about him who understood the way he worked. And he got results: even as an anachronism, that guaranteed his survival.

The hands on the clock in the hall showed 3.17 as Lambert crept past it. He went into the kitchen to make himself a drink, then decided against it as exhaustion wrapped itself about him, crushing him like a great bear.

He did not put the light on in the bedroom: Christine was a light sleeper, and he did not want to disturb her now. That was for his own sake as well as hers; he was too tired even for her sympathy. He left on the light on the landing while he removed his clothes with deliberation and draped them over the chair.

There was enough light through the open door for him to see his wife's head on the pillow. She breathed deeply and quietly. A lock of hair fell becomingly over her left eye, making her look quite young; her hair had no hint of grey, but the oblique light edged it with a silver which made it look as though it were cut from marble. She lay on her back, peaceful, quiet, untroubled by the things he had had to witness. In this half-light he could detect no lines on her forehead; the years seemed to have fallen away from her.

Her position reminded him inevitably of that other woman, whose life had been ended tonight. She had lain as tidily as this; and even more quietly. Creeping between the sheets beside his wife, Lambert thought again of the unknown hands which had composed those dead limbs into that parody of the good religious death.

A murderer who chose to mock them. The kind of damaged mind which was most difficult to detect because it killed without clear motive. His last image as he lost consciousness was of the hands which had arranged that body for him to contemplate. Hands which had killed twice, and would kill again, unless they were arrested.

18

CHAPTER 3

Lambert had five hours of dreamless sleep. It was enough to refresh him, as it had always been. He had few words for his wife at the breakfast table, but that was not significant: he had never been an early-morning talker.

'What time did you get in?' Christine looked at him surreptitiously as she set two slices of toast at his left elbow; she knew that if he saw her assessing the state of his health openly, it would annoy him. Men liked to be pampered once they had decided they were ill, but until then they liked to pretend they were creatures of iron. Or this one did: having had only daughters to contend with, she was never sure whether the schoolboy remained in all men as strongly as it did in her husband.

'Around three, I suppose. I tried not to wake you.' He thought of her unconscious innocence and stillness as he had undressed. She looked altogether more brisk and experienced this morning; despite himself, he found his thoughts returning to that other woman, who had been despatched from life so abruptly when she was still so young.

Christine looked at her watch. 'I must be off. I've got my slow readers first thing, and I want to make sure the right books are there in the classroom for them.'

He nodded, smearing vegetable-fat margarine across his toast with the grimace of ritual distaste he still thought appropriate to it. 'There was another one killed last night.'

Trust him to leave the interesting bit until she had no time to discuss it. 'Another girl?'

'Yes. Not much more than a girl, anyway.' Not for the first time, he wondered what experiences qualified a girl to become a woman; certainly it was not merely a question of age.

'Where?' She found herself hoping it was not anywhere

19

where she moved, that it was miles away, in another county. Her world should not contain such things.

'Out on the edge of the town. Towards Gloucester.'

Too close, then. She felt immediately threatened, and wondered if that small, unpleasant thrill of physical danger was a selfish emotion. Her second thought was maternal, and almost as automatic as her first: she was glad for once that her daughters were married and away from here. Sleepy Oldford seemed suddenly a dangerous place for young women.

She grabbed her briefcase, swept up her car keys from their place above the radiator. 'Where exactly, John?'

'Off Mill Lane. On the road out towards Ditton Farm. They're building a new block of flats there, though God knows when.' He had to force out the little snippets of information. For years, he had said nothing in this house about the work which had once almost divided them. Now he made himself say a little, but that little did not come easily.

'Near the Football Club?'

'That's right.' He should have thought of that immediately. Oldford FC was a flourishing non-league outfit; as the new housing had spread around the town in the 'eighties, so had the 'gates' and the prosperity of the soccer team increased. There was talk among the optimistic about eventual league status for the club.

The football club had a compact little ground, just a little nearer to the centre of the town than where the policemen had stood beside that slim young body last night. Beneath the permanent stand erected six years earlier, it had its own social club, the *Roosters*, which was the nickname of the team. Drinking there was confined to members, but membership was cheap, and the beer was cheaper than in the town's pubs.

As Oldford FC's success and support had grown, the social club had grown noisier and rougher. There were not too many houses near, but the noise was a continual source of complaint from what residents there were. Lately, there had been more serious disturbances: outbreaks of violence

20

between small gangs, the occasional knife, even on one evening open confrontation between a gang of drunken louts and the police called in to control them.

He should have thought of the place last night, was annoyed with himself now that it had been his wife's first thought, when he had overlooked it. Exhaustion made a man inefficient, as he told his subordinates on occasions; he should observe his own dictum. He forced himself to relax, watching his hand as it poured his tea. Rushton and the others would have thought of the *Roosters* club immediately, even if he hadn't; he must learn to trust his team, just as he had had to learn to delegate.

There was no need to say anything else to his wife. Christine's Fiesta was away through the gates before he had finished castigating himself.

Three hours later he had more immediate problems. Cyril Burgess, MB, Ch.B, had that streak of sadism which seemed possessed by all pathologists, in Lambert's experience: he loved to test the stomachs of working policemen with the detail of his findings. Lambert did not find it an agreeable quality; Burgess had long since understood that, and decided that such squeamishness only added to his amusement.

He stood now by the corpse he had just investigated, threatening at any moment to twitch back the sheet and reveal his awful handiwork. 'The stomach contents were interesting,' he said affably. 'I can show you why, if you'd like to see them.'

Lambert shook his head; Burgess, who had known he would refuse, scarcely registered the gesture. 'Who was she?' he said.

Lambert checked automatically on his notes, relieved to look anywhere away from that shape beneath the sheet on the stainless steel. 'Harriet Brown. She would have been twenty-one next week. Unmarried.'

'But not a virgin. Be unusual if she was, nowadays, at that age.'

'She seems to have been on the game. Or starting on it,

21

perhaps. The uniformed lads knew her, but she had no convictions.' It was the usual route into prostitution. Girls tried it for pin money, or because they were in debt, found it lucrative, and were drawn into it full-time. If they lasted, they usually ended up with pimps. Oldford, thankfully, had not yet many of those; organized prostitution was still seen as a city activity.

'Local girl?'

'We don't think so. Word has it that she came here from the Midlands or the North about a year ago. We should know more before the day's out.' He wondered about the girl's parents in some distant town, ignorant as yet of their daughter's death, and pictured some young WPC charged with the duty of breaking the news. Then there would be other relatives; grandparents, perhaps, with a girl of this age. The ripples of suffering spread outwards for weeks; he wondered uselessly if murders might sometimes be prevented if the killers had an overview of the consequences of their acts.

Burgess said, 'I can give you semen samples for the DNA profile. Your victim had had intercourse not long before death.'

Lambert nodded, still picturing the distress of those faceless parents. 'Julie Salmon, the first girl killed, had been raped as well.'

Burgess shook his head. 'You misunderstand me, John. This girl wasn't raped. I said she'd had intercourse, that's all. There's no evidence on the corpse that the act was accompanied by any undue violence.'

Lambert castigated himself for the second time that day, this time for jumping to conclusions. He said woodenly, 'How long before death?'

Burgess shrugged: he was not prepared to speculate as readily as his medical colleague Don Haworth had done. 'I should say in her last hour of life. Very probably in her last few minutes, but I couldn't be certain of that.'

'Are there any tests you could do to be certain?'

'No. Nothing that would provide evidence strong enough for a court of law. Is it important?'

'It could be very important. If she is a girl who sold her favours, your semen sample could come from someone who was nowhere near her when she was killed.'

'There were samples from Julie Salmon. It should be easy enough to compare the two. "Murder, though it hath no tongue, will speak with most miraculous organ."' Burgess smiled benignly, pleased with his mildly improper suggestion. He had an addiction to the crime fiction of the 'thirties, a deplorable weakness as far as Lambert was concerned. It led him to an indulgence in quotations, which he made no attempt to control.

Lambert said drily, 'That might well be the motto of forensic science. Are you quite sure that there was no evidence of sexual assault on this girl?'

'As sure as I can be. Of course, modern advice to girls is to take the line of least resistance. Even the police tell women they should not fight if defeat appears inevitable. The fate is no longer seen as worse than death. But unless you assume that she meekly succumbed to avoid injury, you must accept that she was not assaulted.'

Lambert said heavily, to himself as much as to Burgess, 'Does that mean that these murders were not by the same person?' He had already decided that he would rather that they were not; he would prefer two routine killings to the alternative of a madman embarking on a series of homicides.

Burgess's mischievous grin was in the worst possible taste. 'You're the policeman. You'll have to decide that, John.' Perhaps he saw that the Superintendent was about to explode, for he went on hastily, 'But there might be something to be learned from the method of killing, I suppose. It was very similar in both cases.'

'Strangling.'

'In layman's terms, yes. But not asphyxiation. Vagal inhibition.'

Lambert wondered where he had heard the phrase recently, then recalled the police surgeon using it in the darkness on the night before. That had been only nine hours previously: it seemed like many more. 'By the same man?'

Burgess shook his head, disapproving of this lust after certainty. 'Impossible to say. But there are similarities. Your man—a woman could have done this, by the way, but let's assume not for the moment—applied his thumbs to exactly the same point on the neck in each case. The bruising is almost identical. And death was mercifully swift on both occasions. Technically, it was from heart stoppage, caused by pressure on the carotid arteries in the neck.'

Without warning, Burgess stepped over to the corpse and turned back the top of the white sheet. The girl's face looked even paler in the strong overhead lights here than when it had lain in the undergrowth on the building site. The pathologist said, 'If death had been from asphyxia, her face would have been purple and there would probably have been bleeding from the nose or the ears. You can see the marks of your man's thumbs clearly enough.' He pointed with his ballpoint at the girl's neck, which looked now as if it had been elongated to accommodate the huge, ugly bruises on each side of the slim throat.

Mercifully, Burgess had exposed only the face and neck of the corpse and not his workings lower down the body. Lambert forced himself to take the sheet and pull it back across the unlined face, so unnaturally serene in spite of the violence it had suffered. He turned away, drawing Burgess with him, putting distance between the two of them and the mutilated flesh they were discussing, guarding against any more visual demonstrations from the pathologist. Then he said, 'What about those small abrasions on the neck?'

Burgess shook his head. 'They were made by the girl herself, I'm afraid. When she tried to drag her killer's hands away. It must have been all over in seconds.'

'Anything under her fingernails?'

'Nothing useful. The skin and tissue are the girls' own, from those neck scratches you noticed.'

'Did you find anything on the corpse that might be from the man who killed her?'

'No. He wore gloves, as did the murderer of Julie Salmon.

24

I can't even tell you what kind of gloves, because I've found no fibres on the neck.'

'Leather?'

'It's possible. Plastic of some kind is probably more likely. But I'm guessing—no traces of the gloves have been left on the girl's neck or arms.'

'So this killer was at pains to leave no trace. And he probably went out expecting to kill.'

Burgess was immediately interested as always in the workings of the detective mind. He looked his question, and Lambert said, 'On a warm night, he went out with gloves in his pocket. I can't think of many people in Oldford who would do that.'

Burgess said with uncharacteristic humility, 'Yes, I see that as soon as you say it. Has your Scene of Crime team collected any fibres from her clothing?'

'A few. It remains to be seen whether they're useful ones. They may have no connection with her assailant.' In his present gloomy mood, Lambert felt already that they would not. 'What about the time of death?' It was the question they always wanted answered, but in this case he did not think Burgess would be able to give them much more than they already knew.

'She'd eaten fish and chips about five hours before death. She died between nine o'clock last night and one o'clock this morning.'

Lambert nodded, suppressing a smile at how much wider this old hand set the boundaries than Don Haworth had last night. But the police surgeon was a younger man, enthusiastic to help them. And it was not his evidence which would be quoted and possibly challenged in court. He said, 'You've conducted the autopsies on both Julie Salmon and Harriet Brown, Cyril. Would you say they were killed by the same man?'

Burgess prepared himself for an elaborate series of medical cautions to explain why it was impossible and undesirable to look for such certainties on the evidence available. Then he saw Lambert's strained face and thought better of it; he would like to be as helpful as possible to a man he now thought of as an old friend. Moreover, he was fascinated by the processes of detection, and loved to become involved in them.

'It's impossible to be certain, on the forensic evidence so far available.' The pathologist dropped his voice into an awful American intonation: Hollywood B movie, circa 1950. 'But you're asking me to play a hunch, Lootenant, and I'm gonna do that for you. I'm gonna level with you, and hope you'll do the same with me in doo course.' Whether in response to Lambert's pained expression or because he found the imitation too tiresome to sustain, he dropped back to his normal voice. 'From the manner of the killing, I would be surprised if these two young women did not die by the same hand, John.'

Lambert nodded glumly. That was his own view: he had hoped to hear it refuted. He said, 'And since I've managed to lure you at last into the realms of speculation, have you any other thoughts that might help us in the investigation?'

Burgess looked across at the shape beneath the sheet which he had worked on so carefully for two hours. He preferred the dead to the living, since with corpses he could carry his research to whatever lengths was necessary, a process not possible where life had to be preserved: that appealed to the scientist which was the strongest factor in his persona. Sometimes he spoke flippantly, as though his material was no more than dead meat. But he remained aware always that life had been abruptly and unlawfully terminated, that his work in this laboratory was ultimately concerned with justice and order.

Burgess said soberly, 'I'm not a psychologist, John. But the manner of these killings—swift and apparently motiveless—is too similar for my liking. I think you should expect your man to kill again.'

26

CHAPTER 4

Sergeant Bert Hook was supposed to be good with disturbed girls. It was one of those repetitive station jokes which CID sections love to perpetuate.

He did not feel himself very effective with Debbie Cook, and the WDC he took with him was too young to be of much assistance to him. Miss Cook was too tearful to be coherent, and though he knew she needed physical comfort, Hook was too old a hand to put the fatherly arm he knew she wanted around her narrow shoulders.

'She looked so—peaceful!' she sobbed, for the third time. 'I couldn't believe at first that she was dead.'

Hook could imagine the words being used for weeks to come, when she had ceased to weep and become a temporary celebrity through her association with the dead girl. He said, 'You're upset, love, of course. But we're going to need your help if we're to catch the man who did it.'

She nodded, wiping a tear from her nose with her index finger. She looked very young and forlorn, like a child who sees the end of the world in a broken doll. 'What happens next? What about the funeral?'

'Well, first of all, Harriet will have to be identified formally by her next of kin, even though because of you we know for certain now that it's her.' She looked up at him gratefully at his acknowledgement of her help, and he knew suddenly that it was a long time since anyone had been kind to her. Except perhaps the dead Harriet.

As if she read that thought, the girl said, 'It sounds funny, "Harriet". She never called herself anything but Hetty.' She stared down at her sodden handkerchief, turning it over in her hands as if she could not understand how it had become so wet.

Hook, recognizing the effects of her ordeal upon the girl, took the cardigan he saw on the back of a chair and draped it round the slim shoulders as they gave a sudden shudder.

It was warm enough outside, but this small bedroom was on the second floor of the house, facing north, and the girl was in shock. He had a moment of sudden fear that the woollen might belong to the dead girl and not this one, but then she pulled it about her like a small blanket, without putting her arms through the sleeves.

'My mother used to do that when I was little,' she said. There was surprise in her voice, as though the memory had come to her from a long way away and surprised her.

Feeling rather more like a social worker than a detective-sergeant, Hook said rather desperately, 'There'll have to be an inquest.'

She nodded gravely, studying her bright red nails. 'What happens there?'

'Oh, it will all be over very quickly. And we won't need you for that, I don't think.' He had meant to be comforting, but she looked a little disappointed. 'One of Harriet's—Hetty's—parents will give formal evidence of identification. Someone from CID will say a little about how she was killed. The Coroner will recommend the verdict of "Murder by person or persons unknown". Then we'll get on with finding out who did it.'

She nodded sagely, as if she was digesting new information, then said, 'Hetty wouldn't have hurt a fly.'

Someone nearly always said that about a victim of violence, but poor Debbie Cook wasn't to know that. Hook looked round the room with its faded flowered wallpaper, its two unmatching single beds, its brown stain of damp in the corner of the outside walls. There was a single small and uncomfortable armchair, which he now occupied and overflowed, and two painted blue wooden stand chairs. The WDC sat on one of these. Debbie was sitting on her bed, turning the threadbare candlewick bedspread to try to make its holes a little less obvious. There was a cheap plastic shade on the light which hung in the middle of the room, but someone had put too strong a bulb in the socket, so that one side of the shade was burned dark brown.

He said, 'You and Hetty rented this room together?'

She nodded, crushing the small handkerchief between

28

her palms until it disappeared. The WDC pushed a tissue between her fingers. He thought she was going to break down again, but she said with a touch of defiance, 'We were going to get ourselves something better, before too long.' Then she looked up at him in fear, as though she felt that the little spurt of pride had tricked her into an indiscretion.

Hook said gently, 'How long had you been here, love?'

'Ten months.'

'You didn't grow up down here, though, did you?' The girl's Black Country accent had been stronger in the extremes of her distress than it was now.

'No. I came here from Walsall. To work at ICI in Gloucester. That's where I met Hetty. She'd come from Nottingham, just before me.'

'So you both wanted to get away from home.' He made it a simple statement, and she accepted it as that.

'Yes. I had a stepfather who decided when I was eighteen that it would be more exciting to fuck me than my mother.' She produced the word defiantly; its sudden harshness broke through the monotone of the sentence to hint at the bitterness she felt.

If she had thought to shock the avuncular figure who sat opposite her, she would have been disappointed; Hook heard worse tales than this far too often for his comfort. He merely nodded and said, 'And was Hetty's home situation similar to yours?'

'No, I'm sure it wasn't. Her parents are still together, for a start. But her dad was unemployed, and he wouldn't give her any freedom.'

Hook, who had two boys of his own who were not yet ten, thought of the trials of adolescence which lay ahead of them and him. He said gently, 'What kind of freedom, Debbie?'

She shrugged, looking at him for a moment with a flash of petulance. 'The usual things. When she went out with a boy, her father had to know who it was the whole time. Every time she was in later than they thought she should be, there was a shouting match.'

29

It was a familiar, even a routine story. And now a girl lay dead. But that was just bad luck for the father who had shouted, and the girl who had shouted back. 'So she left home. How old was she?'

'A year older than me. Nearly twenty-one.' That was the child in her, he thought, still wanting to be as old as she possibly could, counting away every day of her departing innocence.

If the uniformed men who knew this area were to be believed, it had been departing rapidly. He said, 'But the work at ICI didn't last long for either of you.'

Again he delivered it as a statement, not a question, and she looked up with apprehension into his round face, wondering just how much these people did know about her. Perhaps those things she had heard about never trusting the police were true; but this kindly man with the fresh red face had seemed so much like the father she envisaged but could not remember.

She said, like one searching for a footing in mud, 'No. We were only temporary, but we thought it would become permanent, if we kept our noses clean. We weren't the only ones made redundant, you know.' It seemed important to her that she should convince her listener that their dismissals had been through no disdemeanour.

'No, of course not.' He looked round the room unhurriedly, fixing his eye upon the battered wardrobe where the dead girl's clothes lay. They would have to be removed for examination and storage in the Murder Room they had set up at headquarters. 'Do you have a kitchen, Debbie?'

'Yes, and a little bathroom—well, a shower room really, but we don't have to share. And there's a tiny little lounge with a telly.' She was like a girl trying to convince her mother that the accommodation was adequate. 'You can come and see, if you like. It might be a bit untidy, but—'

Hook held up his hand, arresting the nervous flow of her words as he had long ago stopped traffic. 'And how much does it cost, Debbie?'

She knew then where his questioning was going, and looked at him with a helpless resentment. He thought for a moment she was going to refuse to answer, but then she said, 'Seventy-five pounds a week.'

'And did you find other work, when you were laid off at ICI?'

'No. We tried, but we had to go on the social.'

'So how do you survive and pay your bills?'

She merely shook her head sullenly, unwilling even to attempt to frame an answer for him.

'Are you behind with your rent, Debbie?'

'No. The landlord wouldn't stand for that.'

'So how did you pay him, you and Hetty?'

'We saved hard.' It was her last defiance, and neither of them thought it worthy of investigation.

'The arithmetic doesn't work, Debbie. Besides, we found as much money on Hetty as she'd have got in a week from the DHSS.'

'The bastard! He didn't even kill her for her money, then.' It flashed out before she could control herself, surprising her as well as him with its vehemence.

While she was still off guard, Hook said curtly, 'You were taking money from men, weren't you? Selling your favours to pay the rent and the bills.'

She drew in a huge, racking breath, and just for a moment he thought she was going to spring at him in her frustration. Then her shoulders collapsed hopelessly beneath the woollen tent of the cardigan and she said, 'What did you expect me to do? Go back to Walsall, to be fucked again by him?' Again she produced the obscenity like a pistol shot, as though shock might be the only weapon she had with which to defend herself.

He said calmly, 'I'm not interested in any prosecution at the moment, though you should be aware that soliciting is a criminal offence. I'm only interested in the girl you've just seen lying dead, and anything that will help us to find out how she died.'

She looked down miserably at her small feet in their cheap silver plastic shoes. 'All right. We took money for it. Hetty said I might as well be paid for it here as be fucked for nothing in Walsall by a man I hated.'

31

It was his first real glimpse of the dead woman. He could see them sitting on these threadbare beds in their poverty, with the older girl being persuasive to this one who feared so much to go home. 'Where did you pick up your clients?'

The phrase alarmed her. She had not thought of herself as setting out to pick up men, nor had she considered them as clients. She had thought of herself as an amateur, beginning to take a little money because she needed it. She attempted the experienced woman's hardness, setting her lips sullenly as she said, 'I can't tell you any more. You lot twist anything to—'

'You can and will tell us more.' His voice was like a whiplash across her face. 'You've just seen your flatmate lying dead in the mortuary. Either we catch the man who did it, or it will be you or some other young fool like you on that slab next week!'

She nodded several times, refusing still to look at him, fearing that the kindly face with its thick, rounded eyebrows would have changed. She sobbed again, producing an involuntary shudder which shook the whole of her body. 'All right.'

'Where did you meet these men?'

'At the *Roosters* Club, mostly, by the football ground. It's a big place inside, you know, and always busy. And the drinks are cheap. Cheap and cheerful, Hetty always said it was.' Another sob racked her thin frame at the thought, but there were no tears.

'Did you bring them here?'

'Sometimes we did, yes. We knew not to come in if the other one was using the room. It didn't take long.'

'And where else?'

'Sometimes the men had a place.' So she was silly and inexperienced enough to break the first rule of prostitution, allowing herself to be led on to alien ground. 'Sometimes it was the back of a car. Once or twice outside, these last few weeks.'

With each new venue, she sounded a little more desperate, as she contemplated her actions for the first time from the outside. Hook wondered as he had often done

32

before why men paid good money for these squalid, loveless encounters. 'And did you ever use that building site off Mill Lane, where they're going to put up new flats?'

She looked up at him at last, divining in that moment where the girl who had slept in the bed next to hers for almost a year had met her death. Her dark eyes were round with fear in the thin, wet face. 'Once. About a week ago.'

'And did you tell Hetty about it?'

She paused, wanting to deny it, knowing that the information might have been her friend's death warrant. Almost in a whisper, she said, 'Yes. We told each other everything, you see. It was a kind of protection.'

But not for Harriet Brown. That thought hung between them for a moment. Then Hook said, 'Who was Hetty with last night, Debbie?'

It was the key question, but she could not answer it. 'I don't know. I had a boy myself you see, early on. He—he doesn't pay me. I like him, you see, and I don't think he knows . . .' She fumbled a little for words, then threw up her hands in a small, hopeless gesture. The tears began again, silently now.

'You left Hetty in the *Roosters* Club?'

'Yes. In a big group of people. She was always popular. She was so lively, you see.'

It sounded like the epitaph for a good-time girl, the parallel to the parents' sorrowful cry of 'Where did we go wrong?' which policemen heard so often after a tragedy. 'We'll need the names of everyone who was around her in that party when you left.'

She nodded, thinking already who they were, the frown on her forehead like that of a dutiful schoolgirl beginning her homework.

'And we'll need the names of all the men you've met in the last few months, those hanging around in clubs or pubs, as well as those who've actually paid for your services.'

She winced at the phrase, but he did not mind that; she was perhaps young enough still to be shocked out of her ways, to be protected from herself. He'd try to get one of the better social workers round here, when the CID had

33

finished with her. She said apologetically, 'I don't know all their names.'

He nodded. 'Descriptions, then, where you don't. We'll have plenty of CID people around the *Roosters* in the next few days, so we can probably pin a name on most of them. And don't leave anyone out, not even the boyfriend you didn't charge last night.'

'Oh, but he doesn't—'

'If he's nothing to do with it, we need to eliminate him. If what you say is true, we can probably do that almost immediately. What we shall be doing with most of the men down there is eliminating them from the inquiry: that's the way we work. So don't leave anyone out, for any reason whatever. Understand?'

She gave him twenty-three names, while the WDC removed the dead girl's clothes, carrying fishnet tights and lurex skirts at arm's length, as befitted the tools of a dubious trade.

It took them almost an hour, and Hook lingered over his examination of the bathroom and the kitchen, hoping vainly to pick up some trace of the man who had dispatched the girl whose presence was still strong in these small rooms. Perhaps the murderer had even been here last night, or on some previous occasion.

Debbie Cook had washed her face before they left. She was sitting on the edge of the bed, leaning forward to use the cracked mirror on the dressing-table, wearing already a bright lipstick, putting blue eye-shadow across her eyelids; donning the uniform which might for a little while longer keep the world at bay.

CHAPTER 5

Charles Kemp was forty-eight and successful. No one called him Charles to his face any more, except his old teacher from primary school and three of the top people in his Masonic lodge.

He paused for just a fraction beneath the big sign which said KEMP'S AUTOS before he passed beneath it and entered the showroom. It always pleased him, that sign; he doubted whether there was a wider or smarter one in the whole of Bristol. Sometimes he drove past at night just to see it illuminated, proclaiming to an uncaring world that Charlie Kemp, sometime eleven-plus failure, street fighter, soccer hooligan, had arrived now, and should be respected as Charles. Some people would have added crook and fraudster to that list, but not in his hearing.

He was a powerful man, just under six feet tall, but broad-shouldered and weighing fourteen stones. That meant he was a little overweight now, but he was hard and strong still beneath the layer of fat that had come with prosperity, watchful and alert to anything which might threaten his well-being. A man who punched his weight, in more ways than one.

He went between the rows of gleaming new cars, running his eyes appreciatively over the stainless steel and walnut, sniffing the strong, uncontaminated smell of new leather upholstery from the biggest of them, calling a greeting to the girl behind the desk at the end of the big hall. In the office at the rear of the building, two men waited for him who were even larger than he was.

They looked uncomfortable enough in their lightweight grey suits to be plain clothes policemen, but they were not. They were Kemp's muscle, though it was not he but other people who called them that. They were on the payroll as part of his sales force, though they had never sold anything in their lives. They could be persuasive, but not with their tongues.

He shut the door carefully behind him, inspected the surface of his desk as if he expected to find it 'bugged', and sat down carefully in the leather swivel chair behind it. The two men who had waited for him sat down only when he gestured towards the stainless steel upright chairs with their leather seats; they were positioned some way on the other side of the big desk. They could see only the upper part of Kemp's body, whereas he could see the whole of theirs, including the feet which coiled awkwardly round the feet of their chairs. The sight seemed to give him satisfaction: he looked at the men's shoes with a small smile for a moment before he spoke.

'Well?'

'It's all right, boss. You can have the site at the price you offered.'

'Fifteen thousand?' It was worth three times as much. Even from his position of strength, he would have offered thirty.

'Yes. He was a bit reluctant, even after last week's accident, but he saw the light of reason when we talked to him.'

Kemp smiled: his secret smile, which was a mixture of satisfaction with his success and contempt for these instruments he had to use. It had no element of mirth in it.

'Was the torched car still there?'

'Yes. He'd had it pushed to the back of the site, but you could still see it. Spoiled the display, I thought.'

The speaker smiled at this rare sally into irony, and his companion, who had said not a word so far, took this as the cue for a snigger. His features were not designed for sniggering, and it came out as a manic chuckle, like the exaggeration of a bad stage actor. He knew it did not sound right, and in an effort to cover his embarrassment he said, 'We told him that, boss, and he turned quite pale. Wayne told him it was a shame it had had to happen to a nice bloke like him.'

The said Wayne gave his companion a look which warned that there was no need for him to give a full account of their meeting with the man who had owned the car sales site. He took the hint and folded his arms, setting his lips hard, as though determined to keep in check the tongue which seemed to arouse his employer's distaste. His formidable forearms were tattooed with a variety of patriotic sentiments, but at the moment they were decently hidden beneath the cheap cloth of his suit, as Kemp had ordered they should be.

'Fifteen k's good.' Kemp would concede so much, even to them. Modern management techniques demanded that you gave successful staff a little encouragement, showed them the carrot as well as the stick; even gorillas like this. Kemp said, suddenly expansive, 'There might be a little bonus in this for you lads, when it's all gone through.'

He picked up the internal phone on his desk, anxious to demonstrate even to creatures like this the power and decision he exercised. 'Eileen, get on to Chris Baker at the solicitor's and tell him the deal for that car sales site in the city's going through. Fifteen thousand, tell him. And tell him to make sure the planning permission for the showroom hasn't run out of time. Get him to get the contract round to Shaw's legal people p.d.q.'

He smiled patronizingly at the puzzled faces across his desk. 'Pretty damn quick!' he explained with a lofty wave of his hand over the phone after he had replaced the receiver. No harm in letting these minions know that he chased respectable professional men about as well as them. Almost respectable, anyway: Chris Baker knew how to cut a few corners, but legally.

He addressed the man who had given his report sternly. 'You didn't offer Mr Shaw any physical violence?'

'No, boss. We were very careful to do exactly what you said.' His large face was pained that there should be even the suggestion that he had not followed his orders carefully.

'And you didn't even threaten him with any grief?' This to the second man, whose broad forehead seemed abnormally short even beneath his close-cropped hair.

'No, Mr Kemp. He didn't need much persuasion. Maybe he remembered how we'd leant on him a little when you first offered to buy the place; maybe he'd seen the light when—'

'That's enough. I didn't ask you that. I know nothing about that. As far as I'm concerned, this was a straightforward business deal. I made an offer and Davis Shaw accepted it. Get that into your heads, both of you. Memorize it. Repeat it in front of a mirror each night before you go to bed, if you need to. Just in case you're ever asked about it.'

They nodded dutifully, and he dismissed them, suddenly

weary of the sight of them. They were caricatures. He realized that: assurances to himself like a lot of other things of the wealth and influence he now exercised. But Kemp never read a book, and rarely a newspaper; his images of power and its trappings were drawn from films and television, from fiction that was always a little out of date. He could have used less obvious hard men than these two, but their very appearance was an assurance to him that he had arrived, just as much as his forward position in the queue to be Master of his Lodge was a reassurance to him elsewhere.

Alone in the office, he permitted himself a slow smile. He had added this latest colony to his motor empire very easily. And it had come ridiculously cheap. Success bred success, like they said. It really was easier after the first million.

He walked over to the mahogany cabinet in the corner of the room and took out the whisky bottle and the cut-glass tumbler. He put a small measure in the bottom of the glass, savoured the fierce, bitter fire on his tongue. He would have liked a little water with it, but they said you had to drink good whisky neat, the ones who knew. He did not even much like it, in truth, but it was the way to celebrate a business triumph. He had seen it on the films.

Two hours later, he turned the big, blood-red Mercedes into the car park of the *Roosters* Social Club. The sign here was not as big as the one over his showroom, but then it made no mention of his name. In theory, he was the humble servant of Oldford Football Club, who could be replaced by a democratic vote of its board. He smiled indulgently at the thought; money talked in football, more than anywhere else. That was one of the clichés he thought he had invented, and he produced it whenever he was short of a sporting thought for the media.

He turned the car carefully into the rectangle on the tarmac which was marked CHAIRMAN, then walked slowly across the half-acre of floor in the main room of the club. There was a bar along the entire length of the wall at one end of this huge room, where eight staff served hundreds of customers on Fridays and Saturdays. A huge red fibreglass cockerel strutted across the wall above the bar. Its comb and the letters which spelt out the legend 'Up the Roosters!' could be lit up with neon lighting in the evenings.

At the other end of the room was a wide dais, with microphones and the standard electronic equipment to support the specialist gadgetry brought by the bands and groups who played here from time to time. On other nights the space was occupied by the singers and comedians who came to this flourishing centre through their bookings on the club circuit.

The rest of the space was occupied by round tables and chairs covered with red plastic upholstery. There were lights high above them which could be switched to a variety of colours, and speakers every few yards along the long walls to relay the efforts of the entertainers or the piped music.

The team played in red and white, and they were the colours which dominated the room. The place was vulgar and noisy, at times even raucous. It was also vibrant and successful. It was Charlie Kemp who had developed it— in his football persona, he was Charlie. He allowed the press to call him that: it was the appropriate name for a man of the people, controlling the people's game and giving it back to them.

He had got the idea for this place from the working men's clubs of the North-East, which he had visited in the earlier days of his career. The beer here was dearer, of course: the profits supported the growth of the football club, though Charlie pretended at every opportunity that most of that derived from his personal beneficence. But the drinks at the *Roosters* were still carefully cheaper than in the pubs of Oldford. That brought people in, and people gave the place life.

Charlie Kemp liked crowds, especially when they were somewhat in awe of him, as they were at the football club. Crowds were good for business, and they offered all kinds of possibilities to a resourceful entrepreneur. Staffing, for instance: he had recruited the two men he had just used in

Bristol here, watching their performance as weekend bouncers for a little while first.

And crowds could become customers. You could sell all kinds of things to crowds, provided you could get the supply. Some of them could be very profitable indeed.

There were other exciting possibilities, too. Girls came here, in a compelling variety of shapes and sizes. With the lights low and the music turned high in the evenings, the place had an excitement and a glamour which disguised its tawdriness from them. After a few drinks, with the presence of fit young men around them—Kemp encouraged the players to mingle here, except on the nights before matches —girls, even women, found this a place of heady excitement.

And Charlie, though officially without an interest in the *Roosters* Social Club, controlled all this. Everyone understood that. And especially the women, whose judgement was not generally clouded by the latest successes or failures on the football field. Power was the great aphrodisiac; Charles Kemp had heard that, and stored it away. He took care to make his power apparent as he moved among the crowded tables of the *Roosters*.

Many of the girls liked his bluff, no-nonsense style, and he was good at spotting the ones who did. He knew very little about women, but in the heady, artificial world of the *Roosters* at night, a world where sweat and cheap scent seemed equally at home, neither they nor he were aware of that fact. Charlie thought he could 'spot a goer', and some of the girls were flattered enough by the attentions of the man the sports pages called 'Mr Oldford' to foster that impression for him.

Charles Kemp had an overweight, unexciting wife at home. They had separate rooms, and he ventured into hers less and less frequently. He thought that in his own way he was fond of her still, but he never investigated those feelings, not being of a reflective nature. She was wheeled out, bejewelled and expensively coiffured, on the occasions when it was necessary to show such a partner. She did not let him down at Ladies' Nights at the Lodge, or at the charity balls where they danced carefully at arm's length and conversed with the respectable burghers of the town. She was one of his badges of respectability.

In the little private suite at the *Roosters* to which he kept the key, Charlie Kemp indulged in urgent and violent couplings of a different kind. They sometimes frightened the girls involved, and they revealed to him a part of his own nature which he had thought safely suppressed. But these girls were there to be used: didn't they come to him of their own free will? Besides, they got money, and sometimes employment: Kemp's extensive range of enterprises could often provide that.

Indeed, he had been preparing in the last few months to offer lucrative employment to a selection of the girls he watched in the *Roosters*. There was money in sex, if it was properly organized. Even some of the punters who came here were prepared to pay for it. Not as many as in Bristol or Birmingham, but enough.

The town was growing, and the oldest trade would grow with it. It was one of Kemp's principles that one should be in on the ground floor with new developments. A little of the organization he was good at would pay rich dividends to himself as well as to the girls.

And he could always indulge his darker side with them. That would be a bonus.

Kemp went into the hospitality suite on the first floor of the building; it had a door at one end which opened straight into the directors' box in the main stand, but that was kept locked, except on match days. Behind a small door on the opposite wall of the room, the Secretary of Oldford FC had his office. He was an employee of the football club, not Kemp's; the man was clear enough about that, but as with other things around the club, the distinction was blurred in other people's minds.

Beside the Secretary's door, there was a neat box with three lights, designed to light up when the button beside them was pressed and the man inside responded. They said

'Engaged', 'Wait' and 'Enter', and lit up when the Secretary pressed the appropriate button on his desk.

Kemp opened the door abruptly without knocking. ''Afternoon, Jack,' he said. 'Has Vic Knowles confirmed his visit?'

If John Castle was disturbed by the manner of the Chairman's arrival in his office, he gave no sign of it. 'He rang about half an hour ago, from his car phone. He should be here in a few minutes, now.' Unlike other people around the place, he never called the Chairman 'sir'. It was one of his tiny assertions of independence.

Kemp noticed the fact, but for the moment it suited him to ignore it. 'Good. I think it would be a good idea if you had a word with the groundsman, Jack. He's cutting the grass on the pitch pretty short, and there's no sign of rain. If we have to water it during this hosepipe ban, we'll have the usual busybodies writing to the *Echo*.'

It was a direction that Castle should be absent when Vic Knowles met the Chairman, and both of them knew it. The Secretary didn't like what was going on, but he knew he could do nothing about it. He nodded, made a face-saving remark about the newly seeded goalmouths, and went downstairs and out into the sunshine. That at any rate felt something of a relief.

Kemp looked after him for a moment with a grin, then made a small redisposition of the furniture in the hospitality suite in preparation for his visitor. In ten minutes, he and Vic Knowles sat opposite each other in big leather armchairs, the atmosphere consciously informal, the Chairman a little more at ease in these familiar surroundings than his visitor.

Knowles sat too far forward to be comfortable in the low armchair. He had a heavily lined face, which made him look older than his forty-four years, and rather prominent front teeth. He had never been handsome, but in his better moments he carried the air of a cheerful Jack-the-lad adventurer. This was not one of those moments.

'So you think you might be interested?' Kemp looked at Knowles across the top of his glass with a conspiratorial

42

smile: this was still a secret between them. 'Do help yourself to water, by the way. I take it neat.'

Knowles reached forward awkwardly to the jug on the low table between them, taking the few seconds to try to size his man up. He had met a considerable number of football club chairmen in his day, and they were not a breed he trusted. But in his profession they were a necessary evil, one you had to live with.

'I'm interested, yes. It would be a bit of a comedown for me, of course, going outside the league, Mr Kemp, but—'

'Charlie, please. We don't need the formalities, at least in private. We find these silly distinctions get in the way of efficiency at Oldford.' He waved a vague and benign hand to indicate the rest of the extensive premises which made up Oldford FC. There would be time enough to make his withdrawals when he had netted his man. 'And don't forget we shall soon be in the league. You'll be impressed with our set-up.'

Vic Knowles had heard that one before, but he had more sense than to say so. He couldn't afford to admit it here, but he needed the money; it was an effort to seem as relaxed as he hoped he appeared. He needed to clear his gambling debts; last week he had even pawned the gold watch he had been presented with after a Cup triumph in his heyday of management. He said, 'Well, I'm open to offers, Charlie. I'm considering one or two proposals at the moment, but . . .'

'Open to offers, yes.' Kemp weighed the phrase. He took a sip of the whisky he had hardly touched, and smiled into his cut-glass tumbler, letting Knowles know that he knew the score. 'I think you'll find ours interesting.'

Ten years ago, Vic Knowles had been one of the biggest names in football management, a gifted but not exceptional player who had made it through the ranks of more gifted footballers to become manager of a big first division team. He had been interviewed often on television then, fingering the lapels of the colourful suits which he had bought as the accoutrements of success, squandering the increasingly

43

generous appearance and interview fees on booze and gambling.

They had been heady days, tarnished eventually by a too-public affair with a player's wife and a fight in a motorway café in front of hundreds of delighted fans. He had moved around the divisions since then, steadily downwards and with varying degrees of success. He did not often last more than a year; initially, he brought discipline to clubs, but he was too careless a martinet for his control to endure in an era of player power.

He had been unemployed since a third division club terminated his contract in April, and Kemp knew all about it. He had taken care to have Knowles's financial background investigated before he approached him through an intermediary. The man must be desperate now. But he was still news, still a big name to land, for a club like Oldford.

And he would be Charlie Kemp's man, if he came. Another coup for Charlie: he could see the *Echo* headlines in his mind's eye already. 'You'd need to move into the area,' he told Knowles. He noticed that the man had already finished his drink, but he did not pour him another one.

'That's no problem. If the deal's right,' said Knowles. He tried to appear laid back—that was the phrase the media still used about him, and he tried to live up to the image—but he found himself swigging automatically at a glass that was already empty.

'We could probably rent you a club house, if it would help.' That would put the new manager more firmly in his power; especially as the said house was owned not by the club but by one Charles Kemp.

Knowles tried not to show his relief. 'It would be a help, I think. In the early stages. Until I sorted things out.'

'That's if we can agree a deal.' Kemp sipped reflectively from the inch of whisky which still occupied the bottom of his tumbler. 'You would be responsible for the team, of course, and for all disciplinary matters.'

Knowles went into the spiel he had used before on such occasions and found effective. 'I think my track record speaks for itself as far as that goes, Charlie. I've managed the best, and got the best out of them.'

Kemp smiled as he might have done at the naïvety of a child. 'Past glories, Vic, past glories. In football, you're as good as your last match. You've been around long enough to know that.'

He produced the clichés with a grave air, as though he were offering a new wisdom upon a troubled scene, and Knowles found himself nodding agreement before he realized that he was making a concession. 'I can handle the team, have no fears about that. Now—'

'I believe you can, or I wouldn't be talking to you, Vic. We'll pay you fifteen thousand.'

'Oh, but I couldn't possibly—'

'And we'll settle your extensive gambling debts.'

The sentence hit Knowles like a blow in the solar plexus. He settled back in his chair, trying to take the deep breaths which were necessary if he was to speak evenly. Kemp decided that he should have a drink, now that he had been softened up. He reached across with the bottle and poured a generous measure, then moved the jug of water two inches nearer to Knowles. 'You will give us an IOU for the amount of those debts, which will be torn up provided that you stay with us for at least a year.'

Vic said weakly, 'I don't think I can live on fifteen thousand a year. I've got responsibilities, you see. Since my divorce—'

'You'll live on it all right, if you cut out your gambling. To assist you in that, our local bookmakers have agreed to inform the club of any . . . investments you attempt to make with them.' He knew the man could still bet with the big firms, but the threat was all he wanted at this moment.

Knowles scratched desperately for an argument. 'But surely some of the players will be on more than me.'

'None of the players will earn more than the manager. We have some promising lads, but they're all part-timers here. Will be until they get into the league. However, they're on a big bonus if we get into the Vauxhall

45

Conference at the end of next season, and so will you be, Vic. We believe in payment by results here.'

A few minutes later it was settled. Kemp conceded what it was not within his powers to deny, that Knowles could keep the fees from any radio and television interviews he was asked to do during the season. They wouldn't bring in much, but the man still had delusions of grandeur. Kemp didn't mind that; they could still be useful equipment in a business which lived on the dreams of supporters. He had the big-name manager he needed to put Oldford FC still more firmly upon the map.

It was not until the deal was agreed that Knowles raised his single, faint, moral scruple. 'What about Trevor Jameson?'

Jameson was the existing manager, the one who would have to step aside to make way for Knowles, an honest, anxious man with a flair for football coaching and none for words. 'Leave him to me, Vic. He's on the Costa del Sol at the moment, I believe. Shame to spoil his holiday; I'll see him when he gets back. He's almost at the end of his contract, anyway.'

Kemp saw Knowles to the door, then watched from the window of the landing outside as the new manager of Oldford FC drove away his Sierra from the almost deserted ground. Then he went back into the hospitality suite and locked away the bottle. He sat for a moment in the big armchair he had occupied for the interview, turning his glass of whisky through his fingers with satisfaction. He had got his man, and cheaper than he had expected. Research, they called it on the telly. Well, he had researched his man; and it had paid off again.

He began to think of the wording of the press release. He thought he would break the news to them before local radio. It was always good to have the newshawks under an obligation. At this hour of the day and in the close season, this place was blessedly quiet, and he enjoyed that.

He was not quite sure how long he had been sitting there when John Castle came into the room, carrying with him an air of subdued satisfaction. 'I'm glad you're still here,

46

Mr Kemp. The police want to see you.' The Secretary enjoyed that involuntary slight stiffening which the word induced in his Chairman.

'If it's about the arrangements for policing our matches next season, I've already told you: you deal with all that, within the budget we've allocated.'

'No, it's not about that. It's top brass, I think. A Super-intendent Lambert. He wants to see you about a murder near the ground last night. A strangling, I believe it was.'

Castle permitted himself the small insolence of a long look at the Chairman's powerful hands.

CHAPTER 6

Vic Knowles did not drive far before he stopped the Sierra. He had set off with no idea where the car was heading, anxious just to get away from the ground. As soon as the floodlights of the Oldford Football Club stadium were out of sight, he stopped the car and put his head in his hands.

His mind raced with a variety of emotions, not all of which he understood. He was glad to be employed again in football. It was the only thing he knew well, and with all his faults he loved his sport. It was still for him the 'beautiful game'; it was still the sport which stirred him, when he witnessed the 'total football' of the Dutch, or the Brazilians' instinctive brilliance and improvisation.

And he still felt himself capable of managing well; he had brought out the best in hardened professionals, he had spotted and developed young talent in the years which were now behind him, and he could do it again. His pulses quick-ened at the thought, as they had done each time he took on a new job over the years. He had the gambler's optimism that each new venture would bring a great success, as well as the gambler's lack of self-knowledge and refusal to con-front unpleasant reality.

Normally, he would have savoured his new post, wanted to stay near the ground which was to be the physical setting for the triumphs which might lie ahead. Yet this time he had driven himself quickly away from any sight of the ground. He had been overwhelmed by the wish to put distance between himself and Kemp, to remove himself while there was still time from the man he was already aware was going to control him.

He felt the meshes of Kemp's net closing already about him. How much did the man know? He had been shaken by that sudden shaft about his gambling debts. Knowles had the feeling that his new Chairman knew everything. Kemp would have been delighted: that was the very impression he had wished to create. Knowles felt as if he was even now under observation, though his reason told him that the notion was absurd.

Perhaps he should not take the job, after all. There was nothing signed. But he had agreed it now with Charlie Kemp, who was not a man to cross. Besides, he needed the money, desperately. He didn't think Kemp had even half-believed that stuff about other offers he was considering. The man seemed to know his every secret. Perhaps he knew he had been in Oldford last night. Perhaps Kemp even knew what he had done last night.

Paranoia crept into the warm car and settled around Victor Knowles.

'Feeling a little under the weather, are we, sir?'

He started violently at the words, snatching his hands from his face. He was so dazzled by the sudden sun that his head swam a little, and he could not immediately focus either his eyes or his mind. It took him a moment to register the dark uniform and the black and white hat; the policeman was in shirt-sleeve order because of the heat, but his tie as he stooped dangled through the open driver's window and almost touched Knowles.

'I'm—I'm all right.' Knowles looked nervously around him; in his distress, he had not worried where he parked. He could see no yellow lines, and he was not near a junction.

The policeman nodded briefly to his left, and his colleague came over from the patrol car to join him. There was a smell of whisky from the driver: perhaps he had been sleeping it off. 'Is this your car, sir?'

'Yes. I'm Vic Knowles.' Once that name had carried weight; now the policeman looked impassive, and Knowles added, more nervously than he had intended, 'The football manager.' It was on the tip of his tongue to say that he had just taken on the managership of Oldford, but he remembered just in time that it was all still secret and unofficial, that he had agreed with Kemp to say nothing until his predecessor had been safely dismissed.

'Could you give me the number of your vehicle, please, sir?'

Knowles frowned, smiled weakly, felt very stupid. 'I never do know the number of my own car. I know there's a five in it, and it's a G registration.' He remembered that, because it grated: once he had had a car with the current registration letter provided free for him every year. He was dimly aware of the second policeman walking slowly round the car, looking at the tyres, examining with interest the small dent in the rear wing and the wisps of dried grass trapped at the extremity of his front bumper. 'I haven't had this car very long, you see.'

'Yes, I do see, sir. Do you happen to have the registration documents for it?'

'Not here, no. I thought—'

'Driving licence? Insurance?'

'No. I don't think so.'

'Well, you can produce them at your nearest police station within five days, if that should be necessary.' The policeman looked at him for a few seconds, assessing his condition, then nodded again to his companion. 'We'll have to ask you to take a breath test, I'm afraid, sir.'

'But look, I haven't drunk much at all. I—'

'Then you won't have any trouble with this, sir. Just an even breath. I expect you've seen these things before.'

The policeman's deliberately unemotional tones unnerved him more than outright aggression would have done. He stood beside the car and blew into the bag, filled with a sudden, irrational fear. Were these officers in Kemp's

49

pocket? Had the man dosed him with drink and sent them after him on some sadistic whim? Knowles was sure he hadn't drunk much in the hospitality suite, but you never knew how much you were taking when spirits were poured from a bottle. And he'd had quite a bit last night, both before and after. Didn't they say it could linger in your bloodstream until the next day?

He was dimly aware of the other policeman using his radio behind the car; the metallic, distorted sounds which came back through it scarcely sounded like words. When he had last done this, there had been crystals in the plastic container. Now, there were lights on the outside of the cylinder: it seemed more final, more damning. But the red light did not come on. He stared at it for a moment, as if he feared it would come on when he relaxed. Then he tried to breathe more easily, even attempted a truculent little smile, trying to see the outcome as a triumph of the individual over police persecution.

The officer was as carefully impassive as he had been throughout. If he was disappointed at this result, he showed no sign of it. 'That's all right then, sir, as far as that goes. But you aren't very much below the limit. We usually point out to people in these circumstances that it really is better not to drink at all if you're going to drive.'

Knowles brought out his most dignified vocabulary and bearing, what he thought of as his collar and tie mode. 'I appreciate your concern, Officer. And of course you have a job to do. But now that we're agreed that I have broken no law, I think it's time—'

'I've been instructed to ask you to accompany us to the station, Mr Knowles.' This was from the other policeman, coming suddenly into his vision from behind the car.

Knowles, who had been concentrating his pompous efforts upon the officer with the breathalyser, was thrown off key by this development. 'But you've just said I'm within the limit. What the hell—'

'It's not in connection with any motoring offence, sir.'

For a moment Knowles toyed with the wild impulse of driving off at speed, leaving the two policemen to gaze after him and make what they could of it. Then words from his childhood which he thought he had long since forgotten came back to him. And with the words, a picture; a picture of a father, dead now for ten years and more. 'Never fight the police, Victor,' he had said to a round-eyed boy in short trousers. 'The police and the Army are too big to fight, even if you think you're in the right.'

He realized with surprise that it was a precept he had always observed. 'Then what on earth do you want with an innocent citizen?' he said. He was sitting in the driver's seat again now; it was difficult to draw himself up to his full height and give the question dignity when the law was towering above him.

'There was a serious crime committed in this area last night, sir. Not half a mile from here. Your car is one of a number known to have been in the district at the time of the crime. The registration number is recorded at the station.'

PC Rogers was slow and methodical in his speech, like a patient uncle instructing a child in the complexities of adult life. Yet he could not have been more than twenty-two, and Knowles felt insulted by his ponderous delivery. 'I had nothing to do with your damned crime.'

'No one has accused you, sir. If what you say is true, we shall still need to eliminate you from our inquiries.'

He was reciting a formula, and they both knew it, but that did not lessen Knowles's irritation as they proceeded with the exchange. 'Are you arresting me?'

'Certainly not, sir. You would merely be helping us with our inquiries into a serious crime.'

Knowles, hearing the last of the necessary clichés, began to wonder how much they really knew about his movements on the previous evening. He said as firmly as he could, 'And of course I'm only too anxious to give you all the assistance I can.'

Rogers noticed that this man had not once asked them about the nature of the serious crime they had mentioned. Odd, that.

*

By the time he had waited ten minutes in the CID section at Oldford, Vic Knowles had recovered enough of his composure to be rather more aggressive.

DI Rushton was younger than him by a few years. He had not a grey hair in sight. And he had kept himself in better condition: that was always an irritating thing for an athlete to contemplate. Knowles said, hoping to establish immediately the goalposts for this exchange, 'Are you in charge of this case, then?'

Rushton's brown eyes regarded him coolly for an instant before he said, 'No. I keep an overview of the material we're collecting, and organize the documentation. Superintendent Lambert is in overall charge of the investigation.'

Knowles riffled through his knowledge of television crime to decide how exalted these ranks were. He let a little edge of sarcasm creep into his voice as he said, 'A Super in charge: this is big stuff, then.'

'It's murder, sir.' If Rushton enjoyed the little frisson of apprehension the revelation brought, he gave no sign of it. 'The autopsy has now established that officially.'

Knowles felt himself already fretting in the face of the Inspector's calmness. How could these men be so matter-of-fact about the ultimate crime? 'And what connection do you think I have with the crime of murder?' He tried to be as calm as the man opposite him, but he felt the slight tremble which came into his voice on his mention of the word.

'I very much hope no connection at all, sir. Perhaps you will be able to demonstrate that to our satisfaction in the next few minutes.' Rushton's steady brown eyes had never left Knowles's mobile face since he had come into the interview room.

Knowles thought: He's enjoying this, the bastard; enjoying having me on the spot; enjoying the fact that he knows more than I do about the present state of the case; enjoying watching me trying to pick my way through this marsh without falling off the path.

Rushton said, 'The DVLC computer gives your name as the owner of the red Sierra you were driving today. It also gives your address as Sutton Coldfield. Is that correct?'

'Yes.'

'But you were in this area both last night and today. Did you stay in Oldford last night?'

'Yes.'

'And what was the purpose of your visit to the town?'

Knowles glimpsed at last the possibility of a little prestige in a situation which had seemed hitherto to have been designed to humiliate him. He leaned forward a little towards the impassive young face on the other side of the table. 'This must be in confidence for the moment, Inspector, but I'm expecting to be confirmed as the new manager of Oldford Football Club in the next couple of weeks.'

The brown eyes widened a little; the rest of the long face remained impassive. A cold fish, this Rushton. 'I see. I thought Trevor Jameson was the Manager.'

Damn! Just his luck to get a soccer fan. 'He is, but not for much longer, I'm afraid.'

'I see. I didn't know that. Mr Jameson is a neighbour of mine.' Rushton allowed his distaste to overlay the simple statement of fact.

Things were going from bad to worse. 'Look. Perhaps I've said more than I should have done. But you asked me why I was here, you see, and I was trying to be helpful. Between you and me, I don't think Trevor knows much about it yet, but that's the way it is in football. I saw Mr Kemp this afternoon—'

'Charlie Kemp?'

'Yes. The Chairman of the club. I had an appointment, you see.' Knowles's fingers stretched up to the thin gold chain beneath his open-necked shirt, twisted it for a moment, then dropped away as he saw the Inspector's eyes upon them.

'Yes, I see, Mr Knowles. What I don't see is why you were in the region of the ground at midnight last night, when your appointment was for this afternoon.'

Rushton, beneath his careful politeness, was enjoying Knowles's discomfort, and both of them realized it. 'I— well, I thought I'd come and look at the set-up here. I had a look round the club, saw how prosperous it was, and—'

'Did you go into the *Roosters* Club?'

'No.'

'Why not, Mr Knowles? That would have given you an even better view of the "set-up", wouldn't it?'

'Yes, but I didn't want Mr Kemp or some official of the club to see me. Didn't want them to think I was spying, you see.'

'Even though that was exactly the purpose of your visit.' Rushton permitted himself a small smile; the observant brown eyes creased a little at their corners.

Vic reached up and tugged at the tie which hung crookedly from his neck. 'Look, you asked me why I was here, and I've told you. It's normal practice, isn't it, to want to know what you're letting yourself in for when you're considering a new job? I was just doing it discreetly, that's all.'

'A wise precaution. Especially when Mr Jameson apparently doesn't even know that his job is at risk.' DI Rushton liked Trevor Jameson; and like the rest of the CID, he disliked Charlie Kemp, a crook who had so far been too elusive for them to pin down.

And he did not care for the man in front of him: Vic Knowles was 'flash', with his smooth suits and his glib phrases about the game. Rushton, who enjoyed his football, did not like the flash operators he saw more and more often within the professional game.

Knowles said, 'Look, I'm just trying to be as helpful as I can.'

'As is your duty as a good citizen, Mr Knowles. So give us an account of your movements last night.'

The tape turned silently beside them, but Knowles's eye had caught the young DC to the rear of the Inspector, with his pencil poised over his pad. He could not shake away the image of a chronicler of his sins, that recording angel that had been planted in his imagination by an earnest Sunday School teacher almost forty years ago.

'Well, I parked near the *Roosters* and watched the people going in.'

'Time?'

'I don't know. I didn't know I was going to be cross-examined about it today, did I?' Rushton gave him no more than the slightest of smiles. 'I suppose it was about half past nine. Look, if you could just give me the details of this crime, I'm sure I could—'

'In due course, perhaps, Mr Knowles. How long were you parked near the *Roosters*?'

'I told you: I can't be precise. I suppose it was about three-quarters of an hour. Maybe an hour, at the most. I had the radio on. I listened to the ten o'clock sports bulletin, and I was there for some time after that.' Knowles ran both hands abruptly through his lank hair, as if he could no longer keep control over them.

'And you watched people going in and out of the *Roosters*. Not a very exciting evening, for an active man like you.'

'That's my business. Are you saying you don't believe me?'

Rushton enjoyed ignoring this man's questions. 'And what did you do when you had completed your vigil of observation on Oldford Football Club, Mr Knowles?'

'I went back to my digs.'

'Where were you staying?'

'At the *White Lion*.'

It was a run-down pub on the edge of the town, which still kept a couple of cheap bed and breakfast rooms, used largely by reps who wanted to make a bit on their expenses.

It was not the location recorded for the red Sierra by the observant beat copper.

'So you were back there from about half past ten onwards?'

'Yes.'

'And you went quietly to bed? Not a very exciting evening for you.'

'I was tired. I had a couple of drinks before I went to bed.'

'Ah! That's useful; it means the landlord will be able to confirm your presence at the time you suggest.'

Knowles looked at him with a hatred that was suddenly

manifest. He had never troubled to dissemble his feelings when he talked to the footballers who had called him 'Boss' over the years, and he could not conceal his emotions now. 'No, he won't. I had a bottle in my room. I didn't know whether I'd be staying in licensed premises or not, you see, so I brought a bottle of whisky in my case. I nearly always do. I've learned over the years to be independent.'

He was talking too much now. Rushton let him run to a stop before he spoke. 'So there is no one who can confirm your story about the time when you returned to the *White Lion*. Unfortunate, that.'

'Look, I don't have to take this. I've a good mind to make a complaint—I came here of my own free will . . .'

He spoke like a man who expected to be interrupted, and Rushton deflated him by refusing to do so. He did not think this man would lodge any complaint, in view of what was still to come.

When Knowles ran out of bluster, he said, 'You have been told that your car was noted as one of the vehicles in the area where a murder was committed last night. It was noted by a constable on his beat at 11.15 p.m. And it was not in the car park of the *White Lion* hotel. It was quite near the spot where the body of a woman was found later in the night. A woman who had been strangled.'

For an instant, Knowles's eyes widened, and showed the bright red veining at the corners. Then he cast them down; a small pulse beat for a moment at the top of his right cheek, and he flicked at it with his fingers as if it had been a fly.

Rushton said, 'Are you telling us that someone else took your car while you were in your room at the *White Lion* and drove it to where it was seen?'

For a moment, it seemed that the lie would be attractive to Knowles. Then he shook his head sullenly. Rushton said, 'Do you wish to have a lawyer present for the rest of our exchange?'

He judged correctly that the suggestion would strike Vic Knowles only as a further threat. When the man had refused the offer, he said, 'I think it's time you gave us a full and proper account of what you did last night, Mr Knowles.'

There was a silence which seemed to Knowles to stretch interminably in the small room, though in fact it was no more than thirty seconds long. His irregular breathing seemed almost that of an asthmatic as his mind raced and he sought to control it. Eventually he said, 'I went to the *Roosters* as I told you. It might have been a bit later than I said; it was going dark.'

'What you are telling us now will form the basis of a statement which we shall ask you to sign, Mr Knowles. In your own interest, you should take care to be accurate. What happened next?'

'I—I wasn't there as long as I said. Perhaps quarter of an hour—I did hear the ten o'clock sports bulletin on the radio, as I said.' He produced this irrelevance as if he had a desperate idea that it might confirm his integrity. Then, as if he realized how futile it sounded, he said, 'But just after that, I picked a girl up.'

'Is that why you waited outside the club?'

Knowles nodded sullenly, twisting the cheap digital watch on his wrist. 'There's no law against it.'

'There are laws against both soliciting and kerb-crawling. Those laws are not my concern at the moment, but—'

'I knew the girl already, I'd seen her before.'

'What was her name?'

Knowles's broad shoulders dropped hopelessly. 'I don't know. I'd only seen her once before.'

'But you had arranged to meet her outside the *Roosters*.'

'No. Well, I had—Oh, I don't know.' Knowles dropped his eyes; they were unable to contend any longer against those relentless brown ones.

Rushton tried to keep his growing excitement out of his voice as he said, 'You went there to wait for her, then.'

'Yes.'

'But you didn't know her name. Was she a prostitute?'

There was another silence: it pained Knowles to admit,

as he knew he must, that he had been reduced to this. 'Yes, I suppose she was.'

'And you had intercourse with her last night? That was presumably your purpose in contacting her.'

'Yes.'

'At her place?'

'No. In the back of my car. It was cheaper that way.' For an instant his searing self-contempt came through the words.

'And where did this occur?' Rushton, who was having trouble with his own wife, was taking a ruthless satisfaction in the exposure of this shabby liaison.

Vic Knowles looked up at Rushton and the officer behind him for the first time in several minutes, and there was fear in those bloodshot eyes. 'I don't know. I don't know this town. I drove to where she told me. Somewhere quiet on the edge of the town, but it was dark, you see.'

'I see. Your car was recorded at just before eleven o'clock, just off the Gloucester road. Would this lady whose name you do not know have been with you at that time?'

He nodded hopelessly. 'The time sounds right. I've told you, I don't know where we were. I just drove to a quiet place, as she directed me.'

'How much did you give her?'

'Twenty pounds. I told you, it was cheaper in the car. So long as all you wanted was straightforward sex, and you didn't take too long over it.' Again his disgust with himself seemed too genuine for a man like him to simulate.

'We shall need a description of this woman.'

He gave them what he could. Young, seeming to him not much more than a girl. Dark hair, cut fairly short; red blouse; skirt navy or black; fishnet tights; a handbag—black, he thought. He was not even sure of the colour of her eyes. It sounded like the murdered girl: it could also be one of a dozen others. And that assumed, of course, that this man who had begun with a string of lies was now telling them the truth. *She had fair hair on page 15.*

Rushton said, 'And where did you drop your passenger off when this transaction was completed?'

58

'I didn't. She got out where—where we'd parked. She said she hadn't far to go and she needed some fresh air.' He could not find the phrases for the self-disgust he had known was in her as well as himself that they should be reduced to this breathless coupling on the back seat; nor the abrupt way she had flung open the door and set off down the road while he had still been struggling with his trousers round his ankles.

He remembered his sudden fury that she should need to be rid of him like that. But he could not tell them that. Not now.

Rushton and his DC were watching him intently, as he eventually realized when he was forced to look up at them. Rushton said, 'Did you follow her in the car?'

'No, of course I didn't. Why the hell do you think—'

'Did you kill the girl you were with last night, Mr Knowles?'

'No. No. Why in hell's name should you think—'

'A girl was found murdered within three hundred yards of where you say this girl left you last night. From your description, it could well have been the woman you say you were with.' Rushton eased his tall frame back in his chair for the first time, as if the better to study his man. 'You say she left you alone in your car. What did you do after that?'

Knowles's voice was very low as he said, 'I stayed where I was for a little while. Perhaps ten minutes, I don't know. Then I drove back towards the football club, until I found my bearings, and drove from there to the *White Lion*. The rest of what I told you earlier was true.'

Rushton waited, but Knowles volunteered nothing else. 'We shall need to examine your Sierra. It will take us a couple of hours, maybe more. I'll get a police car to run you back to your hotel, if you wish.'

Knowles was about to say that he had planned to drive straight back to the Midlands, that one night in the *White Lion* was quite enough. But he thought better of it, and merely nodded. All he wanted to do at the moment was to get out of this place, and gather his thoughts.

Rushton said, 'Do you live alone in Sutton Coldfield, Mr Knowles?'

'Yes. I've been divorced for three years now.'

'So there is no one at your address who could bear witness to your movements over the last few weeks?'

'No. Look, I've told you—'

'You told us a few minutes ago that you had already seen the girl you were with last night—the girl whose name you cannot remember—on a previous occasion. When was that?'

Knowles licked at lips which stayed obstinately dry. 'I came down to the ground when the team played a testimonial match at the end of May. The last match before they went off for the close season. I'd been sounded about taking on the manager's job and it was my only chance to see the ground and the players in action. Oldford was just a name to me, you see.' At this moment, he wished with all his heart that it still was.

'And when would this be, Mr Knowles?' Rushton thought he already knew, but he was determined to keep Knowles under pressure, and vulnerable.

'It was about a fortnight ago. A Wednesday night.'

'And you first picked up this girl on that night?'

'After the match and a drink, yes.'

'That match was on the evening of 25th May.'

'If you say so.'

'Mr Knowles, what do you know about a girl called Julie Salmon?'

'I don't know anything, I've never heard of the girl. Why are you asking me this?'

'Julie Salmon was raped and strangled on the night of 25th May. The last night when you were in this area. Until last night, that is, when another girl was killed in an identical way.'

CHAPTER 7

Crimes like the Oldford stranglings tend to bring together groups of people who normally find themselves on opposing sides.

The few known prostitutes of the area were brought into the police station to be briefed by Detective-Inspector Susan Wild on the need for care in their movements. It was a strange meeting. DI Wild set up a little half-circle of folding wooden chairs and sat on one herself in front of the women, trying to make the set-up as informal as possible. Coffee was served in cups and saucers by a WPC who did not quite know what her attitude should be to the recipients as she handed round the biscuits. Everything possible was done to make these unusual visitors to the station feel at ease.

It did not work. DI Wild wore the two-piece suit which was her normal plain clothes wear in her office and the CID section. The women wore the leather and plastic, the heavy make-up, the tight, short skirts and fishnet stockings which amounted to the uniform of their trade. These were the known prostitutes, and they were as contemptuous of amateurs as were other professions. The housewives who picked up a little pin-money and disguised the fact beneath respectable clothes were both despised and resented by women who saw them as a threat to their living.

Some of these women were no longer young; there was a high proportion of blondes among them, few of whom were natural; in their normal locations, they watched each other suspiciously, jealous of their own territories and any intrusions upon them. But they assumed a common form of dress, and in the face of this police initiative they presented a united front of suspicion and cynicism.

'We know about the killings, of course we do,' said a thirty-year-old who had dropped into the role of their spokesperson. 'What we want to know is what you're going to do to protect us.' She gazed at Inspector Wild with unblinking blue eyes from behind her contact lenses.

'We're doing everything we can, of course, Barbara. You'll get the same degree of protection as any other citizens.'

It was a mistake. There were grins around the group as Barbara said, 'Oh, thank you very much, ma'am. Toms get the same degree of protection as if they were human beings now. Very enlightened, that.' She picked up her cup and sipped delicately with her little finger elaborately crooked, as the others tittered at her daring.

'You know what I mean. As far as our resources go, we'll look after you.' Susan Wild tried hard not to get annoyed with the group: she had had to sandwich this meeting into the middle of a busy day. 'But it's up to you to cooperate with us. You must help yourselves.'

'And how do we do that, pray?' It had been a man who decided that the only female DI in CID should meet this all-female audience, of course. It was a mistake: these women were used to dealing with men, confident with them because they had a wide experience of their weaknesses. They treated the male police with a robust, impersonal distaste which was half way to an understanding. This woman seemed by her very appearance to condemn them, to give off vibrations of disgust for those members of her sex who should choose to make a living as they did.

'All I'm saying is that you should be careful. Don't go into isolated places at night. Don't go with men you don't know.'

The little semi-circle in front of her grinned sardonically at one another. One of them said, 'Tell her, Barbara.' They enjoyed this rare feeling of superiority to a respectable member of the establishment which so regularly pursued them.

The blue-eyed woman said, 'Listen, dear. We make our living by going with men. And most of them don't like doing it with an audience. Bashful creatures, men are. But perhaps you wouldn't know about that.' She let her eyes rest for a moment on the sensible, low-heeled shoes in front of her, then moved her gaze slowly up the strong, nylon-sheathed calves, over the hem of the grey skirt, up as far as the Inspectorial groin, where it stayed.

DI Wild tried not to notice—managed it, indeed, better than most people would have done. The modern police force has much experience of coping with dumb insolence. She stared at the darker roots beneath the light blonde hair and said, 'I know you make your livings by going with men. Soliciting is against the law of the land, but it is also a fact of life. But it is my duty to warn you that you may put yourselves in grave danger by doing so.'

Her careful impassivity made more of an impression than anger. They were quietened by the manner rather than the substance of her words. They muttered contemptuously that women like them had a fat chance of keeping away from men as they filed out, but despite their blasé shrug-gings, they carried a little fear away from the room with them.

And that, in truth, was as much as could be expected. Most of them were not in a position to opt out of their trade at short notice. But the forms had been observed: the Chief Constable was covered, as he had intended when he ordered this meeting. If there were subsequent killings, the press could be assured that all the known prostitutes of the area had been warned about the danger which threatened them.

Amy Coleford had not been called to the briefing at Oldford Police Station. She read the terse press release about the killings in the newspapers and the more lurid speculations of the journalists who sought to develop the story, using the timeworn principles that sex and violence sell newspapers.

Her children were at school; she was able to scare herself with the pronouncements of her older neighbour about the killings as they pegged out their washing and called to each other across the ragged hedge. 'They should string him up when they get him,' said Mrs Price. 'If them that made the law was women, we'd have the buggers hanged, instead of locked up for a few years and then let out to rape us all.'

She shook her head with a thrill of delicious horror at the thought of this mass violation.

'I expect they'll get him, eventually,' said Amy. She realized she was seeking the reassurance of her neighbour's agreement on this.

'How many more women will be torn apart before that happens? That's what I'd like to know,' said Mrs Price, folding her arms as if she was delivering the challenge in person. She was a squat woman of thirty-seven who looked rather older, square of face and resolute in her conventional opinions. All mass murderers were vaguely linked in her mind with the Yorkshire Ripper, about whom she had read every word she could find. There were only two Oldford murders so far, but she was hoping, half unconsciously, for the abattoir glamour that a serial killer might bring to the locality.

She had had her two children when she was young, and they were in their late teens now. Since both of them were boys, she had no qualms about their safety amid the present happenings, though she had little idea of where they got to when they went out. She was secretly amazed by how much Amy paid her to baby-sit in the evenings; she was surprisingly and instinctively competent with the two girls of four and five, and she enjoyed the hours in front of the telly when she had got them off to bed.

She had almost ceased to wonder where Amy got to when she was out, or why she needed to go out so often.

Amy was relieved that her neighbour was so incurious. When Harry had first left her with the kids, she had been at her wits' end. And the maintenance had soon ceased arriving; no one seemed to know or care where Harry was now. It was a mercy that she had kept her looks: otherwise she could never have supported her kids. They would have been taken into care, instead of being well clothed and cared for. She was saving the state expense, as well as keeping her independence and the children she loved.

She was amazed by how easy it was to make money from men, if you had the looks. When Harry had first walked out, she had tried typing envelopes at home, but it hadn't even brought in enough to clothe the children. Now, for a few hours' work on a couple of evenings, she could do all that and more. And most of the men weren't unkind, though sometimes you had to turn your face to the wall and just think of the money. They were like children really, most of them: they liked you to show them the way.

She'd heard that some of the men you picked up could be quite rough, but she hadn't met much of that yet. She didn't think of herself as on the game: it still surprised her that she could get money for this, though she had grown used now to asking for it at the outset. Most of the men seemed to like to kid themselves that she wasn't really a hardened woman, so it worked out quite well, really.

One or two of them had even said that they loved her after it was over, that they would like to take her away from all this. They all said 'from all this', though none of them knew anything of her real life. But they didn't seem to be ones she particularly liked. Perhaps one day, when she'd solved her problems and looked after her children, she would start again properly with some man; a man who wouldn't have to pay her for it.

Meanwhile, the money came plentifully and easily. Almost without her noticing it, the couple of nights a week had become three, and then four.

CHAPTER 8

Charles Kemp was not at all put out by the news that the police wanted to talk to him.

He had recognized it as inevitable, once the news of the death of Hetty Brown became public. He was glad that they chose to meet him on his own ground. At Oldford Football Club he was king, just as much as he was among his hirelings in the less public world of his business enterprises.

When the club secretary, Castle, announced that Super-intendent Lambert and Sergeant Hook had arrived to see him, he took them into the hospitality suite and waved his hand expansively at the armchairs which were occupied on winter Saturdays by the ample posteriors of visiting directors.

Lambert looked round before accepting the offer, but no more formal seating was available. He nodded his acceptance without a smile. Kemp, determinedly affable, said, 'Can I offer you drinks, or is the old rule about being on duty still in force?' He spread his hands a little, his whole attitude saying, 'I am one of those who refuse to be bound in by bureaucracy, but I am understanding of those who are not such free spirits as I am.'

Kemp knew Lambert was the most dangerous kind of copper, shrewd and tough beneath the quiet exterior. But he also knew that when they had tangled before, he had defeated him.

Lambert said, 'Mr Castle offered us tea on the way in, and we were happy to accept his offer.' He sat down in the ample leather club chair, nodding to Hook, who took this as a cue to produce his notebook in his most formal manner. As he did so, a woman of about forty, presumably Castle's assistant, brought in a tray with a china teapot, matching cups and saucers, and a plate of ginger biscuits. Hook laid down his notebook as she left, and poured the tea and milk with the elaborate care of a large man, as though he feared that he might break the crockery if he did not apply his greatest concentration.

'Well, gentlemen, I am at your service, anxious only to help the police in the pursuit of their investigations,' said Kemp, when neither of his visitors showed any inclination to speak.

'Just as you were two years ago,' said Lambert, stirring his tea. He looked at Kemp with a distaste he did not trouble to disguise. It had been a serious business: GBH and a man crippled for life. But as usual they had not been able to assemble enough evidence to persuade the Crown Prosecutor to go for this man.

'Water under the bridge, John. I bear you no ill will for your mistaken allegations at the time.' Kemp's smile might not extend to his eyes, but he was pleased with the way he produced the bland, half-mocking tone he remembered from television villains. He flicked his glance to the Sergeant. He had not met Hook before, but there could be little to fear in this slightly overweight and pink-cheeked time-server.

Lambert could see the victim of that assault in his mind's eye now, depressed and bitter, sitting with a rug over his knees to hide his broken thigh, dependent on social security and the inadequate sum tardily provided by the Criminal Injuries Compensation Board. Better, as the lawyers said as they pocketed their fees, to be libelled than battered; more lucrative as well as less painful.

He told himself he must be objective with Kemp, must follow the old policeman's precept of addressing the case in hand. He said, 'Did you know a woman called Harriet Brown?'

'I might have.' Kemp was suddenly cautious: he had not thought they would be so direct.

'I presume that means you did. She was in and out of your club on most evenings, it seems.'

'Not my club, John, more's the pity. The *Roosters* is the football club's concern. And a lucrative one, I'm glad to say.'

Lambert wondered how Kemp knew his Christian name; it fell from his lips like an insult each time he used it. 'So you knew her.'

Kemp's mind was working fast beneath his calm, wondering just how much they knew. 'Know her would be putting it rather strongly, John.'

'I didn't mean in the biblical sense, Kemp.'

Kemp did not quite understand this. And like most people afraid to admit to ignorance, he moved the conversation on quickly, revealing more than he had intended. 'I like to have a drink in the *Roosters* at night. Keeps me in touch with the supporters. Everyone round here knows Charlie Kemp. You know I have never attempted to be anything but a man of the people, John.'

Lambert decided that he always distrusted men who

67

proclaimed themselves men of the people: to have any validity, the description had to come from others. He looked round the plush hospitality room, wanting to ask Kemp how often the terraces supporters got into here, deciding he must not be tempted. 'So you drink with them. And you drank with Harriet Brown.'

'Very probably. I try to move around to different groups. Show the flag for the club. I'm not very good on names—never have been. But it's very probable that—'

'How well did you know Hetty Brown?' The interjection came like a missile, not from Lambert but from Bert Hook, more furious about the baiting of his chief than Lambert was himself.

Though he employed violent men to pursue his business, Kemp was ruffled when he met even the hint of violence to himself. He said, 'All right, I knew her. What of it?'

Hook knew his Superintendent too well even to look at him now. 'How well did you know her?'

'Look, I'm helping you of my own free will. And I can't say I like your tone. If—'

'Our information is that she was taken into this room with you. That she spent time alone in here with you. On more than one occasion.'

Lambert had planned this differently; he would have withheld the extent of their knowledge for longer, letting Kemp trap himself in a web of his own evasions and then embarrassing him. But Hook's instinct to attack was right. Kemp was shaken. His mind was racing with a string of conjectures about how they had come to know so much, and it was not able to come up with answers. He had always thought he knew more about the clumsy manœuvres of the police than they knew about him, and he was shaken to find that on this occasion he was wrong.

'Hetty did come in here. It's not against the law.'

'No. But you weren't going to tell us that. And now she's dead. It makes us wonder why you wished to conceal your relationship with her.' The positions were suddenly reversed; now it was Lambert who was baiting the man who had felt secure enough to taunt him at the outset.

'I didn't conceal—'

'Come on!' Hook's outrage came out in the shout, which seemed to echo round that quiet, oak-panelled room. 'You were pretending just now that you weren't even certain that you knew her.'

'All right. She came in here. Look, I don't like your attitude—'

'Would you prefer that we had this conversation at the station? With your lawyer present, of course, if you would like that. It seems that might only be prudent, now that you're in the middle of a murder investigation.' Lambert did not trouble to disguise his satisfaction in the thought. They were not on tape yet; Kemp was merely helping them voluntarily with their inquiries. As a responsible member of the public should.

Kemp stood up now, walking over to where the single long, high window gave a limited view of the pitch outside. They watched his barrel-like torso inflating and deflating as he strove to control his breathing. The Chairman wished suddenly that he was not alone, that he had the reassurance of the brains he employed in different sections of his enterprises at his side. Even the two gorillas who were his muscle would have been a reassurance: even the wife he despised would have reminded these hunters of his respectable side. For he thought of himself now as the quarry of these men. They had scores to settle from the past, and he felt unusually isolated.

He tried as he turned back to them to be conciliatory. 'Look, she was on the game. You know that now, and I knew it then.'

'So are you saying you had her in here to warn her about bringing that into the club?'

For a moment he was tempted. Then he said, 'No. I had sex with her, and paid her for it. That was all.'

'On how many occasions?' Hook's voice was for the first time unemotional; he held his pen expectantly above the pad.

'Two, maybe three. Look, there won't be any need to—'

'Was she in here last night?'

69

'No.'

'Did you kill Harriet Brown, Mr Kemp?'

'No. Of course I—'

'Have you any idea who did?'

'No. How could I have?'

'Because you keep in touch with the punters here. Because you're a man of the people, priding yourself on your knowledge of what goes on in the *Roosters*. You told us so yourself.'

Kemp acknowledged with a sullen nod that he had claimed as much. 'All right. That doesn't mean I killed a cheap little tart. Or that I know who did.'

'Did you see her in the club last night?'

'I might have.' Something in Lambert's eye must have warned him of the danger of such phrases, for he said hastily, 'All right. I remember now, I did see her. I suppose it was about nine. I didn't speak to her, though. I challenge you to find someone who says I did.'

Lambert said, 'And who was she with at the time?' It was a habit of his to cloak the most important questions in his most neutral tone.

'I don't remember all of them. But she was in a group of six or eight, on one of the round tables, nearer to the end of the room where the bar is.'

It tallied with the information they already had. So far. 'Was she drinking much?'

'No more than usual. Hetty wasn't a drinker. She'd have one to loosen her up, perhaps another one later. But mostly she drank orange.'

For a man who had claimed he was not certain that he even knew the girl a quarter of an hour ago, this was an admission of detailed knowledge. But there was no point in rubbing it in now. Lambert was anxious not to blow the cover of their source of information, a young officer from the drugs squad who spent most of his nights now at the club, trying to find the big men behind the pushers of coke and heroin whom he had already identified.

'Did you meet Hetty Brown later in the evening?'

'No. Why the hell should—'

70

'The girl was murdered within four hours of when you last saw her in the club. You are among the last people to see her alive. Naturally we are interested in your movements during the rest of that evening.'

Kemp said, 'I didn't see her again after I saw her at that table.'

Lambert stood up, his eyes a good six inches above those of the stockier man, but no more than three feet away; Kemp had not resumed his seat after he had walked so abruptly to the window. 'Our information is that she left the club because she had an arrangement to meet a man. Presumably not far away, since she had no transport of her own; so quite possibly in the club car park. You're telling us that that man wasn't you?'

'No. I was up here.'

'Alone.'

'Yes.' There was just enough hesitation before the word to suggest to them that he was deciding to lie.

'Do you know who it was that she met?'

'No.'

'Can you provide us with any suggestions? It would be in your own interests to do so.'

'No.'

'We shall need details of the rest of your movements during the evening.'

Kemp's face was creased with hostility now; there could scarcely have been a greater contrast to the contrived urbanity with which he had begun the interview. 'I had a drink downstairs. I came up here then.'

'Time?' Hook contrived to sound as though he expected a lie.

'About half past nine, quarter to ten, I suppose.'

'You say you were on your own up here?'

Again there was that momentary hesitation. 'Yes.'

'For how long?'

'Perhaps a couple of hours. About that.'

'And what were you doing?'

'Paperwork.' None of the three men in the room thought it was true, but Hook wrote it down.

71

'Did you have any more to drink?'

'A whisky, I think.'

'So the bar staff could probably confirm your presence here, some time after Hetty Brown had left.'

'No. I have my own bottle up here.

'Gents?'

Kemp shook his head. 'Not downstairs. There's one up here, if I need it. But I drink my whisky neat.' For a moment, the functioning of his bladder seemed to be more important to him than murder.

'What then?'

'I left the club.'

'Alone?'

'Yes. I've told you.' He hadn't, but they let that pass.

'And where did you go then?'

He must have been as aware as they were that this was about the time of the killing. 'I went home.'

'And arrived there when?'

'I couldn't be sure. Some time around midnight, I suppose.'

'So your wife could confirm the time, presumably.'

'No. She was in bed and asleep when I arrived.'

'And you didn't disturb her, of course.' Lambert allowed his cynicism free rein.

'No. We have separate bedrooms. Not that that's any business of yours.'

The two men were still facing each other, not a yard apart. Hook, who was recording the detail of Kemp's replies below them, thought they were like prize-fighters squaring up to one another. Lambert looked abruptly down at the feet that were so near to his own. They were in good shoes, fashioned in better leather than his own. 'What size of shoe do you take?'

'Tens. What's that to you?'

'The Scene of Crime team found the imprint of a shoe near Hetty Brown's body. Size nine and a half or ten, they thought: I had to get them to translate these new-fangled continental sizes for me. A city shoe, by the look of the sole, they said.' He looked down at Kemp's traditional Oxford leather shoes with considerable satisfaction.

Kemp said, 'It might not have been the murderer's shoe. There could have been lots of footmarks in the clay round there.'

'Know exactly where she was found then, do you? Interesting, that; especially as we haven't released any of the details yet.'

They could almost hear Kemp's mind working in the pause which followed. 'I—I heard where she died. On that building site, wasn't it? You can't hush these things up. It's been all round the club today.'

It was Lambert's turn to pause, pretending to weigh this and find it unconvincing. Eventually he said quietly, 'Did you know a girl called Julie Salmon, Mr Kemp?' Though Hook had used it once before, it was the first time Lambert had afforded Kemp the title, and it fell from his lips with the irony of insult, much as his own Christian name had been dropped by his opponent earlier in their exchanges.

'The girl who was killed a fortnight ago? She used to come in here, yes. You're not trying to pin that one on me, surely?' The sense of outrage he wanted did not come through in the words, but his fear did.

'We may need an account of your movements on the night she died, Mr Kemp.' They had already checked before they came here, but it would be useful to know if he thought it necessary to lie. There had been a meeting of Oldford FC Committee in the earlier part of the evening, but no one knew accurately when Julie Salmon had died, because she had not been found for two days.

Bert Hook stood up at a nod from Lambert. 'The forensic team will need to go over this place, and perhaps your office as well, to see if there are fibres from Harriet Brown's clothing present.'

'If you're going to start on police persecution, perhaps—'

'And of course, when we have the report on the clothing Miss Brown wore on the night of her death, we may need to check your wardrobe for any fibres that tally. We tend to be both meticulous and persistent when murder is the

73

crime. And the magistrates tend to be sympathetic to our efforts when it comes to search warrants. No doubt you will let us know if you plan to move out of the area.' Lambert turned abruptly on his heel and was gone, without waiting for any reply.

Kemp poured himself one of his neat whiskies when he was sure they had left, feeling the therapeutic effect of its warm fire as it coursed into his system. Then he went into his office, looked up a number in the notebook in the top drawer of his desk, and tapped out the numbers carefully on the phone.

'The police have been here. About Hetty Brown. They wanted to know about what I did last night. I told them I was in the hospitality room, on my own. They didn't believe me, but that's the story at the moment. If they try to pin it on me, you may need to tell them you were here with me. For the moment, keep quiet about it.'

CHAPTER 9

Back at the Murder Room, Lambert found Don Haworth, the police surgeon. He had called in to check the latest progress on the case. Lambert was pleased to find a busy medic so interested in their work, particularly as Haworth, unlike Cyril Burgess, the pathologist, had no interest in lurid detective fiction.

'No luck with Julie Salmon's boyfriend, I believe,' said Haworth.

'Darren Pickering? Afraid not. Mind you, he's been in trouble with the uniformed boys before, and there was no way he was going to be easily intimidated,' said Lambert. 'He had the duty solicitor there all the time we questioned him, and of course that helpful gentleman kept telling him not to answer leading questions.'

Pickering, a powerful young man with a shaven head and a small earring, had been the boyfriend of Julie Salmon, the first girl killed. Or rather the former boyfriend, since she had broken with him two weeks before her death. No one, least of all Pickering, seemed certain how permanent a break it had been. He had been in a highly emotional state when they had brought him in for questioning, but that might have stemmed from shock or genuine grief at her death as easily as from fear.

'Didn't the search of his room throw up anything?'

Lambert wondered suddenly if Haworth would be interested in Burgess's job when the old boy retired: he couldn't have more than a couple of years to go now. He would welcome this bright, cooperative young man who seemed so interested in their investigations. Maybe, with a failed marriage behind him, he wanted to immerse himself in his work. If so, he deserved every encouragement. 'We found lots of things to connect him with Julie Salmon, as you'd expect, but nothing to identify him definitely with the killing. We've sent some of his hairs off for a DNA test to compare with the sperm sample from Julie Salmon, but we won't have the results for a day or two.'

'What about the second murder?'

'Pickering has no clear alibi for the time of the murder —between twelve and one, you thought—but then lots of innocent people wouldn't have.'

Haworth grinned. 'Don't hold me to that time. As I said, it was informed speculation rather than an authoritative estimate. Have you got anyone else in the frame?'

It was Lambert's turn to smile, at the doctor's adoption of the police jargon. 'One or two possibilities. Nothing more.' He did not want to discuss Charlie Kemp with outsiders at this stage. 'It looks as though our man might be someone who frequents the *Roosters* social club, but that gives us a big field. It's a pity from our point of view that the place is so successful.'

'I pop in there from time to time myself, you know. I'm the official team doctor, though they have a physio who does a lot more than I do. It's the close season, now, but I still use the club in the evenings sometimes. One advantage of being single is that you can follow your interests, and I've always been a football nut.'

75

'Do you come across Charlie Kemp much?' Lambert changed his mind and thought that another perspective might be useful.

'Not a lot. He poses as an amiable tycoon, a likeable rogue who's been lucky enough to make a bob or two. But I should think he could be pretty ruthless if you got on the wrong side of him. The players certainly think so. I'm glad I don't have to work for him, anyway.'

An opinion which would be shared by all right-thinking men, thought Lambert.

Darren Pickering would have been pleased to hear that the police had so far found nothing to incriminate him. But no one had told him that.

He did not like the police, and they did not much like him. He was not the kind of figure which authority finds attractive. He was a large youth, much given to the wearing of T-shirts just too small to contain his heavily muscled torso without tight stretching. He considered his closely shaven head and his single earring part of a uniform of aggression, but he showed his independence by eschewing the tattoos which many of his Saturday-afternoon football companions affected.

His massive forearms looked curiously naked as he folded them across his chest and stared glumly at his pint of special. The *Roosters* was filling up nicely: he didn't like it too quiet. He stretched forward his legs in the tight jeans, wondering as he studied them whether their newness was a little too apparent, whether a little staining, perhaps a couple of small slits around the knees, might produce the effect he thought appropriate. The jeans looked to him a little too pristine above the well-worn blue and white trainers on his size ten feet.

His companion said, 'Leave them alone, Darren. They'll get sullied soon enough when we have a rumble.' It amused him to show the man beside him how easily he could follow his thoughts. He referred to Pickering, sometimes to his face, as 'a bear of very little brain', a description Darren accepted inexplicably as a compliment.

Benjamin George Dexter could scarcely have been a greater contrast to the man beside him. Harrow had prepared him for Cambridge, but he had chosen instead to slum it at the London School of Economics. He worked now in the money markets at Bristol, one of those young men who spent much of his day in front of a computer screen and made a lucrative living out of moving other people's money around.

He had draped his jacket over the back of his chair, it seemed less for comfort than to show off the elaborate patterning of his waistcoat upon its rich purple background. The linen of his trousers was sharply creased, his Gucchi leather shoes looked surprisingly delicate upon his substantial feet. As if to underline the crudity of Pickering's hair, his own blond locks fell in a carefully coiffured casualness over his perfect ears.

Pickering said, 'The pigs had me in again today. There's been another murder, you know. That Hetty you fancied a bit, till you found she was on the game.'

Dexter nodded. 'I heard. Shame, that: useful bit of crumpet getting snuffed out like that.' He was careful to show no emotion, to confine his previous connection with Hetty Brown to a little casual lust. The police hadn't had him in about this one, so far. They had asked him about Julie Salmon, but as far as he could gather that was only because of his connection with Pickering, who was bound to be in the frame for his girlfriend's death.

The police fascinated Ben Dexter: he studied their workings with the fixed attention of a man who watches the movements of a dangerous snake and is unable to turn away. His father, to whom he had not spoken for over three years, had been a senior policeman when he retired. He said as casually as he could, 'Did you find out how much they knew about Hetty's death?' He was anxious to know just what progress the pigs had made with their investigations into the killing of Julie Salmon; he suspected not very much. They had let his bear-like friend go after questioning, to his secret disappointment. Probably they

77

thought Darren Pickering would simply not be bright enough to bring it off.

As in other areas of his life, Ben Dexter's judgement was not as sound as he thought it was. Pickering, despite the appearance he chose to affect, was not stupid. He had little in the way of formal qualifications, for he had always fought the system at school. But Julie Salmon had persuaded him to go to evening classes, and he had found himself taking at last to study, surprising both his tutor and himself by his rapid grasp of engineering concepts. He had not been to the class since Julie's body had been found. And now there was this other death, another corpse of a girl he had seen in here.

He said, 'Hetty hadn't been long dead when the police found her. That Dr Haworth who comes in here had certi-fied her. He's the police surgeon, you know.'

Dexter nodded. 'Funny bugger he is, too.' He knew little of Haworth, but he was feeding Pickering the appropriate reaction: anyone who chose to associate with the police must be a funny bugger.

'He used to be Julie's doctor, you know.' Pickering threw in this apparent irrelevance with a superior air, glad to reveal any snippet of information not possessed by his com-panion. Ben Dexter's unspoken assumption that he was an unthinking prole grated sometimes, even though it was only the acceptance of the image Pickering had chosen to create for himself.

'Haworth could have his pick of the girls in here,' said Dexter. 'I've seen them looking at him. Silly bugger doesn't seem interested. Wonder if he's queer.'

'Shouldn't think so. I expect he has to be a bit careful, being a doctor.'

Dexter's lip curled at the idea of such pusillanimous self-denial, but he said nothing more on the subject. To have done so would have been treating Pickering's opinions as if they were as valid as his own.

They sipped their lager for a moment without speaking. Dexter had in truth been happy to divert their conversation from the subject of Julie Salmon. He found that for reasons he preferred not to confront he was made uncomfortable by any mention of Julie from the lips of this muscular lump who had once been her boyfriend. Danger attracted him, just as violence did, but he resisted the temptation now to come back again to her violent death.

He decided that the excitement they got from football was safer. 'We'll be in the Vauxhall Conference next season,' he said, not for the first time. 'Chance of a few rumbles when we travel with the lads. You could be glad of that Martial Arts course we did before Easter.' He looked down at his sinewy fingers, thinking of the scientific, calculated ferocity which they could now inflict. He preferred to rely on Pickering as his minder in any confrontation, but it was as well to be prepared for all situations. There might even be more individual conflicts, where the big man was not at his side with his ready fists.

Dexter loved organizing violence, manipulating situations and the participants. He had never been arrested himself, even in the days when he and a middle-class group like him had marshalled the battalions of travelling West Ham bother boys. There had been blood then, and even the odd knifing, but he had enjoyed it all from the wings. 'Up the Roosters!' he now said automatically, just as he had once said, 'Up the Hammers!'

Darren Pickering did not react, unless his long pull at his lager could be called a reaction. He looked round the club. This early on a Wednesday evening, it was still not half full. 'Not much action here. Let's go down the town.' He drained his glass and stood up, straightening his powerful limbs ostentatiously beneath the jeans and the over-stretched shirt.

Dexter glanced at his expensive watch, then lounged back, straightening his long legs beside the table and studying his feet. 'No. Let's give it another half-hour and see what turns up.'

Pickering said obstinately, 'I'm going anyway,' turned upon his companion, and walked out. He had suddenly realized that he wanted to be on his own. He felt good as he emerged into the cooler air of the car park. For once, he had made this decision, not Dexter.

Neither of them had seen Charlie Kemp watching their separation from the small glass observation panel above them.

Amy Coleford did not go to the *Roosters* that Wednesday night. Some of the lurid imaginings of her neighbour about the two girls who had died in the last three weeks had stayed obstinately in her mind, long after she had thought she had shrugged them away.

She went into Oldford, hoping secretly to pick up the kindly middle-aged man who had been content merely to fondle her for half an hour two nights earlier. Easy money, that, she told herself; if the silly fool was prepared to pay her thirty pounds for a quick grope, she was certainly prepared to take his money. She was working hard at creating around herself the porcelain-hard glazing of bright indifference she saw in the more experienced practitioners of her trade. Emotions, she knew, must be kept for home: this was business. But she was not finding the distinction easy. A small part of her still wondered about the lives her clients went back to when they left her.

Oldford was quiet. Any experienced street-walker would have told her that it was too small a town to have many good pitches, that a Wednesday evening in summer when dusk was scarcely departed was not a good time. She should have given her phone number to those customers who were affluent and harmless, and waited at home for them to ring for her services. Then, with an eager client on the other end of the line, she could have announced her list of charges for the various services she was prepared to offer. With youth on her side, it would have been easy to build up a list of regular and harmless clients.

But Amy Coleford was new to the game and knew none of this. Without the dubious benefit of a pimp to organize her work, or advice from an older practitioner of the ancient profession, she was learning the hard way. She would learn the ropes in time—if she was allowed that time.

She tried a road which led off the town's main street and down to a shabby inn at the bottom of a gentle slope. There were shops down both sides of the road, most of them with flats above. It was darker here, with only a strip of sky visible between the tops of the three-storey buildings. Men did not like to conduct the first negotiations in a place that was too well-lit.

But she had not been there five minutes when a harsh female voice from a doorway behind her said, 'And what the hell do you think you're doing, you little cow?'

It was an older woman, unmistakably looking for trade in her short black leather skirt. Her peroxided hair bounced with fury as she warned off the young rival, her lined face raw with anger beneath the mask of make-up. Amy had never heard such a vicious string of obscenities before, not even from Harry in their rows before he had left her. It shook her: for the first time in months she felt the need of the mother who was dead.

She walked up and down the High Street for a few minutes, trying to recover the composure the woman had battered away. Then a police car pulled up alongside her. 'What are you doing, love?' the non-driving policeman asked her. He knew well enough: they had been watching her for five minutes.

'I—I'm waiting for a friend. I—I don't think she's going to come,' she said. The man's brown, humorous eyes, shadowed by his black and white hat, seemed to see right through her.

'Get home, love, while you can. And don't let us see you touting for custom here again, or we'll have to take you in.' They watched her walk a hundred yards, looking back twice over her shoulder to see if they were still watching her. Then the car eased quietly forward and stopped again at her elbow. 'Do you want a lift home, love?'

She was tempted. Then something told her she must not let the police know her address. They were the enemy, weren't they? 'No, thanks, I'll walk. I haven't far to go,' she said stiffly.

'Suit yourself then, love, but take care. You know about

these killings we've been having. You stay home at nights, there's a good girl.' He was not from anywhere round Oldford; his Yorkshire accent seemed to her immensely reassuring, so that she did not want to leave the security it suggested. He was older than she had thought at first. She had a sudden fantasy of him as a client, putting his arms round her protectively when they had finished, wanting to forbid her ever to sell herself again. She might even accept. The police car was gone before she had dismissed the notion.

She had thought she might call in at the *Roosters* club after all; she could see the lights of it, no more than two hundred yards away at one point and seeming nearer in the summer darkness. But she was more shaken and depressed than she would admit by the memory of that raddled woman in the town centre. Was this what she must come to in due course? The future stretched blankly away in front of her, impenetrable and ominous.

For once, she would cut her losses and go home. It would mean paying Mrs Price needlessly for her baby-sitting, but she had done well enough in her short career to be able to afford that. She began to think of reasons she could give for her early return, cheering herself up with the thought of her children's sleeping faces.

She did not hear the car which had been following her when it stopped. She heard its driver's door shut quietly a moment later, but she apprehended no particular danger from that.

It was only when she heard the footsteps, a good two minutes later, that she felt the first thrill of fear. She looked back; at the outskirts of the town, the lights were poor and widely spaced. She saw only the silhouette of a figure, intensely black against the yellow light behind him. He looked larger like that, and taller still when he raised his right arm above his head in a single, restraining gesture.

He might be the customer she had given up hope of attracting, and for a moment she thought of turning towards him with the welcoming smile she had practised in front of her mirror. But he had not called out, and his silence was suddenly significant to her.

She began to run, cursing now the high heels she had thought such essential footwear when she went out.

He loped behind her, his footsteps less noisy now that he ran than when he had walked. She wondered if it was really so, or whether her own haste and the wind that rushed past her ears was shutting out other sounds. She could not be more than three hundred yards from home now, but half of it was down a lane with nothing but a straggling hawthorn hedge on one side and a single house, set well back from the road, on the other.

She thought of turning into the driveway of that house, but there were high rhododendrons which shut out the sky for thirty yards beyond the gates, and she could not face the possibility of being overtaken in that darkness. She tried to increase her speed as she passed the gates: they seemed to swim past her in slow motion, as if someone was replaying the scene to study her futile flight at his leisure.

She wondered why the man had not overtaken her yet. He was no more than ten yards behind her, and he must surely be capable of arresting her stuttering progress now whenever he wished. Then came the worst moment of her horror, as she realized that he was merely biding his time, playing with her like a cat with a mouse. He would attack when she was at the least illuminated part of her route.

She wanted to turn and scream at him, to hurl defiance and abuse, to kick and scratch, perhaps even to put him to flight by the fury of her resistance. But the legs which so obstinately refused to flee any faster also would not let her stop. With her lungs bursting, she flung herself on towards the light which marked the first house of her road and possible safety.

She was at the darkest point when the hand fell over her mouth, gagging her, preventing her from flinging forth the wild screams which might still save her if there was anyone to hear them. She tasted the smooth glove in her mouth, tried unavailingly to close her teeth and bite it.

Then she heard the man laugh, hoarsely, excitedly. He

83

was trying to twist her to face him. Suddenly, illogically, she knew that he wanted to see her face as she died. She must not turn round, or let him turn her. She kicked out wildly with her heels, tore fiercely at the strong forearm that pressed so tight across her neck, refusing all the while to see the face of the man who was going to kill her.

It could have been only a matter of time. She was making no forward progress, and he was immeasurably the stronger of the two. But her struggling saved her, by the single extra minute it bought for her.

A car turned the corner at the end of the lane, by the lamp which she had been trying to reach, and came slowly towards them. Her assailant was aware of it before she was; it was not until he released her that she registered that the vehicle was there.

Suddenly, he was gone, half walking and half running back along the way they had come. Amy staggered forward, knowing she should stop the vehicle and secure her salvation, unable in her extremity to utter a sound from the throat which had a moment ago been crushed. She lurched unevenly towards home, expecting the vehicle to stop as it drew level with her.

She realized afterwards that she had assumed that it was the police car she had seen in the town centre: all she could see were the two orbs of light from the headlamps. Perhaps, from the speed with which he had released her, her attacker had thought the same. In fact, the car moved slowly past her, and she did not think to raise her arms in distress until she knew she must be outside the vision of the driver. It was an old blue saloon, its exhaust blowing a little from a hole; it moved on down the lane behind her without even checking its pace.

But it had saved her. The man who had followed her had disappeared rapidly before it. She hastened on, into her own road and towards the sanctuary of her house, looking fearfully behind her but seeing no more of the man who had followed her. He must be back at his car now. She could still taste the plastic of his glove in her mouth.

There was only a forty-watt reading lamp switched on

in the lounge: Mrs Price, concentrating on her television film, had no need of more. She did not notice how white and shaken young Amy was. And she was anxious to get away, so that she could catch the end of the film on her own set next door. Her haste made her miss the only real bit of melodrama that had fleetingly entered her drab life.

Amy found that Harry had left a little of his whisky behind him. There were about two inches in the bottom of a bottle under the sink, where she had hidden it from him months ago. She poured it into a tumbler and drank it like medicine, laughing a little hysterically as she saw her face screwed up in the mirror.

She was careful not to breathe on the children as she checked their sleeping forms before she crept into bed.

The whisky worked quickly: she did not realize that there were about six measures in the glass she had poured. Her last thought before she fell asleep was that there was no point in reporting the assault to the police. She had not seen the man, and she did not want the police asking about how she managed to support her children on her own. She had far better keep quiet.

It was the last and most serious of the foolish decisions she took that day.

CHAPTER 10

'It's our Ladies' Night in two weeks,' Charles Kemp reminded his wife. 'You've got the date in your diary, haven't you?'

'It's been there for months.' Diana Kemp looked in her dressing-table mirror and made a minor adjustment to her right eyebrow, studying her husband surreptitiously as he moved about the room behind her. He was running more obviously to fat now. He had always been a powerfully built man, seeming stocky despite being nearly six feet tall, but in their early days he had been hard and muscular. Now

85

she could see his belly drooping a little above the belt of his trousers.

Had there been love still between them, she could have been quite affectionate about this touch of physical weakness; as it was, she found she rejoiced to see it. She wondered how his other women reacted to it. Perhaps his money would blind them to it for a little while. But she was long past deceiving herself.

'Need a new frock, will you?' Kemp still spoke to his wife as his father had once treated his mother, so that dresses were still frocks to him. Party frocks, they used to call them, when he was a lad. And women could always be bribed to good behaviour by the offer of a new one, in those days.

'I shan't be going.' Diana was pleased with the way she delivered this. It came out calm and clear, as she had intended. Modern women would have had no difficulty with the delivery, but she had been rehearsing it for four days. She could hear the pulse drumming in her head, even now, when the announcement was out.

Charles said, 'What do you mean, you won't be going?' It was like a line in a bad soap, one of those American things she had insisted on watching a year or two back, but he couldn't think of any other reaction. He needed to think; already he was wondering what pressures he could apply to her when ordinary persuasion failed.

'Just that I won't. I don't want to. You can go on your own.' She picked up a nail file and began to smooth some invisible blemish on the nail of the index finger of her left hand. She did not normally spend much time on such things; now she found them quite useful. They saved her from looking at her husband, reinforced the air of indifference which she did not feel but so wanted to project.

'But you've got to, Di,' he said clumsily. 'I can't go to a Ladies' Night on my own. Not when I've got a wife. Not when I'm to be the Master of the Lodge next year.' He realized anew how important to him it was to be Master, how much he treasured that assurance of respectability.

'That's up to you. Sort it out as you think fit. Next time you play your dressing-up games with the other little boys.'

She shocked herself with the words: she had never spoken like this before; had even, in the early days, enjoyed putting on her finery to go out with him to the occasional Masonic functions where women were permitted. But with the surprise that she should speak to him like this came also an exhilaration. Her part in this exchange was not proving as difficult as she had thought it would be in the days of her anticipation.

He came over and stood behind her, placing a hand on each of her plump shoulders. It was a long time since he had done anything like that, and he felt her flesh stiffen under her dress. 'Come on, old girl. Don't go sulky on me. Is it the change giving you problems again? We'll—'

'No, it isn't. Can't you get it into your thick head that you can't write everything off to the menopause?' It was the first time he had heard her call it that. He had let her go her own way too much lately, he thought, been too confident that this section of his life would take care of itself while he got on with the rest. Perhaps the separate rooms hadn't been such a good idea after all. His eyes fell upon a copy of *Cosmopolitan* on her bedside table. She had been filling her head with these silly ideas of independence.

But she'd come round, if he gave her a little attention. She always had done. 'Listen, why don't you go and get your hair done, and we'll talk about this later?'

'I had it done yesterday. You just haven't looked at me.' She was triumphant in her grimness, not afraid to look at his face in the mirror now, enjoying his disconcerted reaction.

'Sorry, old girl, I should have noticed. It's just that I've been rather busy at work these days, with—'

'It isn't. And I'm not your "old girl". Not your girl of any kind. I'm a woman, and one that's fed up with you and your ways.'

He tried stroking her hair, another half-forgotten gesture from their youth. It was dry and hard now beneath his fingers, where once it had fallen soft and lustrous over the back of her neck. 'I need you, Diane. These blokes sneer at me behind my back. You give me credibility.'

87

It was so near to the truth that for a moment she weakened. It took her back to the old days, when the streetfighter making his way had needed both her support and the cloak of respectability provided by a wife who knew nothing of his more dubious dealings. He so seldom told her the truth now that his vulnerability almost won a concession from her.

Then she thought of the last twelve months and hardened her resolve. 'They won't stop sneering at you because of me. They're sorry for me, those who know anything about you, because they know the way you use me. Wheeling me out to be examined whenever you need to show a dutiful wife, ignoring me the rest of the time.'

'It was your idea to have separate rooms.' He felt himself being drawn into the argument he did not want, the one he could not win.

'Only because I was sick of you coming home stinking of a different whore every night.' She checked herself, feeling herself being persuaded into anger and resentment. She had intended to be cool as ice about this. She didn't think he'd hit her, not any more, but she didn't want the kind of row where they flung obscenities and accusations at each other. He was better at that than she was; she would fight this battle on her own ground.

'You've always enjoyed our Masonic do's,' he said. He was not used to having to get his way simply with words. He was used to having weapons to make people do his business: muscle or money or knowledge which could be used to apply the necessary pressure. Without them here, he felt himself powerless to crush her stubborn opposition.

'How do you know what I enjoy any more? I might have enjoyed them a little once—I can't remember any more. But for years you've tarted me up like a Christmas tree and brought me out to be inspected.' It wasn't completely fair, she knew: she had gone along with it willingly enough for too long. But she was no longer interested in being fair to him. 'I've had enough of being afraid to open my mouth, in case I reveal something I shouldn't about one of your shady deals before you've pulled it off.'

'I need you, Di. Go with me this time, at least. Then we'll talk about things, see if we can put it right.'

It might have worked, if she hadn't heard the echo of the phrases he had used on her so often before. 'No, we won't. I've tried to talk to you plenty of times in the last year, but you've never had time for me. You're only trying now because you want to parade me at the Masons.' She was surprised how calm, how logical she sounded, despite the pounding of her heart. She drew strength from that.

It was her logic that was defeating him. He had not expected this, had never invited her to reason with him in his life. Confronted with it now, he was at a loss. He clenched his powerful fists, resisting the impulse to try to beat her into submission. 'It's my fault, I admit it. You're right to bring it to my notice.'

He used the phrase he had picked up as a standby when people began to complain about his business operations. He could hardly claim here, though, that some unthinking underling was at fault, that he had not been personally involved. 'Now that I know you're unhappy, my love, we can begin to do something about it.' He made a clumsy grab for her hand, trying to cushion it between his own broad paws. It was another gesture from the past, but she easily avoided him.

'I'm not your love, and I haven't been for a long time —perhaps I never was. And I no longer want to be your love.' She had picked up that phrase he never used, and contrived to deliver it back to him with a sneer that became more pronounced with her repetitions. This was easier than she had thought possible.

'Doesn't all—all this I've provided mean anything to you?' He gestured vaguely round the bedroom, trying to take in the big house and the garden beyond it with the movement.

She looked at the long velvet curtains, the wallpaper with its small blue flowers, the long range of built-in wardrobes, the double bed with its bedside cabinet, its elaborate reading lamp and Teasmade, as though she was registering them for the first time. 'I've never asked you for any of this.

89

And God knows what you've done at times to get it. But I'll have my share, when I go. I reckon I've earned it.'

She had never before even hinted that she might leave him. He could not cope with the idea. But he had the sense not to continue an argument where she was scoring all the points. He would get away; think over her bombshell; marshal whatever resources he could to help him. Perhaps he could get their daughter over from Norwich to paper this over: he found it difficult still to think beyond the short term. 'I've got to go, Di. We'll talk later. Whatever it is, I'll make it up to you.'

He still thought in Hollywood clichés that were already generations out of date. He left her studying her face in the mirror; like an ageing Rita Hayworth, he thought.

In his reserved car parking slot at the *Roosters* Kemp stood for a moment collecting himself, thinking himself back into the dominant role which he and others expected him to play here.

He locked the door of the blood-red Mercedes, drew himself sternly erect, pulled down the cuffs of his jacket until he was sure that it hung upon him uncreased. Diana had shaken him, more than he cared to admit. But in this place he was all-powerful; and it was a power that extended to women, as well as to more important things.

He went and spoke for a moment to the bar manager, letting the man know that the boss was around, but making the effort to be affable, jovial, understanding of the problems of the workers. This was Charlie Kemp, man of the people, in touch with the Oldford FC supporters, providing the success and the excitement they wanted. And controlling them, of course.

The tables were filling up as he went across the floor to the hall, acknowledging the greetings of the drinkers, smiling the smile he reserved for this royal progress to his own rooms. 'Just another supporter like you,' his bearing said, 'just another soccer-mad boy at heart, who happens to be lucky enough to indulge his passion for football and bring you fortunate people into it at the same time.' But beneath the affability he had pinned on at the door, he was as observant as a hungry shark.

His eye picked out the vulnerable, attractive figure of Amy Coleford. It was a fateful moment, for both of them.

He stopped for a moment to check that she was alone, then spoke quietly to her. 'Come up and have a drink with me, if you like. I enjoy meeting our supporters.' It was his standard line, almost a formula by now, which most of the girls knew as well as he did. Charlie Kemp didn't care if they spotted it for what it was; didn't have to care, he thought.

Amy Coleford did not recognize it as a limp chat-up line. A few moments later, she mounted the carpeted stairs beneath the little hanging sign that said PRIVATE. She was not so naïve that she thought she was going just for a drink. But had she exchanged notes with other practitioners of that trade she scarcely realized she had entered, she would have known better what to expect.

Kemp watched her cup her hands round the tumbler of gin and tonic, then sat on the arm of couch beside her and fondled the back of her neck. With the back of his knuckles, he felt her hair. It was soft and gossamer light, as he remembered Diana's had been once. At about this girl's age, he thought vindictively.

Amy did not look up at him. She still found these opening movements in the sexual exchange difficult; she supposed she would get over the embarrassment in time. She always told herself that it must be worse for the men on the other side, having to think up the things to say. But on this occasion she did not think that could be so; this man must be very experienced. The drink was useful; she stared into it with her small, glassy, uncommitted smile, resolutely avoiding the eyes of the man who had poured it for her until he should make his intentions clear.

He said, 'A girl like you could cause a lot of trouble.' It was a line from one of his favourite old movies. Robert Mitchum, he thought, or Humphrey Bogart. The girl didn't seem to think it was corny, perhaps because he didn't himself: he delivered it with complete confidence.

She said, 'I'm not out to do that, Mr Kemp.' Sitting in his chair in these lavish surroundings, she found herself on new, exciting ground. They said that all women had a little of the courtesan or the temptress in them; she switched into what she thought of as her tartish mode. Using the hand which now did not have a wedding ring, she brushed her hair back over her left temple, looked up at him for the first time, and said, 'I'm sure I wouldn't want to give you any trouble.'

'You won't do that, I'm sure, my dear. And it's Charlie, when we're together up here.' He slid down beside her and put his arm round her shoulders.

She liked that gesture. It reminded her how much she missed the protection of a man—had missed it for a long time now, because Harry had been a threat rather than a shield for months before he actually went. She nestled into the large shoulder next to her. 'It's nice up here, Charlie.' She had to force herself into the boldness of using his name, but it sounded easy enough on her ears as it came out. They liked you to use their names, if they gave them to you: it made it seem less of a commercial transaction, more personal.

He kept his left arm around her, drew her closer to him, holding her against his side like a gentle bear. He could feel the warmth of her through her thin dress, fancied that he could even feel the pulse in the slim thigh as it pressed against his. He ran his right hand over the nylon of her knee, up on to the unresisting thigh beyond it. Both their eyes were on that large, muscular hand as it moved and stroked. She kept a small, unchanging smile on lips that were parted just enough to reveal a very regular set of white teeth.

He moved his hand up her thigh, taking with it the skirt that was too tight to allow this movement, feeling the suspender at the top of the nylon, lingering there for a little to savour the moment, the lack of resistance he might choose to interpret as pleasure.

She was pleased with herself when she felt that pause. They said, all the magazines, that men preferred stockings to tights, and here it was being proved. She allowed herself a little shudder, hoping he might take it for pleasure, moving herself still more tightly into his side. She allowed herself to move her hand on to his arm, caressing him lightly where the muscle bulged above his elbow. She might even grow to like this trade, if it could be as gentle, as unhurried, as this.

She wondered when she should broach the question of payment. It was always the moment which gave her most difficulty, particularly when men had been considerate to her, like this. Something told her that she must be careful this time, must not rush it. She even had a wild, vague hope that this man might want her for a mistress, rather than a quick bang and away. You never knew, when you were still young. He seemed at this moment as if he wanted to care for her, and he certainly had the money. And a kind of glamour: to be Charlie Kemp's mistress would certainly carry a little excitement.

Amy Coleford was still very young.

He moved his hand up on to her hip, then round to the softness behind it, pulling her round to face him so that he might explore her secret areas the better. As she buried her face in his chest, she gave a little whimper of pleasure; at that moment, she was not even sure herself whether it was genuine or a part of the technique she was fashioning as she gathered experience.

He felt her pliancy, her femininity, against him, thrust his face into her soft hair. As a punishment in his mind for Diana, he thought of his wife's harshness, of her hard, unrelenting face in the mirror of her dressing-table, trying to contrast her ageing with the youth and femininity he held against him.

It was a fatal juxtaposition. For some reason he could not fathom, lust forsook him when he felt the need of it most. With the thought of his wife, he wanted only to humiliate the whole of her sex. If he had been able to order this soft creature to strip before him, to lay herself out to be taken violently by him, to name her price as if she had been so much meat in the market, he might still have taken

93

her. Harshly, and with no pretence at love; as a mere sating of an animal appetite, with what was going on clear to both sides.

But he had begun in the wrong way to do that now. He would not mind shocking the woman at his side: that might even add to the pleasure, once he had begun the process of humiliation. But it was himself he could not switch on. He could not find the words, and he could not operate without words to initiate him, few though they might be.

He eased himself a fraction away from her, withdrew his hands from her body. 'If you're going to make money at this game, you need to be organized, dear, same as in any other business.'

The change in his tone was so abrupt that at first she did not fully comprehend that he was talking about her. Men often talked about their own business worries, the stress they were under, as though they had to excuse to themselves the fact that they were paying for sex. She must encourage him to talk about it, if that was what he wanted. She looked up at him with round blue eyes, misting with a little moisture in her bewilderment. Innocence and vulnerability were always the best cards to play with men when you were confused.

But not this time. Kemp thought of his wife's phrase about him coming home smelling of whores and decided that Amy Coleford represented whoredom. 'If you're going to peddle your wares like this, you'll need to be put into a proper set-up. Oldford hasn't got any brothels yet, but they're coming. You stick with me, babe, and you could be in on the ground floor.'

It was his absurd, outdated Hollywood dialogue that freed her tongue and her anger. 'I don't need your help, I can look after myself. I—I thought you wanted me, or I wouldn't have . . .' The words tailed away and she gestured hopelessly with both hands at her body and his, the couch, the drink on the table beside her, the silent, thickly carpeted room with its rich wood panelling.

'Come off it, Amy. You were offering your fanny for money, and we both knew it.' He watched her wince, saw

94

the tears forming, and was exultant. He stood up, towering over her, dominating her. 'You've got a nice little body there. Slim and healthy, but still plenty of what the punters like to get hold of.'

He liked that: it made it sound as though his earlier moves on the couch were no more than a sampling of the goods as a preliminary to the proposition he was now about to put to her.

She said, 'If you don't want me, Charlie, there's no need to insult me.' She wanted to get up, to face him, to give him as good as she got if the insults were going to fly. But her legs were like water and she was suddenly bereft of all energy. She felt the hotness of tears in her eyes, and was furious with herself for her weakness, when she so wanted to be furious with him.

He looked down at her, contemptuous now as he saw her tears. 'I didn't say I didn't want you: I might, in time. That might be part of the deal. What I'm telling you is that if you're planning to open your legs up for money to all and sundry, you want to make sure it pays. And you need protection. What I'm offering you is the benefit of my organization. We'll set you up with a base, set the rates, vet the clients, make sure you have protection. At a price, of course. Nothing is for nothing, especially sex; we shall take our percentage, that's only fair.'

'I don't want to work for you.' She was scrambling to get up, but he stood very near her, and she could not manage to raise herself from the low, softly sprung couch.

'Be sensible, dear. You won't have much choice. In a few months, you'll be working for us, on our terms, or you won't be working at all. Not with that.' He gestured obscenely at her groin.

She managed at last to get to her feet, staggering a little with her emotion. 'You can't stop me. I'll do my own—'

'Fight us, will you? On your own? Don't even think of it, my dear!' He managed to snarl out the term of endearment as though it were another obscenity. He was on his own ground now, threatening a weakling with the power of the thugs ranged unseen behind him. 'You won't make much of a hooker with your face slashed to ribbons.'

She faced him but could not look at him; her damp, pretty face was a mask of frustration and rage. 'I don't need you. I'll manage. There are people who'd like to know about what you're doing . . .' She stopped, realizing too late that she should not have threatened him.

'You need me far more than you know, Amy Coleford.' His voice had dropped to a growl. 'You must have heard about these girls who've been killed. The last one at least was on the game. Dabbling in it without protection, like you. You'll end up like those two before long unless you come to heel, I can tell you. Now get out!'

She raised her hands a little in front of her, as though to protest, then turned hopelessly to the door where she had come in.

'Not that way.' He could not have that face with its rivers of eye-shadow going through the club. He took her out of the other end of the hospitality suite and showed her the top of the outside staircase, which except on match days was almost his private access to his rooms here.

She looked him in the face before she went out into the air, for the first time since he had decided he did not want to take her. Was it one of this man's men who had followed her last night? Or even Charlie Kemp himself? She wanted to say something, to fling some last defiance before she slunk away from him. But she saw his features set like flint against her, and the words would not come.

He shut the door upon her and watched through the small window beside it as she went down the iron steps and into the car park. She walked a hundred yards across the tarmac, turned for a single backward glance of resentment at the tall building where he stood, and was gone. He stood watching for a moment, reviewing what he had said to her in the excitement of crushing her. It was too much, too soon. She could do him damage now, if she talked. The last threat he had thrown at her came back to him, and he looked at the spot where she had disappeared with a cold smile.

It would quite suit his purposes if the Strangler was to get her.

96

CHAPTER 11

The new Chief Constable had his reservations about John Lambert. He liked his superintendents to play things by the book. In the modern police force, that meant they remained at the station, the visible head of a murder investigation, the focus for all the streams of information that flowed in from an extensive team. There were now over sixty officers involved in varying degrees in the Strangler case, and the officer-in-charge should be the man who coordinated the efforts: the man who bullied, cajoled and informed the troops, using whatever means were necessary to keep morale high.

Lambert did not work like that. He let the Scene-of-Crime team and the house-to-house men get on with their necessary routine work, reporting in the main to DI Rushton, who enjoyed the painstaking documentation and checking for discrepancies much more than he did. He headed the CID investigation himself, spending most of his hours away from the Murder Room, interviewing important witnesses himself wherever possible, using a detective-sergeant, rather than the more normal inspector, to accompany him, to support him; even, when he thought it necessary, to conduct key interviews.

It was irregular, but it worked. The old Chief Constable, Douglas Gibson, had told his successor all about Lambert when he handed over. 'He has his own methods. You'll find yourself calling him old-fashioned, though I'm not sure that's the right phrase. Stubborn, certainly. But not threatening: I believe him when he says he wants to stay exactly where he is as far as rank goes. And he gets results.'

It was the last phrase which struck home with George Harding. In an era where crime statistics are public property and a senior policeman's job can depend on clearup rates, Detective-Superintendent Lambert's record was

second to none. That was bound to win him a little indulgence. And Harding found that he had assembled a team
around him who seemed to accept his methods. Policemen
generally did, if the villains were nailed. That was in everyone's interest, including those young thrusters for promotion who occasionally found Lambert treading on their
toes.

For his part, Lambert found that the new CC had one
great advantage: he had no exaggerated reverence for the
media.

He did not dissolve into apology and explanations at the
sight of a television crew; still less did he extract Lambert
from the urgency of his investigations to confront the media
representatives. When the official Press Officer could no
longer hold them at bay with his routine announcements
on police progress, George Harding saw them himself.

His Chief Constable's uniform and badges sat easily upon
him, whereas Douglas Gibson had always looked and felt
like a station sergeant in fancy dress. He took the questions
of press men and television women calmly, refusing to
answer if he thought them not in the public interest, dealing
equally with those queries which were disguised insults to
the force, giving precisely the information he had planned
in advance and no more.

It was all a great relief to Lambert, who sat beside his
Chief at the morning press conference on what the tabloids
had already dubbed the Cotswold Strangler. He had needed
to do little more than reinforce the Chief's highly articulate
account of the investigation and explain a little of police
procedure. Where Douglas Gibson, an honest cop of the
old school, had usually looked shifty and defensive in front
of the cameramen, Harding gave the impression of a Chief
Constable and a force that were operating smoothly and
were confident of success.

It was only when he sat down to compare notes with
Lambert and his team leaders in the Murder Room afterwards that he allowed the strain to show. No one liked a
serial killer. The police like everyone else were left wondering where the next strike would be, how many victims there

would be before the murderer was identified. The mistakes made in the pursuit of the Yorkshire Ripper were never far from policemen's minds, and they knew that the press would be delighted to hark back to those confusions if the CID did not get a result quickly in this one.

'I've just told the organs of enlightenment how much we're on top of the case,' said the Chief Constable with a sardonic smile. 'Now tell me how much we really know.'

Rushton, at a nod from Lambert, took this as his cue to report on the findings he had been gathering together at the centre of operations. He would normally have been in his element with the CC in his audience, taking the opportunity in his slightly officious way to demonstrate his grasp of detail, his efficiency in documenting and cross-referencing the bewildering collection of data the men on the ground were bringing in, his insight into what might be key areas for further investigation.

Instead, he was for once a little hesitant. He looked white and strained, almost as though he wished this task had fallen to someone else. He was having to work hard to summon the concentration necessary to summarize a mass of information. Lambert wondered if he was sickening for something, or whether the absence of any definite lead made him nervous of the new Chief Constable's wrath.

Rushton said, 'We have accumulated a lot of knowledge, but as yet nothing that would point to an arrest, sir.'

'You mean you've produced bugger-all as yet. Don't try and fob me off as if I were Joe Public, lad. I was putting out statements like that when you were in nappies.' By police standards, it was a gentle rebuke, amiably delivered; a modern Chief Constable has no need of vehemence.

'Yes, sir.' Rushton coloured and looked at his notes. 'We still haven't got a definite time for the death of Julie Salmon, the first girl. She wasn't found for a couple of days, as you know. She was last seen at seven o'clock on the evening of Wednesday, 25th May, and the autopsy confirms pretty certainly that she died that night. We don't know what time: it could be any time within about eight hours. We may never know more precisely than that.'

'Not until we arrest her killer,' said Harding drily. 'What suspects do we have for Julie Salmon?'

'There's an ex-boyfriend. A Darren Pickering. Neanderthal type, not averse to a bit of violence. We've had him in before. Once in connection with football hooliganism— a punch-up between rival groups of so-called supporters— once for a fight outside a pub. Neither came to court.'

'How recently?'

Other officers would have gone to the computer, where Rushton had made sure the information was available to anyone who pressed the right button. Instead, he pulled out a card covered in his own neat handwriting. 'The football incident was during last season. The pub fight was almost two years ago. The officer who interrogated him is still here; as I say, neither incident came to court.'

'Any history of violence towards women?'

'Not as far as we've been able to ascertain, sir. But he did admit in interview that it was the girl that had ended the affair. And it was only ten days before she was killed.'

'And off the record, Inspector, would you put him in the frame for these killings?'

Rushton was thrown a little by the direct question. He never liked to commit himself: you could end up looking very silly if your opinions were thrown back at you later. And this might be the CC's only contact with him in months. He said, 'I couldn't say, sir. I didn't conduct the interviews with Pickering myself.'

'I saw him, sir. I'd rate him a possible, along with several others with no alibi for either of the killings. Nothing stronger than that.' It was Bert Hook, the most junior officer in the room of high ranks, who had spoken up unexpectedly. 'He's rough, and I don't mean a rough diamond. You'd prefer him to be on your side in a fight: he's strong and hard. I don't know whether he's a man who'd go round killing girls: I've been trying to answer that ever since I saw him.'

'How did he react to being questioned about the girls?'

'He was shaken. He pretended not to be, that it was police victimization and no more than he expected. And he had the duty solicitor summoned pretty promptly, so that he said no more than he had to. But he was shaken when we questioned him about Julie Salmon. Less so about Hetty Brown. That's what you might expect, of course. He knew Julie Salmon well, and Hetty Brown hardly at all, according to his statement. And we haven't found anything to connect him with her. He doesn't seem to have been among her clients.'

'Is there anything to connect the two girls?' Harding knew the CID men would have asked themselves this, investigated exhaustively all the things he was asking about. But he was briefing himself on the investigation: these were the most serious crimes so far on his new patch, and he would have to account for the police reaction to them in various contexts. He had better be fully informed, even if his days of direct contact with detection were far behind him now.

Lambert said, 'Beyond the fact that they were killed in the same area and in the same way, not very much. Julie Salmon was an attractive girl, living at home with her parents. They reported her missing that first night, though she wasn't found for another forty-eight hours. She worked in an estate agent's office. Her parents didn't approve of her relationship with Darren Pickering, as you might expect, and were quite relieved when it broke up.'

'No suggestion that Julie Salmon was on the game? Or dabbling with it?'

'None at all. She was on the surface rather a shy girl, without many boyfriends before Pickering. She kept a diary, but there's nothing in it that seems significant. She appears to have had a brief relationship with an older man before Pickering—there's a reference to this man calling Pickering 'a lout' after she took up with him. Sounds like a professional man; we went through all her associates at work, but came up with nothing.'

'A married man?'

'Quite possibly, though there's nothing to indicate that

101

definitely. The meetings seem to have been only sporadic, from the diary. But it's very vague anyway, like most of the other entries. She never refers to the man by name. Her mother produced the diary for us immediately, and I wonder if Julie was a bit guarded in writing because she suspected her mother might get hold of the diary when she was out. Of course, they may be nothing more than a young girl's fantasies about an older man: she was only nineteen when she died, and these entries are a few months before her death.'

'What about Hetty Brown?'

'No diary to help us there, I'm afraid. Be useful if there was, even if it was no more than a list of her meetings with men.'

'No mysterious professional man there?'

'None apparent, no, sir. Our source of information is mainly her flatmate, Debbie Cook. They worked together at ICI in Gloucester for a while, then were laid off. Took to the game to pay the rent, according to her. It certainly looks like that: they've neither of them been at it long.'

There was a little silence in that room of hard professionals. It was a familiar enough story, more frequent in these days of the slump which the government still called a recession. A prospect of easy money in hard times. And now a girl of twenty-one was dead.

The Chief Constable voiced the question which had nagged at them all as they gathered information. 'Similar killings. Same murderer?'

Lambert smiled wryly; in this situation, any kind of certainty was a comfort, but they were difficult to come by. 'The method of dispatch is identical. Dr Burgess is away, but our police surgeon, Dr Haworth, has been good enough to come in this morning.'

He nodded to the only man in the room who had not so far spoken. Don Haworth took it as his cue to summarize his findings. He had been sitting on the edge of his chair, apparently fascinated by his first view of routine police procedures. 'I was the first medical man at the scene of both killings, in my capacity as police surgeon. Both girls

102

were killed by vagal inhibition; gloved hands were expertly applied to both throats. Probably plastic gloves of some kind, since I understand forensic have found no traces of material on the skin.' He looked interrogatively at DI Rushton, who nodded confirmation.

'My opinion would be that it would be the same pair of hands in each case, but I could not swear to that in court; you would need other evidence, which it seems at the moment you do not have.'

It came out like a suggestion of police negligence, so that Lambert, who was the man who had sanctioned Haworth's rather irregular presence in this group, was moved to say, 'It was Dr Haworth who helped to pinpoint the time of death in the case of the second murder.'

Haworth smiled that boyish, self-deprecating smile that made him seem younger than his thirty years. 'I thought between twelve and one on the morning of the eleventh of June. Again, I couldn't make that more than an opinion in court. I'd have to go with the four-hour period the pathologist came up with after the PM.'

Harding looked for a moment at the eager young man with his slightly untidy mop of fair hair. It was useful to have a medic in on this session; typical of Lambert, that, he thought. 'Any other thoughts, Doctor? Now is the time to speculate: we won't throw your thoughts back in your face later, even if they prove to be wildly mistaken.' The words were intended as much for the policemen in the room as for Haworth. There was nothing like the fear of being wrong in front of top brass to keep ideas bottled up.

The police surgeon shrugged. 'Nothing to add to forensic findings, I'm afraid.'

Lambert said, 'It's useful to know that Don thinks it probable the same man killed both girls. There are some differences as well as the obvious similarities. The first girl was violently raped. The second had had intercourse, but there were no signs of violence.'

Rushton, anxious now to get back into the discussion, said, 'The first girl obviously resisted fiercely. The second one was a prostitute. Maybe she had the sense to take the line of least resistance with a sexual assault. Perhaps if she'd resisted, there would have been the same marks on Hetty Brown as there were on Julie Salmon.'

Rushton, terse and strained, sounded almost as though he was delivering a moral judgement. Perhaps the Puritan in him thought that Hetty Brown should not have allowed intercourse without a fight.

Lambert said, 'Despite her struggle, there were very few signs of the killer left on Julie Salmon that have so far proved useful to us. No skin under her fingernails. A few clothing fibres, but even those not necessarily from her killer. She was murdered in a derelict house, which was why she wasn't found for a couple of days.'

'But you have semen samples?'

'In both cases, yes. The first one doesn't tally with any of the few DNA records we have for violent criminals. It will be useful when we get our man, but perhaps not until then, except for eliminating the innocent. The semen from Hetty Brown is still being tested at Chepstow. We shall know within twenty-four hours whether it came from the same man as raped Julie Salmon before he killed her.'

'First one in a house awaiting demolition. Second one on a building site. Any connection there?' Harding's mind still worked like a detective's, seeking out any connection which might narrow the hunt.

Rushton said, 'We've combed through all the construction workers in the area: easier than usual because temporary workers have almost disappeared in this recession. It didn't produce anything definite. One or two we're still watching because they were around without an alibi at the time of both murders, but there are plenty more like that, unfortunately.'

'No motive common to both deaths?'

'Not that we've found so far. Darren Pickering was Julie Salmon's rejected lover, of course, but no obvious motive for Hetty Brown.'

Don Haworth said, 'He did know her, though. I've seen both of them in the *Roosters* club.'

Rushton nodded. 'He admits to a nodding acquaintance,

but nothing more. And we haven't dug up anything closer, yet.'

They were silent, contemplating the bleak probability of an unbalanced mind which had struck without reason and might do so again at any time. Lambert said, 'The bodies were found within a mile of each other, both in deserted places which yet were not far from the town. It might argue a local man. But of course, we don't know that it wasn't the girls who sought out the location: they may have had no fear of being killed when they went to these places.'

'That could apply to the one strong suspect we've so far turned up from outside the district.' Rushton looked at Lambert, wondering whether he should bring this out in front of the police surgeon, and received his nod of assent. 'A certain Vic Knowles.' Don Haworth, with his football club connections, leaned forward involuntarily at the mention of the name.

Rushton checked his notes. 'He admits to picking up a prostitute from the *Roosters* on the night Hetty Brown was killed. He had intercourse with her in the back of his car, according to his story. Forensic confirm from an examination of his car that that is probably true. He claims not to know her name, and he claims that she chose the spot where he should park. It was within a few hundred yards of where Hetty Brown was found dead. Incidentally, we're now certain she was killed where she was found, so he didn't kill her in the car and dump her. If, of course, it was Hetty Brown and not some other girl altogether in the car, as he'd prefer us to believe.'

Lambert said, 'The sooner we have that semen analysis, the better.'

Rushton said, 'One thing that we do know is that although Knowles lives a hundred miles away, he was also in the area on the night when Julie Salmon was killed.'

'Reason?'

'He says he was watching a testimonial match at Oldford. The match did take place that night. But even if he was there as he says, he could still have killed the girl later.'

'Have the Scene of Crime team turned up anything that might tie him in with the first murder?'

Rushton rustled through his notes again, though he knew the answer: he had tried hard to pin these killings on the man who was to be the new manager of Oldford Football Club. 'Nothing from the first killing, as yet. There are various hairs and clothing fibres from the house where Julie Salmon's body was found, which forensic are in the process of comparing with the materials the boys gathered from Knowles's car yesterday.'

Lambert said, 'The SOC stuff from the Julie Salmon house is proving very difficult to use, so far. Lots of people had been in and out of that house—it's been empty for months—and it's very difficult to isolate what was there before the night when she was killed. We're looking for stuff common to both sites, but there's nothing significant as yet.'

Harding looked grim. 'What about the Hetty Brown SOC findings?'

Lambert said, 'Again, far too many people have been in and out of that site: kids mostly. The team did find one footprint, of a city-type shoe, in the clay near where the body lay. We don't know for certain that it was connected with the crime, but forensic think it was made not more than twenty-four hours before we found it. Needless to say, we haven't found a Prince Charming to fit it yet, or I'd have let you know before the news conference.'

'Not enough evidence to warrant a search warrant for any of your suspects, yet, I presume.' Harding was more conscious than anyone of the way investigations could be hindered by the necessary safeguards of the law. 'Sergeant Hook said you had a few men in the frame.'

Lambert nodded. He might not be worried about promotion, but he was human enough to want to show that his team had not been idle, even though there was no sign of a result for them yet. 'We've mentioned Darren Pickering and Vic Knowles. Both of them have changed their stories in the course of interrogation. We're still gathering more information on both of them. We've got their fingerprints, but one of the things about this business is that there's a notable absence of dabs at both scenes of crime. It suggests that our man didn't kill on impulse, but went carefully prepared, knowing what he was going to do.'

It was a thought which brought a moment of silence even to experienced policemen, hardened to bloodier deaths than these. The Chief Constable drew a hand over his frizzy grey hair. 'Who else?' he asked curtly.

'A man we'd love to pin a serious crime on. Charlie Kemp.'

'You can say that again.' Harding was well aware of the villainy perpetrated without retribution by the elusive Kemp. 'It's not just wishful thinking?'

Lambert smiled grimly. 'I'm trying to guard against that, sir. But one of the threads running through the crime seems to be the *Roosters* club at the football ground. Kemp controls that, whether or not the licence says he's officially in charge.'

'What's his connection with the two victims?'

'He knew both of them, though at first he tried to deny it. Our one bit of luck so far is that we have a drugs squad officer operating in the *Roosters* club. Drugs are being bought and sold there. It's the usual tale: the drugs squad sergeant's biding his time, hoping to get at the suppliers behind the pushers. I haven't confronted Kemp or anyone else with him so far, and unless it proves really necessary we certainly don't want to blow his cover. But he's observed quite a lot of interesting comings and goings at the *Roosters*, apart from the drugs traffic.'

'Including Charlie Kemp's.'

'Exactly. Incidentally, it seems quite possible that Kemp is part of this drugs ring, but he's far too astute to be seen at the front of things. But that's not our concern at the moment. He could have committed both murders, from the timings we know about. Julie Salmon had been in the *Roosters* with Darren Pickering, so Kemp would know her at least by sight. He had sex with Hetty Brown in what he treats as his private suite at the *Roosters* on at least three occasions: he's admitted as much. On the night of her death, he says that he saw her, but that she wasn't with him. He has no alibi from nine o'clock onwards on that evening. He says he was alone in his office for two or three hours—most unlikely—and that he arrived home at "about midnight". He and his wife sleep in separate rooms, so that she is unable to confirm that.'

Kemp had been able to thumb his nose at them for far too long. But the knowledge of the satisfaction it would give to Lambert and his team to pin this one on him sounded a note of caution in Harding's Chief Constabular brain. 'Anything at the scenes of crime that suggests Kemp was there?'

Lambert shrugged. 'Not so far. But then there isn't anything definite for anyone, or we'd have pulled them in. The shoeprint near Hetty Brown's body could be Kemp's, but we haven't enough evidence yet to ask for a search warrant.'

'Anyone else I should know about?'

'There are various people we are still keeping an eye on: most of them are regulars at the *Roosters*. But I'm afraid we're working on negative rather than positive evidence. They're people who can't give convincing accounts of themselves for the nights of either murder, but who were also not sighted anywhere near the places of the deaths.'

It was Bert Hook who said, 'Has anything further come up on Benjamin Dexter?'

Harding raised an eyebrow at what was a new name to him. Unexpectedly, it was Don Haworth who enlightened him. The police surgeon said slowly, 'Ben Dexter spends a lot of time around the *Roosters*, much of it in the company of Darren Pickering, whom you discussed earlier. They make a very odd couple, and I think young Dexter rather likes that.'

Lambert said, 'Dexter enjoys baiting the police. His father was a chief superintendent in the Met Police. He's retired now: his son was born when he was forty-seven. They have no contact with each other, but it does mean that young Dexter knows more than we would like him to about our procedures. We could pull him in on minor drug charges any time we want. He's a user. As far as we are aware at the moment, he may be no more heavily involved than that. But he was heard exhorting Pickering not to take Julie Salmon's rejection lying down. And we think he's one of the people who's been helping to organize the hooliganism which has grown with the success of Oldford FC. He's never at the centre of it, but he always seems to be somewhere around.'

Haworth said, 'Dexter is a strange young man. Well educated, with a lucrative job. He seems to enjoy what he calls "slumming", which perhaps accounts for his association with Darren Pickering. They usually seem to be together when I see them at the *Roosters*.'

Harding said, 'Girlfriends?'

Rushton said, 'No regular ones that we've been able to find. And no boyfriends either. He strikes you as an unpleasant young man with a capacity for violence, but enough intelligence to cover his tracks. Of course, we haven't taken him to task about the drugs yet—that's drugs squad business, and they'll move when they think the moment's right. When we had him in here, Dexter was polite, even cooperative on the surface, but he was ready to sneer at you as soon as you turned your back.'

Lambert said, 'He has no previous convictions, of any sort.'

'I'm no psychologist,' Don Haworth offered, 'but it would be interesting to see what one made of Ben Dexter.' He looked around the table, waiting for the routine police winces at the mention of this branch of medicine, but received none on this occasion. Perhaps that was a measure of the anxiety. 'It may be that the drugs account for the oddities in his behaviour, but I have a feeling you may be dealing with an unbalanced mind there.'

There was a little pause while they weighed the thought, looking to the cabinets behind the doctor which held the clothes of the two dead girls. Then the Chief Constable glanced at his watch and said, 'Anyone else?'

Lambert said, 'One of the troubles with killings of this kind is that there may be no apparent motivation. That makes it difficult to narrow the field by elimination. No one

109

else seems as strong a candidate at the moment as the four we've mentioned. Equally, I have to say that the evidence is not so strong against any one of those as to stop us looking further. I'm afraid it's quite possible that our man may be someone else entirely, someone we've hardly considered as yet. I've told the team as much, and emphasized that they must remain vigilant for any new leads.'

It was a bleak but realistic thought on which to break up the meeting.

Lambert was dealing with the mountain of paper he had pushed aside to pursue the Strangler when there was a discreet knock at his door.

Rushton came in quietly, almost apologetically, not at all like the erect and confident bureaucrat he usually presented to his chief. Lambert concealed a spurt of irritation, which derived as much from his dissatisfaction at their lack of progress as from the interruption. 'What can I do for you, Chris?' He made himself use the Christian name, prepared himself to squash the 'sir' which Rushton persisted in allotting to him, even when they were alone together.

The Inspector, who usually would have had to be asked, sat down absently without invitation in the chair opposite Lambert. 'It's personal, sir.'

It was the one thing John Lambert had not been prepared for. Rushton usually behaved as if he did not have a private side to his life; even if he had problems there, they did not have the kind of relationship which would have made Lambert a natural confidant.

He pushed aside his papers, leaned forward a little. 'What is it, Chris? Illness?' He sought desperately for the name of Rushton's wife. Christine would have been able to tell him; for a policeman, he was very bad on names, and getting worse as the years passed.

In this case he need not have worried. Rushton, clasping his hands for a moment on his knee in front of him in a gesture which was so uncharacteristic that it made him

110

seem strangely vulnerable, said, 'No, nothing like that. It's Anne. She's left me, you see.'

There was really no reason why Lambert should feel so shocked. It was common enough anywhere now, and commoner still in the police force. Everyone knew that. Broken marriages were a hazard of the job. But it was still a shock when it happened to someone working with you. 'It may be nothing permanent, Chris. We're all working under a lot of stress at the moment.'

'She's gone off to her mother's and taken Kirstie with her.'

Again, he would never have got the name for himself. The child couldn't be more than two years old; he remembered Rushton with the first pictures of the baby, surrounded by WPCs. He said, 'It may not be too serious. Most women do that at some time.'

He could think of nothing but clichés. He wanted to tell the man in his suffering how even Christine Lambert, the wife everyone said was the perfect police wife, had almost left him twenty years and more ago. How she had screamed her frustration and isolation at a man too immersed in his work, had demanded that he choose between her and the force. But he did not know how to start, and in the end he said nothing: it seemed like a treachery to Christine even to attempt it.

Rushton said dully, 'We've had a few shouting matches. I hadn't thought it would come to this.'

'Take some time off. Go and speak to Anne. Tell her you need her. Women like to feel they're needed.'

He wondered why he was so reluctant to use the word 'love'. It had seemed an effrontery to bring it into lives he scarcely knew; was that what had driven him into that stupid generalization about a whole sex?

'That's good of you, John.' Rushton brought out the forename self-consciously, even amid his pain, like a grown-up child who is told that he must address a parent thus for the first time. He seemed absurdly grateful for the offer of leave; it was a concession which would have been no more than his right, in these circumstances.

111

Lambert found that any advice seemed presumptuous to the point of fatuity. Yet his inspector, normally so assertive, sat there as if waiting for it. His head was bowed, and there was not a sign of grey in the dark brown hair. Should he tell Rushton to plead with her? From what little he had seen of the lady, that hardly seemed right. Should he reason with her, putting his need for dedication to his work, the progress he was making in the force, the home he was able to provide? He knew Rushton well enough to know that he would have done that fully already; perhaps too often. He said, 'Tell her you're a family unit. That Kirstie needs you, that the three of you together are more than you can ever be apart.'

Was that what had saved him and Christine when the children were small? He had a dim idea that it was, though he had never framed any argument on those lines. 'Don't tell her what she needs or you need, but what Kirstie needs, what the three of you are together.'

Rushton looked up into his face for the first time since he had sat down. Lambert saw surprise, and wondered if he was going to be rebuked for his presumption. But Rushton said, 'Thank you. I will go and see her, but I don't need time off. I'll leave it until the weekend.'

A part of Lambert's mind breathed a sigh of relief. This Strangler business was stretching his team to the limits; Rushton's efficient grasp of the steadily accumulating documentation would have been sorely missed. 'Well, play it by ear, Chris. You only have to ask. A cooling off period might be a good idea. I'm sure the damage isn't irreparable.' Even the use of that multi-syllabled word seemed a mistake, distancing him, when he should have been close and spontaneous.

Rushton didn't seem to notice. 'I'll go up at the weekend. Her father should be there then; I've always got on well with him, and Anne listens to him.'

'That sounds like good tactics. I'm sure you'll find in the end that it's not as serious as it seems now.'

He had dropped back into conventional assurances to cover his embarrassment, and Rushton's response came like a slap of rebuke. 'Sometimes I think I hate all women. They're so damned unreasonable!' His voice for an instant was raw with passion. Then he dropped quietly back into his normal mode to say, 'She's talking about a legal separation.'

'I'm sure it needn't come to that. Tell her that Kirstie needs a father, almost as much as you need a daughter.' Lambert forced a smile.

Rushton nodded absently and stood up. 'I'll get back to work then. I—I just thought you ought to know, sir.' He looked to Lambert absurdly young, like a boy being brave about a cut knee. It was almost a surprise when he did not limp from the room.

He had got to the door when Lambert said, 'You did right to come in and tell me, Chris. Keep me posted on the situation.'

Rushton managed a small smile that might have been gratitude. 'I will. Thank you, sir.'

He had gone out, as he had come in, on that 'sir'. And both of them in the end had been happy with it. Lambert resolved to think more deeply about Rushton's situation, to provide real rather than token support over the weeks to come. In that naked moment when the inspector had cursed all women, he had seen the strain behind the mask of professional efficiency.

It did not take long for events to thrust that resolution to the back of his mind.

CHAPTER 12

Amy Coleford was a brave woman. Foolhardy, as is often the unfortunate way of these things, but undeniably brave.

She had been badly scared by her experience near home, but she decided that if she did not venture forth the next night, she might lose the confidence to do so at all. Her father had always said you had to remount the horse immediately when you fell off, or you would lose your nerve.

Amy still remembered many of her father's sayings with affection; now that he was no longer around to offer his advice, it seemed even more necessary to take heed of them. It was a kind of homage, after all.

She selected her very best dark skirt, put on a new pair of fishnet tights and a little more make-up than usual, and went forth determinedly into the world which had so nearly seen the end of her on the previous night. She kissed the children with more than her usual fervour, but she was an affectionate mother, and Mrs Price noticed nothing unusual as she settled down in front of the television. She was still too full of the excitements of the American melodrama she was following to give Amy her full attention.

'You watch out for that Strangler, dear,' she said. 'Should be strung up, he should, when they get him, but he won't be. Them do-gooders will see us all raped before they've done.' She smacked her lips in salacious horror at the idea. It was no more than a ritual reaction, a revelation of her own vicarious excitement in the killings rather than a real warning to her neighbour.

Mrs Price had decided that young Mrs Coleford must have got herself a boyfriend, to be going out so regularly now in the evenings. So no doubt she was safe enough. There was a touch of naïvety about this middle-aged woman who thought herself so worldly-wise.

Amy was brave and foolhardy, but not completely stupid. She had the sense to realize that Oldford was going to be a dangerous place until the Strangler was caught—hadn't she had evidence of that last night? For the moment, she would look for trade somewhere else. It was a pity, for she liked the *Roosters* and knew enough people there to feel comfortable. But Charlie Kemp had ruined all that for her, when he had taken her up to that wood-panelled room and treated her like dirt. She decided that she would go back to the club in a few days, when she had got over that horrid episode. For the moment, she could not face it.

Perhaps unconsciously, she turned towards somewhere with happier associations. Years ago, she had been with her father to the ancient docks at Gloucester. She remembered standing with her small hand in his large one, watching the barges and the men stripped to the waist who unloaded them. She thought it had been beneath a blue sky and flying white clouds, but most of her childhood memories seemed to be framed in such a context. They said the docks were a beautiful place now, quite a tourist attraction, with a glass-topped building full of shops and a museum. Perhaps, if it was as good as they all said, she would take the children there during the day, when the holidays arrived in a week or two.

She did not see the man who watched her leave the house.

Amy had not realized how long it had been since she had visited the docks as a child. She had some difficulty in finding her way down to the water over the newly paved approaches. Everything had been tidied up, and looked different from the way she remembered it. Where once there had been interesting dirt and disorder, there was now an almost clinical tidiness, especially on a quiet, still night like this.

But it was beautiful. She decided that as she came quite suddenly upon a wide stretch of water and wandered between the huge silhouettes of former warehouses. A bridge ran over the broad canal which connected this water to the main basin of the docks. She found herself beside a big, brightly painted boat. The water scarcely moved against its hull, so still and warm was the night. *Queen Boadicea II*, said the letters near the bow. You could take boat trips on this spruce vessel during the day. She would treat the kids to a sail, if the weather was good. She smiled at the thought of their eager, open faces. They would love it, and it would be educational for them, too. She could afford it, now that she had found out how to make money so easily.

The thought reminded her why she was here. She had somehow expected the docks to be rather sleazy, with dubious pubs and an even more dubious night life, where a girl might pick up men who had money and were anxious to spend it, where the authorities might turn a blind eye because they expected such activities here.

But it was not like that at all. There was a new shopping centre, which seemed in this light to be constructed entirely of glass—not a material to encourage surreptitious dealings. And the building beside which she now moved was actually a church. She grinned at the thought of the transactions she had proposed to conduct in its environs.

The only pub she could see was called *Doctor Foster's*. It looked as innocent as its nursery rhyme name suggested—not at all the sort of hostelry where girls like her might operate profitably. She noticed how that phrase 'girls like her' had crept into her vocabulary. Well, she might as well accept what it was she was doing; perhaps Charlie Kemp's brutal words had brought a necessary touch of realism to her thinking.

The pub was brightly lit, but quiet; it was but thinly patronized tonight. She walked past it and along the quay, heading automatically for the more dimly lit part of the area, though she knew now that she would do no business here. The black water of the main basin of the docks was as still as a mirror; the reflections of the lights in it almost as clear as the real lamps at the tops of their columns.

It was as beautiful as Venice. And the silent warehouses which cast their tall shadows across the water might have been palaces upon the Grand Canal. She had never been to Venice, but she had read about it many times, and promised herself that she would go there one day. She had been in a scene from *The Merchant of Venice* which her form at the comprehensive had done for a parents' concert. How long ago that seemed now! But she could still remember some of the words:

> The moon shines bright! in such a night as this,
> When the sweet wind did gently kiss the trees,
> And they did make no noise . . .

The moon shone here too, white and full and round, reflected in the water, larger and more beautiful than any

116

of the lamps around her. She walked slowly to the far end
of the great expanse of the main basin, her heels ringing
loud in the silence which seemed to come seeping like mist
from the water. There she found a seat beneath a lamp
whose bulb had failed, and sat in a pool of darkness to
appreciate the still water, the vast sky which was so exquis-
itely reflected in it, and the pleasing shapes of the manmade
architecture, which seemed from here to have been built to
complement the heavens and the water.

Somewhere, in a flat she could not see, hands she would
never know were playing a piano. When she arched her
head back and listened, she could just hear the occasional
sequence of notes, though she could distinguish no tune.
She remembered more of the scene from that play;

> How sweet the moonlight sleeps upon this bank!
> Here will we sit, and let the sounds of music
> Creep in our ears; soft stillness and the night
> Become the touches of sweet harmony.

Shakespeare must have written that on such a night as
this. She threw her head back, looked at the same sky that
he must have seen all those years ago, then shut her eyes
and basked in the soft stillness of this magical night. In a
moment, she would open them, run them over the Venetian
stillness of the water which lay everywhere around her
among the tall, silent buildings.

She would not look tonight for men with money to spend
upon her. She would let this peace and beauty work their
own therapy upon her troubled soul. She acknowledged to
herself for the first time how disturbed she was by the life
she was adopting, how febrile she was in her planning and
her thinking. Perhaps it was on such a night as this that
many people began to take stock of themselves.

The man's feet fell very softly behind her. He was almost
upon her before she turned. She knew him, so that her first
reaction in that quiet place was one of relief. By the time
she found his two thumbs pressing like iron upon the sides
of her throat, it was too late.

117

Her killer watched her face as she died, as he had planned to do on the previous night. Most of all, he watched her eyes, almost bursting with the pressure of the blood behind them. Quickly, as he knew it would be, they saw and felt no more, though they bulged more widely than they ever had in life. Her arms dropped limply to her sides and her assailant put her carefully, almost primly, down on the bench from which she had scarcely risen. He closed her eyes, as he had closed those of Hetty Brown, and put her hands together in her lap. She looked as though she had closed her eyes to pray, as quietly composed in death as Hetty had been. He liked that.

Amy Coleford's short life was over. On such a night as this.

CHAPTER 13

It was well after midnight when a distraught Mrs Price dialled 999 and the police learned that another Oldford girl was missing.

The body of Amy Coleford sat cooling through the night in its pool of darkness by the docks at Gloucester. The late-night walkers ignored the dark figure on the bench beneath the lamp which shed no light. Once they would have been driven by curiosity or charity to investigate it. Now the dogma said that you minded your own business. The figure might be one shattered by drugs or drink, or driven to some other craziness by the pressures of our civilized society. It might even be the bait in a trap, waiting to snap shut on those unwary enough to approach it.

So the corpse stiffened into the parody of repose in which its murderer had placed it, with its hands set gently one on top of the other in its lap, while the police combed each street and lane of the quiet town of Oldford. No one thought in those first hours to extend the search those few miles further into Gloucester.

The body of Amy Coleford was covered with a light dew

when it was found at six-forty by a pensioner walking his spaniel around the docks on this bright summer morning.

John Lambert, coming hastily into the CID section with his mind full of black thoughts, almost collided with the police surgeon. Don Haworth had already completed his brief report on the death before he went off to his morning surgery.

'Killed by the same man as the other two?' said Lambert. He had already heard enough of this latest death to assume it was murder.

'Almost certainly. The same method, certainly. The bruising on the throat is identical with the other two. It's almost as though he took a pride in making it so.'

'Time of death?'

Haworth shrugged. 'Last night. Impossible to be more precise than that at this stage. It's a pity she wasn't found earlier. The PM might give you something, but I doubt whether it will be able to point up more than a three or four hour period. It's a shame I couldn't have got to her last night: I could probably have pinpointed the moment for you then.'

Lambert nodded at the young, eager face. It was good to have a man who thought in terms of the problems they had to meet. 'No other significant medical evidence at the scene, I suppose.' He might as well use the enthusiasm and energy of this helpful medical man if he could.

'Afraid not. Rather like the other two in that. It will be interesting to see if your Scene of Crime boys come up with anything in the way of fibres on the body. I couldn't see anything when I examined her. I'm sure you'll find your man wore plastic gloves again.' Haworth looked down at his own well-manicured hands, which before long would be examining living flesh, trying to prolong life rather than establish the reasons for death.

'Thank you, Doctor. We'll keep you in touch with any developments. And if any further thoughts occur to you, please pass them on to us. We need all the help we can get with this one.'

He was treating the police surgeon almost as a member of his detection team, but he had known medical men in his time who could be as surly and uncommunicative as defence lawyers, a breed notoriously obstructive to CID work.

Meantime, they had better check quickly on their suspects for the previous two killings.

Kemp was in his office in Bristol when they tracked him down. In this place, he was Charles Kemp, entrepreneur and industrialist; Charlie Kemp, man of the people, was strictly for the more public context of Oldford Football Club and the columns of the *Echo*.

In happier times Lambert might have enjoyed the discomfiture of Charles Kemp, but this morning he had neither the time nor the inclination to savour it. He glared at the two heavy, muscular men who stood like Tweedledum and Tweedledee on each side of the door of Kemp's inner sanctum as he passed between them with Bert Hook. They were Hollywood heavies; like so many of the things with which Kemp surrounded himself, they carried the air of an earlier era, when films were made on celluloid and there were long queues outside a thousand Odeon cinemas. No doubt their fists were real enough; he wondered what other armoury they carried beneath the suits which sat so awkwardly upon those wide shoulders.

Kemp gestured widely at the chairs opposite his desk. 'No doubt you are pursuing your inquiries into the death of Amy Coleford,' he said. With the sharp thrill of the hunter, Lambert noted that he knew the name and wondered if there was significance in that. As if he read the thought, Kemp said, 'Her name was given out on Radio Wyvern as I drove here.' His smile became a taunt.

Mrs Price, thought Lambert. The police hadn't released the name of the latest victim, but there was no defence against a babysitter with a taste for melodrama. 'Curious that you should remember the name. Not many people would have done so—unless, of course, it already meant something to them.'

120

Kemp smiled. These palookas—he treasured that word —had gone straight down the avenue where he had directed them. 'Oh, but it did, you see. I knew the girl from the *Roosters*. Not well, of course, but I knew her.' In this small moment of triumph, he must be careful not to overplay his hand.

'I see. There seem to be no signs of resistance on the corpse, Mr Kemp. That might indicate, of course, that she was killed by someone she knew. Someone she was not expecting to attack her.'

Kemp thought that Amy Coleford would scarcely have regarded him as a friend. He remembered how he had reviled her and sent her weeping from his private suite at the *Roosters*. But these men knew nothing of that meeting, and now they must not even suspect it. 'That's an interesting thought, Superintendent. But I didn't kill her.'

'Where were you last night, Mr Kemp?'

It was too much to hope that an old hand like Kemp would be made nervous by Bert Hook's elaborate turning to a new page in his notebook in preparation to record his replies. He looked at the sergeant with a small, humourless, smile and said, 'I don't have to answer that, of course. But I'll tell you; I'm always anxious to help the police.'

Hook raised his eyebrows elaborately, but made no comment. Kemp, a little disappointed that he had not risen to the bait, said, 'There's no problem about my whereabouts, you see. I was with my new Manager of Oldford Football Club.'

Not 'our' but 'my' new manager, they noticed. It was probably no more than a recognition of the real situation; the affluent Chairman ruled his board with a rod of iron in many clubs nowadays. 'You were at the club?'

For the first time, Kemp looked uneasy. 'No. We were in a pub. We haven't announced his appointment officially yet, you see, and—'

'Where was this pub, Mr Kemp?'

Kemp's narrowed brown eyes looked from one to the other of the impassive faces which confronted him. 'It was in Gloucester.'

Lambert told himself there was no need to feel such satisfaction at this reply. It was probably no more than the prologue to a perfect alibi. He let the moment stretch, watching Hook write with elaborate care in his notebook. Without further prompting, Kemp said nervously, 'It was the *Dog and Partridge*. There would be plenty of witnesses.'

'One of them would interest us more than most, Mr Kemp. Your new Manager would be Victor Knowles, I presume?'

'That's right. Vic has the charisma which an ambitious club like ours needs. He was a good player, of course, but more important than that, he knows the game through and through. He's been around, and managed some of the big clubs, and he'll bring us—'

'I'm sure he will, Mr Kemp. Unless of course he's arrested on a murder charge.' Lambert shouldn't have spoken of one suspect to another like that, but he had been unable to resist the chance to deflate Kemp.

'Vic Knowles? You must be joking!' Kemp couldn't get quite the contempt he wanted into his voice.

'He may well be innocent, but we are certainly not joking. He was in the Oldford area on the nights when Julie Salmon and Harriet Brown were killed, and his account of his movements is not substantiated by any reliable witness in either case.'

Kemp looked astonished. Perhaps it really was the first time that he had known that Knowles had even been considered as a candidate for the murders. Lambert followed up while his opponent was still shaken. 'In other words, he is in exactly the same situation as you, Charlie Kemp.'

Kemp's surprise turned to anger. 'You're trying to pin this on me? After I've done my best to cooperate? I'll have you know—'

'We're not trying to pin anything on anyone. All I've said is that we've so far been unable to eliminate either you or Mr Knowles from our inquiries. It's interesting to us that you should be together in the vicinity of last night's killing. No more than interesting, at the moment.'

Kemp looked furious, but had enough sense to say

nothing while his mind worked furiously. It was Hook who looked up from his notes to say formally, 'And what time did you leave the *Dog and Partridge*, Mr Kemp?'

Kemp looked again at the two grim faces, wondering what the safe answer might be. He and Knowles could alibi each other, if he could get hold of him before the police got to him. But he couldn't rely on doing that. If he lied now and Knowles didn't support him . . . 'It must have been about ten o'clock, I think.' It had been earlier than that, but the staff in the pub restaurant wouldn't be able to be precise. And if what these buggers said was true, Knowles would surely realize it was in his own interest to stretch the time they were together as far as was possible.

'And did Mr Knowles leave with you?'

'No. We went our separate ways. We didn't want to be seen together until after the official press release about his appointment. The *Echo* is sending a photographer along to the ground tomorrow. Vic left just before me, by a different exit.'

'And where did you go then?' Lambert, who was keeping silent while Hook rapped his series of factual questions at a man they both disliked, caught the slightest hesitation before Kemp said, 'I went home.'

'And could anyone confirm this?'

'My wife might be able to. But I told you when we spoke at the *Roosters*: we have separate bedrooms.' He wondered if the wife who was still refusing to accompany him to the Masons would support him in this. Surely she would not let him down in anything so serious? He tried to dredge from his reluctant brain the law relating to wives testifying against their husbands.

Hook said relentlessly, 'And what time did you arrive at your house, Mr Kemp?'

'I—I couldn't be precise. I didn't know then that you lot would be badgering me, did I?' His confident affability had dropped away with their questions. 'I suppose it would be some time before eleven.' He knew that he had left the pub at just after half past nine, but probably no one would be able to pin him to that.

123

'Is there anyone who could bear witness to your movements after you had parted company with Mr Knowles?' Lambert made it sound like an accusation.

Kemp should surely have reiterated that he went straight home. Instead he said sullenly, 'No. There's no reason why there should be, is there? What time was Amy Coleford killed?'

'We couldn't possibly reveal that. With your intimate knowledge of police methods, you surely wouldn't expect us to.' Lambert felt a petty delight in his insulting reference to Kemp's previous brushes with the police. He certainly did not mean to reveal that they could not pinpoint the time of this death, perhaps would never be able to do so.

They had not sat down throughout this exchange. Urgency as well as hostility to this man had kept them standing. Lambert, preparing to leave, said, 'Presumably you deny any connection with the killing of Mrs Coleford?'

'Of course I do.'

'Have you any reason to think that Victor Knowles might have killed her?'

For a moment, Kemp toyed with the idea of implicating Knowles in some way. It would get him off the hook, and there were plenty of other football managers around. But he rejected the idea. It was dangerous to be over-subtle. And besides, there was a part of him that resented any alteration to his plans as a result of police activity. He had researched Knowles's weaknesses well before approaching him to take the job; it might be a long time before he turned up anyone whom he could so easily dominate with his knowledge. He said, 'No. I'm sure Vic wouldn't do any harm to anyone.'

Lambert waited until the door was open and the two gorillas outside could hear before he said, 'Don't leave the area without informing us of your plans, Mr Kemp.'

DI Rushton left Darren Pickering alone in the airless cell of the interview room for ten minutes before he saw him. If the wait made the man a little more nervous, so much the better: he might well be a triple murderer, and this was no time for delicacy.

During those ten minutes, Christopher Rushton made his first attempt of the day to contact the wife who had left him. Once again, the bland voice of his mother-in-law in the high elocutionary style she reserved for the answerphone came back at him through the earpiece; it sounded like a deliberate mockery and he banged the instrument down in frustration. He sat very still for a moment, grinding his nails into the palms of his hands, cursing all women and the pain they brought to hard-working men. Then he summoned a detective-constable and went white-faced into the interview room.

Pickering wore a white T-shirt with 'Ancient Order of Piss Artists' printed across the inches which stretched tightly over his chest. He didn't wait for them to speak. 'There's been another one, hasn't there? And you want to pin it on me.'

Rushton did not even look at him. He pressed the button on the recorder and said to the instrument, 'Interview with Darren Pickering began at 10.13 hours on Friday 17th June. Present were DI Rushton and DC Muirhead.' Then he looked sourly into the broad features opposite him, willing the man to lose his rag, to say something, anything, which might be indiscreet. Indiscretions usually led on to more significant revelations in interview rooms.

Perhaps Pickering understood that, or something of it. He said more quietly, 'Who was she?'

Rushton said, 'Where were you last night, Mr Pickering?' It was the last time he would give this thug that title: he always liked to use it once, so that his courtesy to the suspect might be recorded.

Fear passed like a summer cloud across the tough young face. 'I was at home. At first, that is. Then I went for a burn on the bike.'

'You have a motorbike?'

'A Honda 500.' There was a flash of pride, a suggestion that this was more than merely a motorcycle.

'Did you have a pillion passenger?'

125

Pickering looked puzzled. 'No. I was alone.'

'Then you have no witness to your movements in the later part of the evening?' Rushton tried to keep the satisfaction out of his voice.

'I suppose not.'

'What time did you go out?'

'About nine o'clock, I suppose.'

'You'd better tell us where you went.'

'A48, A38 up to Tewkesbury, M50 down to Ross, and back home.'

Pickering rapped out the numbers as though they were a challenge, folding his arms and resting them on the small table so that his brown forearms faced his questioners. Rushton wondered if the road numbers came too pat, like a prepared statement. Then he pictured the route on the map, and had to control his excitement. 'You went to Gloucester.'

'Round it, yes. Why?'

Rushton studied him for a long moment before he spoke, watching the anxiety grow in the twenty-year-old face. 'Do you know a woman called Amy Coleford?'

Fear flooded now into those too-revealing blue eyes. Pickering said unexpectedly, 'Yes. I've seen her at the *Roosters*. Why? Has she—'

'She was strangled last night. In Gloucester. At the time for which you can give no convincing account of your whereabouts.' Rushton enunciated the three staccato facts with satisfaction. 'Now, stop pissing us about and tell us what you were really doing in Gloucester last night.'

Pickering was shaken, but he knew enough to say little and stick to his story. 'I didn't even stop the bike in Gloucester. I went on up to Tewkesbury.' And then he had done the ton down the M50. He had thought he would need to conceal that from the fuzz; it was curious that it should now seem so unimportant.

'Witnesses?'

'No. Why should there be?'

'To preserve your delicate skin, Pickering. Think about

126

that. We're going to leave you for a while, now. You would be well advised to consider your position.'

Rushton announced to the recording machine that the interview was suspended and swept from the room before Pickering could say any more. They would leave him for half an hour or so. Then DC Muirhead could try his luck with the softer, friendlier approach, offering fags and sympathy, emphasizing the advantages of confession.

Detective-Inspector Rushton was increasingly persuaded that he could pin this one on Darren Pickering.

Vic Knowles was preparing to leave his hotel in Gloucester when he was told that the police wanted to see him.

The eyes of the chambermaid who brought the news were wide with speculation, for the news of the corpse which had sat dead through the night beside the docks had already raced around the old town. Visits from the CID would be attended now by even more than normal interest.

The two large men who came quickly into the small reception area did not disappoint the staff. With their sluggish imaginations urgently stirred, they saw Superintendent Lambert and Sergeant Hook as menacing presences, surely about to arrest a psychopath who had spent a night under their roof. Headlines leapt luridly into a dozen minds; minds which were already beginning to exaggerate their proximity to the monster who had dwelt unsuspected in their midst.

They were disappointed when Lambert elected to see Mr Knowles in his room. The hotel was less than half full, and he had been given a double room. The detectives sat carefully on bedroom chairs that were patently too small for them, looking to Knowles like birds of prey on rickety perches. He positioned his buttocks experimentally on the edge of the double bed, like a man who feared that an old-fashioned hospital sister would denounce him at any moment for the liberty.

There was a battered suitcase with a strap round it behind him on the bed; in another ten minutes, he would have been gone. But he had risen and breakfasted late. For a moment, he regretted his tardiness; then the voice of reason told him that he would have been sought out a hundred miles away within a few hours, when the case was as serious as this one.

'Is it about the strangling by the docks? I'm sure I can't tell you anything that will help you.' The girl who had served him at breakfast had brought news of the crime with his bacon, setting his nervous stomach churning and spoiling a meal he usually enjoyed.

'She was strangled, yes. We haven't yet released that detail.' Lambert dwelt heavily on the words. He had only read the reports of Rushton's interview with Knowles about the earlier killings; this was the first time he had seen him.

'The girl must have told me. The whole place seems alive with this murder.' Knowles wondered why his explanations seemed so guilty.

'That is good to hear. If the town is so interested, no doubt we shall soon turn up someone who saw the man who killed this young woman.' Lambert had no great confidence about that, but it did no harm if suspects thought that the police machinery was infallible. 'We shall need to know about your movements last night, Mr Knowles.'

'I—I was with Charlie Kemp. The Chairman of Oldford Football Club.' He leant forward, trying to give his announcement some of the import it would have had when he was playing and managing in the First Division. 'I'm going to be their new manager. It's going to be officially announced later today.'

If he had hoped to impress them, he could not have been more disappointed. Hook wrote carefully, then said, 'I thought Trevor Jameson was the manager at Oldford.' It was impossible to tell from his expression if he was trying to be provocative.

Knowles said, 'Trevor's been in football long enough to know the score. I understand from Mr Kemp that he's now been told that he is out of a job. It was nothing to do with me, of course.'

'Of course not,' said Lambert drily; his eyes had not left his man's thin, too-mobile face since they had come into

128

the room. 'Are you telling us that you were with Charlie Kemp for the whole evening?'

'Depends what you mean by the whole evening, doesn't it?' For a moment, Knowles recaptured the buoyancy of ten years ago, when he was often interviewed on television and never at a loss for a word. 'The Max Miller of football', one of the tabloids had dubbed him, and for three years he had tried to live up to the image, with a series of check jackets and quips that were never quite as good as he thought they were. There had been a lot of experience since then, most of it bad.

He saw now that these men were not seeking to be amused, that he had struck the wrong note already. 'Charlie Kemp and I had a meal together and discussed the way we saw things at Oldford.' At least he needn't tell them that the meal had been largely a monologue from Kemp about the way his new servant would do his job; that he had been made to crawl for an advance to clear his debts in the Midlands before he moved south.

'Where was this?' Lambert decided that it would be better if Knowles did not realize that they had already seen Kemp.

'At the *Dog and Partridge*.'

'And how long were you there?'

'From about seven-thirty to nine-thirty.'

They noted the slight difference in timing from what Kemp had given them. 'Did you spend the rest of the evening with Kemp?'

'No. He went off in his Merc.' They caught the whiff of envy and resentment. Oldford FC was going to be run by a pretty uneasy partnership—if other events allowed it to come to fruition.

'And you came straight back here?'

They watched his too-revealing face as he wrestled with the temptation to lie. Lambert said, 'No doubt if you did we can find someone in the hotel to confirm it.' He had not the time to spend on exposing false stories.

Knowles said dully, 'No, I didn't come straight back. It was probably after eleven-thirty by the time I got in here.'

He looked at the bed behind him, remembering how he had tossed through the night in one of his periodic bouts of self-disgust. 'I went for a drink. In a pub in Southgate Street.'

Hook looked up from his notes. 'Down near the docks, then.'

'Is it? I don't know Gloucester well.'

Lambert said, 'So you were in this pub for approximately an hour and a half. Are there any witnesses to that?'

Knowles hesitated, then said, 'No, I don't think so. The bar staff might remember me, but the place was pretty crowded.'

Lambert said wearily, 'We're talking about the time when a girl was being brutally murdered, within a few hundred yards of where you've admitted you were. Later today, we expect to have the results of the forensic tests on materials found in your car after another, similar murder. We now have three killings, almost certainly by the same man. You appear to have been in the areas of all three of them at the relevant times. If you had anyone with you last night, you had much better tell us now.'

The words had been delivered in a rapid monotone, which Knowles found the more unnerving because it was dispassionate. He switched his eyes from Lambert to the cheap Turner reproduction on the wall behind him and said dully, 'I talked to a woman for a while.'

'Name?'

His shoulders dropped hopelessly. 'I don't know. She was on her own. I think she'd arranged to meet someone who didn't turn up. I—I tried to get her to come back here with me, but she wouldn't.'

'You'd better give us her name.'

Knowles's lined face looked back to them. Hook, who was within four feet of him in the cramped bedroom, caught a whiff of stale breath. Probably he had drunk too much last night in the moment of his rejection. Or in preparation for the latest of his killings. 'I didn't get a full name. She called herself Rose. I wouldn't be certain even of that—

certain that it was her real name, I mean. I think she was a married woman.'

They got a rather vague description from him, then went over the details of his divorce and his situation back in Sutton Coldfield. As he lost confidence in himself, he became ever more frank with them. On his own admission, he, who had once been able to pick and choose his conquests, had not had much success with women lately.

By the time they left him, he had shown his abhorrence of his own conduct as well as his resentment against unresponsive women. It could be the background of a man with a grudge against a whole sex.

If Knowles was a man on the way down, everything about Ben Dexter proclaimed that he was rising steadily.

To his colleagues in Bristol, he gave the impression that he welcomed the CID as simply one more excitement in a life that was crowded with incident. The young men wore their uniform of braces and shirtsleeves as they crouched in front of their computer screens, studying the movements of the money markets around the world, making an excellent living not by producing goods but by moving other people's money around. When they were not speaking rapidly into the phones at their sides, they would occasionally put their feet up on their desks, not to relax but to demonstrate to their colleagues and rivals how simple the whole business was.

Intruders into this strange world were treated as being of a different and lower species. And most of these young men thought policemen so far behind them in their speed of thought that they must be positively retarded.

'A couple of PC Plods to see you, Ben,' said one of Dexter's acolytes. He took them into the small outer office which was reserved for those members of the public who were tiresome and thick-skinned enough to penetrate thus far into this strange world.

'And what can a simple lad like me do to assist our guardians of the law?' said Ben Dexter. He poured himself a coffee from the Pyrex jug on the hotplate, then, as an insulting afterthought, gestured an invitation at them with the jug. Then he sat on the edge of the big desk, sipping his coffee, his every gesture proclaiming that they were lucky to have a little of his time and that they must not presume too far upon his goodwill.

He was either very confident of his innocence, or had that manic presumption of superiority which often characterizes the criminally insane.

'We require a detailed account of your movements last night,' said Lambert, made more formal by the insolence of this gilded young man. 'Take your time, because it's important, to you as well as to us.'

Dexter glanced down at his Rolex. 'I may not have much time to spare.'

'You will have as much as is necessary. We'll do this at the station, if that proves more appropriate. No doubt you are aware that you can have a lawyer present while we question you, if you consider that that would be appropriate.' The deflation of this creature promised to give John Lambert his first moments of pleasure in a trying day.

'Hoity-toity,' said Dexter, as though he was delivering a good-natured rebuke to fractious children. But he was already a little shaken. His fingers crept up unconsciously to entwine themselves in his carefully cut blond hair where it caressed his delicate ears. He kept a smile resolutely upon his wide mouth, but he was consciously acting a part now. 'I expect there's been another of these murders that you can't solve, hasn't there?'

'We shall get the man responsible. However secure he affects to feel himself at this moment.' Lambert looked steadily into the blue eyes, until they blinked and looked briefly away from him to Hook.

'Cleverer than he is, are you?'

Hook looked up from his notebook in time to catch the derision in the young face. He said, 'Cleverer than you, lad, anyway. And much better organized. Where were you last night?'

'There's been another one, hasn't there? And you lot haven't—'

'Answer the question!' Hook rapped out the order so loudly that it could be heard in the big room on the other side of the wall, where the young men in front of their flickering monitors were speculating on what that mysterious Ben Dexter had been doing to excite the CID. Hook, who had never hit a suspect in his twenty-two years as a policeman, gave the impression that he might hit this one at any moment.

Dexter was thrown by the aggression concealed beneath this village-bobby exterior. He did not realize what Lambert had learned long ago, that Bert Hook was an unexpectedly good actor when interrogating, perfectly prepared to simulate whatever emotion he thought most useful. He said sullenly, 'I was at the *Roosters*. I usually am in the evenings. Do you—'

'With Darren Pickering?'

'No. I'm not his keeper, you know. Perhaps you'd better tell me what that bear of very little brain has been doing.'

'Were you in the *Roosters* club until closing time?'

'No.' Dexter turned back to Lambert, suddenly conciliatory in tone, the educated young man conversing with his intellectual equal. He was well aware of this man's exalted rank: it was almost that attained by Ben's rejected father. He said, guying himself like a man in a bad stage thriller, 'Perhaps you had better tell me what this is all about, Superintendent.'

Lambert studied the young face for a moment before he said, 'No doubt you knew a girl called Amy Coleford.'

'I know Amy, yes. Husband's left her, silly bugger. She's a useful little number, Amy. Been putting it about a bit since he left her, too.' He stopped suddenly then, as if the Superintendent's use of the past tense had only just struck him: he brought off the effect quite well. 'Look, you're not telling me something's happened to Amy now? I—'

'Amy was strangled last night. Just as Julie Salmon and Harriet Brown, whom you also knew, had been strangled before her. What time did you leave the *Roosters* last night?'

Dexter's hands ran quickly up and down his bright red braces. It was not the affectation it might have been a few

133

minutes earlier. He was nervous now, for his fingers would not stay still, even when he dropped them down on to his thighs. He wished after all that he had sat more normally behind the desk, which would at least have afforded him some concealment; perched absurdly against the front of it, he suddenly felt very much exposed. 'I left about nine o'clock, I think. It might have been a little later.'

'And why did you leave at that time? Our information is that you usually stay until last orders are called.' Lambert blessed again the good fortune which had given them a drugs squad officer working at the *Roosters*. The background material which Paul Williams had been able to provide on their suspects was one of the few bright spots in the present darkness.

Dexter was shaken by the extent of their knowledge. 'I just felt like an early night. It was too quiet in the *Roosters*.' He was not going to tell them, indeed could hardly admit to himself, that the place had seemed empty without the considerable physical presence of Darren Pickering.

Lambert paused to study Dexter's right foot, with its highly polished Gucchi shoe. It was big enough to have made the print they had found near the body of Hetty Brown. The foot was swinging backwards and forwards in what had begun as a casual gesture, but had now lost its rhythm and become a series of irregular jerks. 'And where did you go then?'

He put the query so quietly that it seemed invested with nuances of suggestion beyond its simple form. Perhaps it was these which made Dexter's reply sound even in his own ears like a lie. 'I—I went home. Back to my flat.'

'You share a flat?'

'No. I live alone.'

It was Hook, taking it upon himself to deliver the final blow to this golden-haired young Apollo gone decadent, who said, 'Is there anyone in the building where you live who could confirm the time when you arrived there last night?'

'No. I shouldn't think so.'

134

'Pity, that. We shall ask, though. It's surprising what people see or hear sometimes. Even late at night.'

Lambert said, 'You have a blue Porsche motor car. Registration J143 FCV.'

'Yes.' Dexter was shaken anew by the extent of their knowledge. He did not know that it was one of the cars which had been reported parked within half a mile of the place where Hetty Brown had been killed three nights earlier.

'How long would it have taken you to drive from the *Roosters* club to Gloucester in that car last night?'

At the beginning of the interview, Dexter would have ridiculed the question. Now, he moistened dry lips before he said, 'No more than a quarter of an hour at that time, I suppose.'

'Did you in fact drive to Gloucester?'

'No.'

'Because, you see, Amy Coleford was strangled by the docks in Gloucester last night. At the time you cannot account for, after you say you had left the *Roosters* club.'

'It wasn't me.' The denial was almost an appeal.

'We shall be checking the whereabouts of your car last night. No doubt such a distinctive vehicle will be remembered.'

Dexter looked from one granite face to the other. It was Hook who said, 'Did you kill Amy Coleford, Mr Dexter?'

'No.'

'Have you any idea who might have killed her?'

'No.'

'We shall require you to sign a formal statement later. In the meantime, you should consider your position and any other information you might be able to offer us.'

Ben Dexter said dully, 'These killings all seem to be connected with Oldford Football Club and the *Roosters*.'

Lambert said, 'That has already occurred to us; even PC Plod can sometimes make connections.'

CHAPTER 14

In the echoing rooms of the big house on the outskirts of Oldford, Diana Kemp was listening to the radio. She moved restlessly from kitchen to dining-room to lounge; she had a set on in each, and the sounds of the news bulletin rose and fell as she wandered about her house.

She sat down on one of the dining-room chairs to listen to the earnest tones of the Chief Constable, who came on at the end of the report on the attempts to trap the Strangler. 'Somewhere, someone is shielding the man who killed these women. Perhaps it is a mother or a wife; perhaps it is a brother or a sister. Perhaps it is a landlord or a landlady, who has let a room. Whoever it may be, I beg them to come forward before more lives are lost. This man has killed three times in two weeks, and he is almost certain to kill again if he is not checked. The man who has brutally strangled these women needs help. It will be in his own interest if whoever is shielding him comes forward now. Please, don't wait to be certain; if you have any reason for suspicion contact us immediately. The police are dependent on your help if further bloodshed is to be avoided.'

Diana Kemp went into the hall and looked at herself in the mirror. She saw a plump, unexciting face—perhaps because that was what she was prepared to see. Her features were still almost unlined, the grey was not unbecoming in her carefully coiffured hair. Her make-up was light but, she thought, reasonably effective: she hated those American women who fought the advance of age every inch of the way. The crow's feet were beginning to appear around her grey eyes, but that inexorable bird had trodden but lightly as yet.

All in all, it was not the face of a traitor.

She went back into the dining-room, pulled her chair up to the round table, and picked up the phone.

The number had begun to ring before her nerve went.

She could not go through with it when it came to the point; not dispassionately, not with no one to persuade her mouth into treachery. She wished she could ring the man she had just heard on the radio and let him convince her that she should speak, speaking personally now rather than in that general, blanket appeal. He had sounded like an understanding man.

Mrs Kemp sat by the phone for a full ten minutes without moving. That was the name she would use when she rang: she was too schooled in the ways of her generation to announce herself in any other way. But that very title made what she was going to do seem more like a betrayal.

She went into the small cloakroom and put on her light summer coat, examining herself again in the mirror, this time more to put off what she was going to do than from any access of vanity; her life had long since rid her of that. She hesitated a moment when she had shut the front door behind her, then went straight past the doors of the double garage, giving a little, unconscious nod to herself. She would not use the car because he had provided it; besides, she was fighting an obscure fear that he might see it parked near the police station.

She did not have to wait long at the bus stop. But the bus seemed to take ages to reach the centre of the small town; it was so long since she had used one that she had forgotten how circuitous was its route. Each stop was a temptation to leave it, to abandon the resolution which had seemed so firm when she had made it that morning. She was beset now not just by the notion of treachery, but by the English fear of looking a fool in public. Surely it couldn't be Charlie who had . . .

She sat looking steadily and unseeingly ahead of her, trying to stiffen her resolve by thinking of the pictures she had found in the drawer of his desk at home.

She had expected to wait at the police station, had steeled herself not to walk out when she was left sitting on the bench a few yards from the station sergeant. Instead, she was ushered straight through to see the man in charge of the investigation. She did not realize how her very name was an immediate passport through the barriers of police bureaucracy.

The tall man with the iron-grey hair said that he was Superintendent Lambert. He sent for tea and took pains to seat her comfortably in the stark, untidy office. He reminded her of the specialist who had explained the need for her hysterectomy. She wondered if all those papers which were spread across the big desk could really be connected with the Strangler case.

He was kind to her, trying hard to put her at her ease when she realized that he could really have very little time to spare for such niceties. She wanted to tell him that there was no need for that, that all she wanted to do was to spit out her poison and have done with it, leaving them to make what they might of it.

She started in herself without any prompting, long before the tea came. 'It's about my husband, Charlie Kemp.'

Lambert nodded calmly. 'I thought it might be.'

He gave her the impression that he had been waiting for this, that it had been inevitable that she should come, that wives came in like this on every day of the week. That made it easier. 'It may be nothing, of course. Probably it isn't.'

Lambert smiled at her and nodded. 'We understand that. We're following up all kinds of information. If yours proves to be irrelevant, there's no reason why your husband should even know that you've been here.'

She nodded, trying to produce a small answering smile to show that she understood and appreciated his concern. The smile was very reluctant to come; she could feel a tautness in her lips which she never remembered before. 'Well, I've been reading about the times when these girls were killed. I know you've seen Charles, and you must have asked him about where he was when these things happened.'

For a moment, Lambert thought that she had come after all to do her best for Kemp, to render him the wifely service of an alibi for the times of the killings. They might not believe her, but that would not matter, unless they could prove beyond legal doubt that he was elsewhere at the times she specified.

Then he looked at her troubled, hesitant face, and divined that he was wrong. 'Would it be easier for you if I simply asked you a few questions? Then you could answer them and add anything you thought might be useful afterwards.' She nodded her gratitude, just as Bert Hook carried in a tray on which he balanced two mugs of tea and a cup and saucer for her. Lambert marvelled at his sergeant's resource: he had not seen a saucer around the CID section for months. 'Sergeant Hook will just make a note of what you have to tell us. If we think it's useful, we may ask you to sign a statement later.'

It was not possible to be sure how much she understood of this. Her hands trembled a little as she took the cup, and she looked down at them in surprise, as though they belonged to someone else. Lambert moved briskly through the first killing, where she could surely have little to tell them. 'The first girl killed was Julie Salmon. Our problem is that we are not sure exactly when she was killed, because her body was not discovered until some time afterwards. Your husband was in the area on the night of her death, and cannot account for his movements for two hours or so of it. But it's only fair to say that there are several other people in the same position.'

Diana Kemp said, 'I've thought about that night a lot. But I can't be sure what time he came in.'

Lambert said, 'Forgive the intrusion, but your husband has told us that you have separate bedrooms. Is that correct?'

She smiled now, a sad, bitter smile that spoke of lost hopes. 'It is correct. But the rooms are next door to each other. I'm usually aware of when he comes in. But sometimes, when things are especially bad, I take a sleeping tablet.' She looked at him apologetically. 'I think the night when Julie Salmon died must have been one of those.'

Lambert felt a little burst of anticipatory excitement. 'Well, as I say, we haven't been able to pin down a definite time for that death yet. But we know fairly certainly just when the second girl, Harriet Brown, was killed.' He turned to his notes, trying to project to her the air of calm routine which would make her answers seem a small part of a larger pattern, although he knew by heart the details he was about to put to her.

'Mr Kemp admits to seeing Harriet Brown at the *Roosters* club at nine o'clock on Tuesday night. She was dead within four hours of that time. Mr Kemp cannot account for his movements in those hours. He says he drank on his own in his room at the club for about two of them, and then went home alone. He's not sure when he got in, but he thinks it was around midnight.'

Diana Kemp trembled a little: this was the moment she had anticipated during those difficult hours when she had built up her resolve. 'That isn't correct. It was about half past one when he got in. I have one of those digital illuminated clocks by my bed. It said one thirty-three.' The detail seemed to her like the last twist of the knife in her betrayal. But he had betrayed her often enough over these last few years.

'You're certain of this?'

'Yes. I've thought about it carefully. I'm sure.'

'Thank you. There may be another explanation of where he was, as well as the obvious one.'

'I know that. I just felt—felt that you ought to know.' She wondered how much that was true, and how much she was motivated by the hatred which had lain dormant for so long within her and now burst out like a cancer.

'Have you any idea where he might have been?'

'No. At least—well, I don't know where he was that night. I do know there have been other women. At the *Roosters*, mainly. He's come home smelling of them often enough.'

Lambert glanced at Hook, who took over readily. 'Mrs Kemp, we see a lot of the more unsavoury side of life in our work. Lots of men, unfortunately, are unfaithful to their wives: some of them with several women, as your husband seems to have been. It doesn't usually make them into murderers.'

140

'No.' The monosyllable did not reveal whether she found that a comfort or a disappointment.

'Is there anything that makes you think his sexual behaviour might be connected with violence? Anything . . . well, unusual about these sexual liaisons?'

She nodded. She had thought she might never get this out, but their quiet questioning, their assurance that nothing she could say would shock them, were drawing her on. She would not stop now. 'I found photographs last week. In his desk at home. Girls fastened up. And Charlie too, in one of them. Whips, handcuffs, ropes.' She stared resolutely at the carpet between them, determined to go on until she had rid herself of all this knowledge.

Sergeant and Superintendent looked at each other, then back to the conventional figure between them. Bondage. It was not as unusual as Diana Kemp seemed to think, nor even necessarily connected with violence. But sometimes it was, and the incidence was certainly interesting in this context.

Lambert said, 'Thank you for telling us. Again it may be merely unsavoury, rather than sinister, but it is certainly something we need to know about. We appreciate your honesty. Let me assure you that you've done the right thing —but I think you already know that.'

She nodded again, still looking at the carpet, like a small girl concentrating fiercely on the words of a recitation. 'I think he's trying to start up a call-girl racket. I don't know, but I heard a bit of a conversation when I came in one day. He was laughing about what he called the perks on the side.' She looked up at them at last, as if she feared she might catch them laughing now at her.

'If you're right, Mrs Kemp, that is a serious crime. It is a matter we shall certainly have to investigate, and we thank you once again for doing your duty as a citizen and coming forward. But, serious as it is, it doesn't make a man necessarily a murderer, any more than adultery does.'

'I know that. But I felt that if I was going to say anything, you should have the complete picture.'

'What did you do with the photographs?'

'I put them back where I found them. Do you want—'

'No, not at present. You did much the best thing in putting them back. He won't realize they've been disturbed?'

'No.' He was too arrogant even to think that she might spy on him.

'Does your husband know that you've come here today, Mrs Kemp?'

Suddenly there was fear in the grey eyes that had been so still. 'No. He mustn't—'

'We shall do our very best not to reveal our source of information. But these things will have to be followed up, as you're aware, and Kemp is no fool. He may realize, or at least suspect, that we have talked to you. Do you think you need protection?'

'No. He won't hurt me. Not seriously.'

'Can you be sure of that?'

'Yes. He'd have more sense, wouldn't he? As you say, he's no fool.' From many women, that observation on a husband would have come with a touch of pride. Perhaps it might have done once from Diana Kemp. Today it came out as a bitter irony.

'Very well. Needless to say, it will make our work of investigation easier if he's not alerted to it like that. But if your views change, please contact us immediately.'

'I'm going to stay with my sister for the weekend in Harrogate, anyway. It was arranged months ago.'

So he won't be aware of his danger. The thought lay between them for a moment. Then Lambert said, 'You know that a third girl, Amy Coleford, was killed last night? She left two young children behind.' He threw in the detail to encourage the woman opposite him to any new revelations she might make, but his own outrage sprang out for a moment with the phrase.

'I know that. In Gloucester. Charlie was in Gloucester last night. I think he was meeting the new manager he's putting in at the football club.'

'That's correct. We've already talked to your husband, and to Mr Knowles, who is the man you mention. What we'd like you to tell us if you can is the time when your husband came home last night.'

'I can indeed.' The information had been burning in her brain ever since she had heard of this latest killing on her radio in the kitchen. 'It was just after midnight.'

They thanked her politely, watched her leave, a composed middle-aged woman in a muted but expensive summer coat, who might have been reporting a lost dog.

Instead of a woman who had just revealed to them that Charlie Kemp had lied twice about his whereabouts when two girls were killed.

CHAPTER 15

On that weekend at the beginning of July, a lot of police leave was cancelled. There was not much grumbling from the team. They expected it, and with the prospect of a fourth killing at any moment, no one was inclined to argue.

Detective-Inspector Christopher Rushton, assembling his documentation for the team conference on Saturday morning, had put off his visit to seek reconciliation with his wife. That did not disappoint him: he was glad that the urgency of the hunt for the Strangler gave him the excuse to avoid a conversation he felt unable to handle. Those other women, the three dead victims of the Strangler, occupied his mind more and more. He wondered more acutely than most where the next victim might be found.

Lambert picked up Hook on his way to the station. It was still only nine, but Hook had been at work since six-thirty on his studies with the Open University. 'It's when they have to transmit a lot of their broadcasts,' he said. 'I don't mind making way for the test match, but I sometimes think the latest American sit-com shouldn't take priority.'

'It's the advance of philistinism,' said Lambert portentously. 'We import everything that is dire from America, and ignore their better facets.'

143

'It isn't their fault, but the OU certainly isn't user-friendly,' said Hook. He knew how his chief deprecated Americanisms, and was rewarded by a snort of derision from his right.

'No good language ever came out of America,' said Lambert firmly. 'Remember that, Bert, if you aspire to masquerade as an educated man.' They ran through the suburbs of Oldford, still only beginning to stir on this weekend morning. 'Anyway, it's good of you to come in to this con ference when I said you needn't. Old-fashioned and un-American of you to be so conscientious.'

' "Labour to keep alive in your breast that little spark of celestial fire called Conscience," ' quoted Hook with heavy solemnity.

'A very English sentiment,' said Lambert approvingly. 'Bunyan, I expect.'

'Chap called George Washington, actually,' said Hook.

There was a pause before Lambert said rather desperately, 'Sanctimonious little sod who cut down fruit trees and then boasted about it.'

It was Hook's only moment of amusement in a dark weekend.

Lambert was not as conservative in his views of policing as he often pretended to be. It was he who had arranged for a forensic psychologist to be present at their conference on that Saturday morning.

In the courtroom, psychiatrists are the traditional enemies of policemen, called by the defence to introduce doubts into cases that seem open and shut, producing views on the personalities of those charged with criminal offences which seem naïve and unhelpful to those charged with the preservation of law and order. During the course of investigations, however, their views on the likely personalities and psychological make-ups of people who have committed serious crimes are sought more and more readily by the CID, particularly in the case of so-called 'motiveless' offences.

Stanley Warboys was not at all vague or unworldly. He was a small man, with a neat beard, closely cut reddish-brown hair and alert brown eyes. He reminded Lambert of a highly intelligent squirrel. But instead of nuts, he stored information, and when he had eventually digested it, he came up with useful and original ideas. He was not afraid to go out on a limb, and though he often emphasized that his ideas on the kind of person they might seek out for particular crimes were quite speculative, he had not so far been made to look ridiculous when criminals had eventually been discovered.

He joined a small but highly informed group. There were no more than seven in all; even the Chief Constable had agreed to content himself with a mere report on their exchanges. Lambert and Hook, Rushton and 'Jack' Johnson, the officer who had taken charge of the Scene of Crime team, were the policemen representing the sixty officers who were now involved in the search for the Strangler.

The only policeman from outside the team was Sergeant Paul Williams, the drug squad officer operating under cover at the *Roosters*. He was twenty-four, a slight, nervous-looking man with jeans and a shirt streaked with white paint; his chin was covered with a two-day growth of stubble. Serial killers transcended even the boundaries of police bureaucracy, so that Lambert had met no difficulties in having him attend this meeting. To preserve his cover, Williams had come to the station crouched beneath plastic bags in the back of Johnson's car, and would depart in the same way.

The only other person there was Don Haworth, the police surgeon who had shown such a lively supporting interest in their work. To Lambert's secret relief, Cyril Burgess, the pathologist who might normally have brought his irritating interest in crime fiction to their deliberations, was on holiday in Austria.

'The idea,' said Lambert in his role of unofficial Chair, 'is that we put together the information we have and add to it our own ideas. I want no one to be diffident because he is afraid of looking foolish. We have a murderer who is almost certainly deranged, no discernible motive, and a string of killings which is going to become longer if people like us don't come up with some ideas. Ideas, not answers

—I don't want anyone to hold back on suggestions for lack of evidence at the moment. Let's have your thoughts, however bizarre: they needn't go down on paper or even be retailed outside this room.'

Despite this invitation to be adventurous, Rushton began with a cautious thought, checking his own conclusions against those of the others. 'The case seems to be connected in some way with the *Roosters* club. All the victims frequented the place to some extent. Our leading suspects have connections with either Oldford Football Club or the *Roosters* itself.' He was beginning to check things off on his fingers, in his normal, rational way, though he looked as if he had not slept for days.

Hook said, 'But our list of suspects isn't exclusive. Our man may be someone who watches for girls leaving there and follows them. Someone we haven't even identified yet.' Rushton frowned, irritated at having his thoughts interrupted. He felt an old tension with Hook, partly because the Sergeant was an older man, partly because Hook had refused promotion and preferred to remain as Sergeant, conferring upon himself that totally unwitting superiority which comes from integrity in an ambitious profession. Rushton could now add Hook's late but happy marriage and family to the list of his resentments against him, though he was totally unconscious of that.

He said brusquely, 'I take it we are agreed at least that we are looking for a man?'

The meeting looked automatically to Warboys, who simply nodded and didn't enlarge. Rushton said, 'Then perhaps we should go through our list of suspects before we indulge in any lateral thinking.' He had not intended this as a dig against Lambert's encouragement of speculation, but it came out as such. The DI was white and tense.

He said, 'Let's start with Vic Knowles, our only non-local suspect. That perhaps makes it more significant that he should be in the area of all three killings on the nights they occurred. Sergeant Johnson now has the forensic reports on the examination of his car, which most of you probably haven't yet heard.'

Johnson took his cue, reporting sensational material in an even, unexcited voice, almost as if he was in court. 'These findings relate mainly to the second killing, that of Harriet Brown. We gave Knowles's car a detailed examination the next day. Fibres from the back seat of Knowles's car are certainly from Hetty Brown's clothing: there are samples from both her skirt and sweater. There were also fibres from Knowles's trousers and shirt present on the clothing taken from the body.'

Rushton said, 'This is good to have, but it isn't a clincher. When I interviewed Knowles about that night, he admitted to picking up a prostitute outside the *Roosters* and having sex with her in the back of his car. According to him, she then got out and left him there. Said she was near home. His story is that he didn't even know her name. We've been to the spot and it is very close to the place where she shared a flat. He's told us a pack of lies earlier in his interview, though; all I'm saying is that these findings don't contradict his story.'

Johnson said, 'We took hairs of Vic Knowles from a golf cap in his car and the forensic boys did a DNA test on them. We also now have the test on the semen samples from the corpse. They are from the same man.'

There was a little stir around the room. Lambert said, 'What about other findings from the Scene of the Crime team for Harriet Brown's murder?'

'Precious little that is useful, I'm afraid. That empty house where she was found was too popular a venue for us to pin things positively to the time of the murder. There was a print from a formal city shoe which was fairly recent, but of course, we couldn't say definitely that it relates to the death. It might have been made earlier in the day. Size nine and a half or ten. A size which could be worn by Vic Knowles, but also by Charlie Kemp, Ben Dexter or Darren Pickering.'

'And by me, Sergeant,' Don Haworth reminded him with

147

a sheepish grin. 'Don't forget I was there very soon after the discovery of the corpse.'

'But you went in with bags over your feet, Doctor. And in any case, you were wearing trainers, not city shoes.' If Johnson was pleased to be able to demonstrate his efficiency as a SOC officer, he gave no outward sign beyond a small, answering smile. 'There is one other thing about the killing of Hetty Brown, though. The pathologist's examination of the corpse showed no sign of violence beyond the strangulation marks on the neck. There had been intercourse within the hour before death, but it was not rape, unless we assume that the victim had been passive to avoid injury. There was also no sign of robbery. The girl's purse was intact, as in the other two killings. There was almost forty pounds in it; Knowles says he paid her twenty for sex in the back of his car.'

Lambert said, 'So Knowles had had intercourse, probably as he told it, but we don't know yet whether he killed her or not.'

Stanley Warboys said, 'From the point of view of the psychologist, the most significant difference between the first two killings is that Julie Salmon was violently raped before she was killed, whereas Hetty Brown was not.'

Lambert said, 'Does that imply two different killers?' His mind was reeling with the prospect.

'Not necessarily.' The forensic psychologist looked round at the other six men, like a teacher sizing up a seminar group and wondering how much knowledge he could take for granted. 'You probably know that ninety per cent of rapes are really about power rather than sexual gratification. When further violence follows, as it did in the case of your first victim, it is usually for one of two reasons. The first is simply panic: perhaps the girl is screaming, or the man knows that she will reveal to others what he has done. He commits the still greater crime of murder in an attempt to silence the only witness to the rape.'

Rushton said, 'Would that indicate that the rapist was known to the victim?'

'Often: far more often than not, indeed; but not exclusively. Again, the majority of people who kill because they panic are of low mentality; with few personal resources at their command, they lose their heads and silence their witness in the only way they can see.'

Lambert said, 'You mentioned a second reason why murder might follow immediately upon rape.'

Warboys turned his shrewd brown eyes upon the Superintendent, rested them there for a moment, then flicked them around the other expectant faces. 'An extension of the most usual reason for rape: the assertion of power. Men may either find the rape insufficient to assuage that urge, or be so inflamed by the rape that it excites them to further demonstrations of their physical supremacy.'

'Like a drug?' said Hook.

'If you like. There are certain chemical reactions within the body, indeed, which produce their own stimulations: the best-known one is the production of adrenalin.'

It was Don Haworth, as if indicating that doctors as well as policemen could be in deep waters when it came to psychology, who said, 'But why should our man rape and kill Julie Salmon, then kill the other two girls without raping them?'

Warboys smiled. For a moment, he was a scientist intrigued by a problem, not an expert called into the investigation of a chain of grisly murders. 'He might have known the first girl personally, but been hardly acquainted with the others. Or he could simply have found himself more excited by the killings than the rape. Murder made him feel even more powerful, even more the master of these women, than rape did.' He stopped smiling and looked apologetically at the grim faces around him. 'If I'm right, that would also help to explain the accelerating rate of the killings. There are nineteen days between the deaths of Julie Salmon and Harriet Brown, but only three between those of Harriet Brown and Amy Coleford.'

'Which means he might kill again very soon?' asked Lambert glumly.

'I'm afraid so. If I'm right and he sees the opportunity. It's all hypothetical, as you realize.'

149

Rushton was very white. He said, 'Yes, it is. Is there anything else you can tell us about the man we're looking for?' His voice was unexpectedly harsh in the quiet room; it was impossible to be certain whether this stemmed from a contempt for psychological speculations or from some other kind of strain.

Warboys was completely unruffled. He said, 'I'd prefer to hear the rest of the forensic findings before we go any further.'

Sergeant Johnson, who had been waiting to speak for some time, said, 'Now that we can compare the reports on the semen samples from the first two murders, we know that they were not from the same man.'

There was a long silence round the table. Eventually Rushton said, 'Does this put Knowles in the clear for murder?'

Lambert said, 'No. It doesn't really help us. It means that Knowles didn't rape Julie Salmon. But he could still have killed her, if he found her in a distressed condition after the rapist had left. Alternatively, he could be telling the truth, in which case the murderer of Julie Salmon might have killed Hetty Brown after she had left Knowles.'

Rushton said slowly, 'Knowles was in this area on the night of the killing of Julie Salmon, although he lived a hundred miles away at the time. It's the most damning fact against him. When you put that together with his presence at the time of the other two murders, it seems a remarkable coincidence. But perhaps it isn't all that remarkable. We've investigated over a hundred men so far in connection with these killings, but found only four who apparently had the opportunity to commit all three of them and have no convincing alibi for any one of them.'

Don Haworth said, 'You mentioned that the man who raped Julie Salmon might have had some previous relationship with her. Darren Pickering was her boyfriend until a week or two before she died. I was her GP, and I know how unhappy her parents were about the association.'

'And he had opportunity to commit the other two killings,' growled Rushton.

The drugs squad sergeant, Paul Williams, found himself at last with something to contribute. 'Pickering isn't as tough as he pretends to be—I've seen plenty of him at the *Roosters*. I'd say he was genuinely very upset by the death of Julie Salmon.'

Stanley Warboys said, 'I'm afraid that wouldn't eliminate him as a suspect. It's quite common for people who kill after they have been rejected as sexual partners to be overcome with emotion afterwards. Sometimes it's remorse; more often it's a complex of feelings. As I think we agreed at the outset of this meeting, we are looking for an unbalanced mind. Our problem is that such minds, particularly those suffering from schizoic disturbance, often display quite normal reactions once they are operating away from the immediate area of the killings. That's why even people close to them sometimes don't suspect them of their crimes.'

Williams turned to Rushton. 'Was there anything among Julie Salmon's possessions which would implicate Darren Pickering?'

Rushton shook his head reluctantly, but it was Johnson who spoke. 'No. There was one strange thing, though. I said there was nothing at the scene of crime to indicate robbery, and Julie Salmon's purse was left in the pocket of the jacket she was wearing. But her handbag was missing, and it's never turned up. Her parents were sure she had it with her, and it certainly wasn't in the house. We've rather assumed that some person unknown removed it from the scene of the crime well after she was dead—remember she wasn't found until some two days after she was killed. But it could have been the murderer, if the bag contained something to connect him with the crime.'

Hook said, 'Her parents were not as down on Darren Pickering as I expected. Apparently Julie had had some dealings with an older man—no one seems sure whether there was a sexual relationship or not and she never revealed his identity to her parents. I think they thought Darren Pickering was the lesser of two evils. At least he was about her own age: she was only nineteen when she died, don't forget.'

151

Don Haworth said, 'I understand Pickering has a history of violence.'

Rushton said, 'Various punch-ups, yes. He also left the *Roosters* shortly before Harriet Brown was killed, and he was out on his motorbike at the time when Amy Coleford died, without any witnesses as to his whereabouts.'

Paul Williams said, 'For what it's worth, I wouldn't make him a leader in the football hooliganism you're going to have to snuff out next season. I should keep your eye on Ben Dexter in that respect: he fancies himself as a manipulator of puppets. Incidentally, both of them have used pot, and I think Dexter's dabbling with heroin. It's possible he's dealing, but we're after the big boys, so please don't raise it with him yet. I mention it only because it might have some bearing on this case.'

They looked expectantly at Stanley Warboys, but he shook his head. 'I haven't seen Dexter, so I couldn't venture an opinion. If he is of a violent disposition, those tendencies of course might be released as any others might be by the administration of drugs.'

Lambert said, 'If he confines his drugs to his leisure hours, that might explain why he was so easily deflated when we saw him in his working environment. He started by being derisory about our efforts, but he collapsed pretty quickly. But he does seem to look for kicks in outwitting the police. I suppose there could be an element of that in these killings.'

Warboys said, 'Yes. It's a factor in most serial killings, especially as time goes on and the murderer remains undetected. It has led several killers to ever more daring and shocking crimes, particularly when press coverage has increased and dwelt on the bafflement of the police. I notice that your man is now universally known as the Strangler. It could be worse: there is some evidence that animal soubriquets—the Black Panther and so on—excite minds which are already disturbed to great displays of violence and what they consider invincibility.'

Williams said, 'Making fools of the police would certainly be attractive to Dexter: the father he claims to hate was a senior policeman. I've listened to him in the *Roosters* and it isn't just a front. He seems to have a contempt for all authority; perhaps it stems from his days in a public school.' He looked quickly at Warboys, as if in apology for this outbreak of amateur psychology. 'That's what's behind his preoccupation with organizing football mayhem—which incidentally he claims he did on a bigger scale at West Ham before he came down here.'

Hook said, 'Dexter's Porsche was sighted within a quarter of a mile of the spot where Hetty Brown was killed, at the time of the murder. He also left the *Roosters* at about nine o'clock on the night when Amy Coleford was killed— much earlier than usual. No sightings of his car in Gloucester yet, but the uniformed boys are working on it.'

Hook tried to keep his rubicund features suitably impartial. He very much wanted their man to be Dexter: he only realized that as he spoke. No doubt it had something to do with his Barnardo's boy background: Dexter's schooling and higher education could hardly have been more different from his own. But he did not feel guilty about his feelings. Someone had done these killings, and was looking to do more: it had as well be that gilded young psychopath Dexter as anyone else.

Lambert said quietly, 'Charlie Kemp is just as much in the frame as Dexter or the others. More so, in fact, in that we know from his wife's statement that he's lying about his movements on the nights of at least the last two killings.' There was a murmur of satisfaction among the five policemen around the table: Kemp was a villain who had got away with far too much in the past. They would all be pleased if they could make this one stick.

Sensing the mood, Lambert went rapidly through the facts about Kemp, surprising the team as he had done often before by not referring to a note at any point. 'We know that he knew the first victim, Julie Salmon, because she frequented the *Roosters*, often with Darren Pickering. But that is all we have been able to pin down. The case is strongest against him on the second and third murders. We are fairly certain that Harriet Brown was killed in the hour after midnight on 12th June—'

'I did emphasize you shouldn't take that as gospel, you know,' put in Don Haworth with a modest grin.

Lambert's acknowledging smile was briefer, a mere disguise for his irritation at the interruption. 'We aren't in a court of law yet. When we are, no doubt we'll have enough evidence to make sure that you're not embarrassed under oath, Doctor. We now have Mrs Kemp's word that her husband was not in the house that night until one thirty-three, despite his earlier statement to us that he was home by midnight.'

Paul Williams said quietly, as if reluctant to reveal information on a man he had been watching in another context. 'Kemp took Amy Coleford up to his suite at the *Roosters* two nights before her death.'

'Why?' The monosyllable came like a pistol shot, reflecting Lambert's annoyance that the information should have been held back until now.

Williams said, 'It didn't seem important until a few hours ago, when I heard that Amy had become a Strangler victim. Kemp has always taken girls up there in the three months while I've been operating at the *Roosters*, to have it away with them—there are various rumours among the regulars about how kinky it gets. I think he's planning to set up some of the girls who are already on the game in houses he will control.

'You will understand that this information is secondary as far as we're concerned: our primary concern is with the drugs operation. We have an interest in Kemp because we think he may be involved in that, but we haven't enough evidence yet to be able to move in. It's the big boys we want, and they're the most shadowy figures, as always.'

It was a long speech, and he gave the impression that every word was wrung grudgingly from him. The drugs squad operated with autonomy from normal CID work. Now Williams had the complication that his investigations were being overtaken, his cover threatened, by the oldest and darkest crime of all, and he did not like it.

Lambert understood all this, and knew also the tension under which this taut, unkempt-looking young man was operating. Drug barons were powerful and unscrupulous men; discovery could mean disappearance and death for those who sought to hunt them down. But Lambert had his own tensions, with a serial killer who had struck three times and might do so again at any moment. 'Have you any suggestions as to how Kemp's sexual activities might be linked with these killings?'

Williams, who looked as though he wished the discussion could become more general again, said, 'Harriet Brown had been up there as well. I don't know about Julie Salmon: she wasn't on the game. But if all three girls had turned him down, that could be a link, I suppose.' He looked rather desperately at the forensic psychologist, but Stanley Warboys neither confirmed nor denied his suggestion.

Lambert said, 'Kemp lied to us about his movements on the night of Amy Coleford's death, as he did with Harriet Brown. He was in Gloucester with Vic Knowles. He told us he left the *Dog and Partridge* just before ten, whereas Knowles tells us that it was at half past nine. More significantly, he says he was home before eleven, but his wife tells us he was not in until almost midnight. That leaves two and a half hours unaccounted for, and it covers the period when Amy Coleford was killed.'

He looked round the table, his expression inviting comment. Rushton said, 'I suggest we get all these four in again and grill them. Using people who haven't seen them before.'

Lambert looked at him for a moment, conjecturing about his pallid cheeks and his intense air. Rushton seemed more determined than ever that this crime should be pinned to one of the four quickly. That was understandable, but he would have expected him to be cooler, more objective. 'We can do that, certainly, and see if we can unearth any discrepancies in the stories they tell. Kemp for one will demand his lawyer, which means he will say nothing and challenge us to charge him before we go any further. We must keep our minds open: it's still possible that the Strangler may be none of these men. I'd like to hear what

155

our forensic psychologist thinks, now that he is aware of what we know at this point.'

Stanley Warboys put both his hands on the table in front of him, studying his closely pared nails for a moment, as if he used them as an aid to concentration. 'I have listened to what you say about your main suspects. We have to bear in mind the Superintendent's last remark, that it may be none of the men we have been discussing. So I think it would be best if I couched my thoughts in general terms.' He had the air of a man launching a dry academic treatise, but there was no lack of attention among the six men who listened to him.

'Anything I have to say is obviously hypothetical. But perhaps I should emphasize that I do not work in isolation; I try to put together the scene of crime findings and other forensic evidence with any thoughts I might have on the psychology behind a crime. One thing I would be reasonably certain of is that you are looking for a man living alone —but not necessarily physically alone. This man does not seem a likely killer in his normal working and social life; that is probably why you have had no useful suggestions yet from the public. He may well be living with a companion who does not suspect, or has not yet cared to confront, the possibility that he is a killer. The Yorkshire Ripper had a wife, but he lived a completely different life outside his house.'

Rushton said, 'Should we expect our man to have previous form? A history of violence?'

'Not necessarily, I'm afraid. No doubt you've had men combing criminal records in the last week, but the trouble with serial killers is that by definition they have embarked on a new kind of crime for them. I think we would agree that this mind is unbalanced, and the things which throw minds off balance don't confine themselves to those who've been in prison. I think you're probably looking for a highly intelligent man, but that doesn't necessarily mean someone with a lot of formal education.'

'Why do you say that?' Don Haworth's question had a ring of professional curiosity.

'For a start, he's outwitted an intensive search by a police machine which is experienced and highly efficient, whatever the popular press might be saying about you this morning.' Warboys permitted himself a small, ironic smile. 'Moreover, he seems to be taking a delight in outwitting your efforts. When you concentrated your resources upon the Oldford area, as all the previous evidence suggested you should, he killed in Gloucester. Either he watched your precautions, or he anticipated them. His third murder was a taunt to the efforts of the sixty officers detailed to catch him. And the way he laid out the second and third corpses, like ritual sacrifices or pious emblems, is another form of black humour.'

'It's almost as though he was familiar with our methods.' Sergeant Johnson looked embarrassed as the faces turned to him; he had voiced the thought even as it came into his mind, without weighing it. He was a stolid figure, with short, carefully cut hair, a conscientious scene of crime officer whose normal work involved the patient accumulation of scraps of physical evidence. He found this more tentative and oblique approach fascinating.

Warboys looked at Johnson, then slid his bottom lip thoughtfully beneath his front teeth. It made him look more than ever like an alert red squirrel. 'It's possible he does know police work. And possible also that he has a degree of medical knowledge. All three girls died by vagal inhibition within a few seconds. They were expertly despatched, and that efficiency probably appeals to our man: I think he will have a perverted pride in the swift competence of his killing.'

Rushton said harshly, his words almost treading upon the calm phrases of the psychologist, 'Are you saying that we should be looking for someone with medical training?'

As Warboys shook his head, it was the police surgeon, Don Haworth, who said, 'Not necessarily. I examined all the bodies. I agree about the efficiency of despatch: not more than a few seconds in each case, with the girl probably not permitted a single scream. But the degree of medical knowledge required is minimal. It could be someone like a

157

male nurse, but it could also be someone who's learned how to kill: there are plenty of people who have been taught a little karate and become very dangerous to the rest of us. It could even be someone who's simply read it up.'

'Like a professional man,' said Hook.

'Yes. Or someone who comes into contact with violence and death in the course of his work,' said Warboys quietly.

'Someone like an ambulance driver,' said Johnson.

'Or a policeman,' said Warboys.

It is not easy to shock the kind of group to whom the forensic psychologist addressed this thought, but for fifteen seconds there was an electric silence in the room. The policemen looked to Lambert to speak, but he said nothing. It was the hoarse voice of DI Rushton which eventually said, 'Is that a serious suggestion?'

'Perfectly serious. But not exclusive.' Warboys chose his words as primly as a man eating cherries with a knife and fork. He lifted the fingers he had studied at the beginning of his exposition and steepled them six inches in front of his eyes. 'To summarize my thoughts, for what they are worth: I think you are looking for an intelligent man, who enjoys the thought of outwitting his hunters; a man who knows how to kill quickly and silently, and has a pride in that efficiency; who has a degree therefore of medical knowledge, but one he could have acquired in a variety of ways; who has been so excited by his first killing that he has been led on to others and is unlikely to stop at three.'

The silence this time was one of assimilation rather than outrage. It was the first time that Lambert had spoken in many minutes when he said, 'Does that exclude any of our present suspects?'

Warboys said heavily, 'Not from what I understand. Neither Kemp nor Pickering has much in the way of formal qualifications, but neither of them is stupid: in their different ways, they have the kind of shrewdness, and certainly the delight in outwitting police procedures, that I have suggested.'

Rushton said, 'And Knowles likes to give the impression of being a rough diamond, but he was actually quite well educated in his youth. Could have gone to university apparently, if he hadn't become a professional footballer.'

Williams said, 'The best fit for your profile is probably Ben Dexter. He's sharp, loves violence, and delights in outwitting the police. And he's a drug user. On a trip, I could see him strangling girls.'

Warboys said, 'I agree he seems marginally the most likely of your suspects. The way the last two corpses have been tidily arranged for inspection—Harriet Brown like an effigy on a mediæval tomb and Amy Coleford like a woman sitting quietly in a chair by the fireside—argues both an insolence and a need to taunt those pursuing him. It also reinforces the view that the first killing, where the corpse was not treated like that but left as it fell, stemmed from a more personal hatred of Julie Salmon. That suggests in turn that there was some sort of previous relationship between killer and victim. But I must reiterate that the psychological profile I have outlined doesn't exclude any of your four. Nor does it mean necessarily that your killer must come from within that group.'

Lambert was not sure whether it had been a good idea to bring this precise, almost pedantic man, into their discussions. Probably his observations would be useful, once they had had the chance to digest them and put them together with the more normal work of a murder investigation. He wound up the meeting quickly.

It was when they were preparing to depart that Warboys, gathering his papers into a neat folder, said, 'There is one further thing. It is impossible that with three murders already you should not intensify police pressure and activity, both in Oldford and further afield. I do not see that you could do otherwise. However, I have to warn you that this may well incite your killer to a further demonstration of what he considers his superiority.'

CHAPTER 16

On that eighteenth day of June, a belt of rain came in from the Atlantic and worked its way slowly but steadily across the West Country.

Late in the day, it would reach the area around Oldford which the tabloids had dubbed 'The Strangler's Stretch'. But it was still fine there when the rain reached Bristol. It was a soft, gentle rain, which the farmers welcomed in the rich agricultural tracts around the city. But in the area of the old city where nothing grew but weeds, it fell as a depressing drizzle.

The district through which Charles Kemp drove was quiet, even apparently deserted. Warehouses are rarely busy on a Saturday afternoon, and on this damp summer day they were silent indeed. He watched his rear-view mirror carefully as he moved the blood-red Mercedes cautiously over the shining acres of tarmac. Only when he was satisfied that he was not being followed did he turn the car into the narrower street which led to the building where the meeting had been arranged.

There were two cars there before him, parked unobtrusively below street level. He ran the Mercedes down the steep concrete ramp, turned its nose so that it was ready to move off swiftly when they had finished their business, and left it alongside the other two vehicles.

He could not resist a look of satisfaction at the car before he left it. It gleamed sleekly beneath the droplets which had gathered on its polished surface; rain always enhanced that effect. It might have been brand new rather than eighteen months old and due for a change. Perhaps he would keep this one a little longer. His cars were still the visible reassurance he gave himself that Charlie Kemp had made it to the big time. That was the phrase he always used, to himself as well as others.

But if his slang was stuck in a 'fifties time-warp, his

villainy was entirely up to date. Heroin, cocaine and that lucrative derivative of cocaine known as crack yielded rich profits to the modern criminal entrepreneur. And Kemp prided himself on being one of those. He took a last, automatic glance up towards the corner of the street before he went inside the building. It was deserted, as the whole of the industrial estate appeared to be on this wet Saturday afternoon.

They met in the basement, in a room without windows, as though they used the earth itself to cover their designs. There were only four men at this subterranean gathering. The Greek, who had made a legitimate fortune from shipping and a much larger one from supplying more sinister substances, was the biggest importer of crack into the UK. His muscle would not be far away, but they never came with him into meetings. They were always at hand, but rarely visible: Kemp thought that an impressive touch of class.

The Greek spoke perfect English. The Levantine beside him spoke very little English, but that little was all he needed. He hardly spoke during the entire meeting, but his nod was an acceptance of the price of a million dollars for the heroin he was overseeing on its roundabout route through the Middle East.

The other man on Kemp's side of the table was a 'wholesaler', as Kemp was planning to be. He operated somewhere in the Black Country. He and Kemp did not know each other's names, and did not want to learn them. Anonymity meant safety when the police across the world made their occasional indentations into this wall of vice.

Ostensibly the four met to fix a price. But each of them knew within five per cent what that price would be when they came into that low, airless room with its harsh fluorescent lighting. They were token negotiations, and not much time was wasted over them.

What Kemp did not know was the quantity he would be offered. It was three times what he had expected. The quality was 'guaranteed', though both he and the man beside him were too eager to acquire the drugs to digest

161

quite what that word meant. They had dealt with these men before, and showed handsome profits. They knew they were the ones taking the greatest risks, for it was they who had to set up the network of retailers, and every extra person involved was a potential leak. But that was the way of these things, when the demand they had created outstripped the supply.

Kemp tried hard to conceal his excitement as he arranged for three hundred thousand dollars to be transferred to a Swiss bank account which he knew only by number. His quick brain calculated even as he agreed the deal that he would make two hundred per cent profit if he sold on the streets at the rates he intended.

The Greek could have told him that more experienced middle men would have expected more.

But Kemp drove away happy. The Greek and the Levantine would be out of the UK before midnight. But the stuff he had bargained for was already in the country; he must alert his network of dealers. Charlie Kemp was in the big time now, all right.

The big red Mercedes was well out of the city before he remembered that other business which the excitement had temporarily driven from his mind. He had better get on with the task of arranging an alibi for those hours when Hetty Brown and Amy Coleford had died: it was obvious to someone of his experience that the police were suspicious.

But he had outwitted them before, and he would do so now. Pigs were stupid, and he would prove it again.

Whatever Charlie Kemp's views might be, the Chief Constable was no fool. Media conferences called for four o'clock on a Saturday afternoon were not likely to be prolonged, with cynical pressmen and television staff anxious to get away to relax in what remained of their weekends.

George Harding kept it as low-key as possible, for he had nothing worthwhile to report. He dealt courteously but briskly with the expected questions. No man was 'helping the police with their inquiries', though the press officer would give them the impressive numbers of those who had

162

been interviewed. No vehicle which had been seen near the scene of the crimes was being sought. No woman other than the three victims had reported being threatened. (The tabloid reporter who had just agreed to give a local lady of ill repute a thousand pounds for a story headlined WAS IT THE STRANGLER WHO HAD HIS FINGERS ON MY THROAT? decided that Monday's edition could still carry the piece.)

The Chief Constable and the press officer did most of the fencing with the members of the third estate. Lambert's main role was as a tangible link with the routine of the investigation itself, an assurance to the media that the men engaged in detection were anxious to keep the public informed about their efforts as well as determined to give women whatever protection they could against further bloodletting. He gave a terse account of the progress of his team, explained with a grim smile that of course he could not give the names or other details of the men who particularly interested them.

Trying to ignore the hand-held television camera which seemed to be moving right into his face, he said with confidence that they were hopeful of an arrest 'within the next few days'. He could almost feel the Chief Constable's eyebrows rising behind him. He told himself resolutely that George Harding was too skilled a diplomat to allow himself any facial expression which might be so revealing.

Lambert wondered if the killer would be watching the telecast that night, and what he might make of that statement. Would he be watching alone, or with some unsuspecting woman at his side?

It was when he was called up to the Chief Constable's office after the conference that Lambert received the shock which drove such conjecture from his mind.

George Harding introduced the woman with brisk formality. 'Superintendent Lambert, this is Detective-Sergeant Ruth David.'

She was tall, with the willowy figure of an athlete but a shape which must have given her some difficulties with the raw young constables who had been trained alongside her. She had ash-blonde hair and eyes of a deep green, set either side of a nose which was a fraction too definite for perfection. Even in her sensible police issue shoes and dark stockings, her legs were inescapable as she settled herself in an armchair at the Chief Constable's bidding. She looked to Lambert no more than nineteen.

He learned in the next few minutes that she was a graduate entry to the force, that she had served three years, that she was in fact now twenty-six: he was getting old. They sat in three of the armchairs in the CC's panelled, well-furbished office, nibbling biscuits and drinking tea, while Lambert waited for Harding to reveal to him what connection this attractive member of the force had with his investigation of the Strangler killings.

Was there to be the suggestion of a reconstruction of one of the crimes? Hardly likely: they had decided earlier in the week that such an exercise would be a dissipation of their resources, with little chance of anyone coming forward with new information. And this striking girl did not look much like any of the victims, even allowing for the addition of the right wig and clothes. She was too tall, for a start.

The CC was probably watching him and taking a small pleasure from his uncertainty, for he eventually said, 'Well, John, time to put you out of your misery. We have a suggestion to offer, Sergeant David and I. The right of veto is yours, as always, but we'd like you to consider the idea very seriously before you decide whether to use it or reject it.'

Beneath his easy, almost teasing urbanity, he was a little uneasy. He had not so far had many dealings with this most senior of his superintendents, and he did not want any public outburst from him about the unorthodoxy he was proposing. But then you could hardly call anything public when it was said in front of one sergeant in the Chief Constable's office.

Lambert felt as though he was trying to help things on when he said, more stiffly than he would have liked, 'We're willing to try anything, sir. You know the state of the inquiry. We have four leading suspects, but still no absolute certainty that our efforts should be confined to them.'

'We also have a suggestion that our killer might even come from within the ranks of the force,' said Harding grimly. Probably he caught Lambert's involuntary glance at the woman opposite him, for he said, 'I have taken the decision to brief Sergeant David fully on the state of play. If she is to be involved in an attempt to trap your murderer, she needs to know everything we know.'

Lambert said without looking at her again, 'May I ask exactly what part it is suggested that Sergeant David might play in our investigation?' He was disconcerted again by the stuffiness of his own reaction: this development had caught him off guard.

'I thought we might plant her at the *Roosters* and see what she can pick up.' Harding smiled at the grim ambivalence of the phrase, which he had not intended.

'With respect, sir, I think that is far too dangerous. I shouldn't like to take the responsibility for putting anyone in that situation.' Let alone an inexperienced young girl like this, he thought; he had just enough sense to realize he should not offer up any such hostage to feminism, but only just.

George Harding smiled. He had relaxed from the brisk, confident chief he had presented in the media conference; he looked older and more tired. His frizzy hair was almost white at the temples, more untidy than it had been in front of the cameras. He was a fit man for his age, in a well-cut uniform, but beneath it what had been hard muscle was relaxing a little into a natural plumpness. He said, 'That was my reaction too, at first, John. I didn't think the risk was justified. But now that we're in private, we can agree that this is a pretty desperate situation, warranting desperate remedies.'

'Hardly desperate, sir, surely. We're—'

'We're no closer to an arrest than we were two days ago. And we all think time is the key factor on this one. If we go another week, we'll have another woman dead—perhaps more than one.'

165

'All the same, there must be other possibilities. If I could just discuss this one with some of my senior officers—'

'No!' The negative came from Harding like a pistol shot. 'Look, John, I've read your report of your conference this morning. I noted the views of your forensic psychologist. He suggests we might have a professional man involved: possibly a police officer. Do you disagree with that?'

'No. Not as one possibility among others. It was I who brought the forensic psychologist in. But that wasn't the only thing he said.'

'I'm aware of that, John. But if there's even the possibility that one of our officers might be a psychopath, it means that we must keep any new initiatives we take within as small a group as possible.'

Lambert nodded glumly. While the two men stared at each other, Ruth David finally spoke. 'May I be permitted a word or two? First of all, the suggestion that someone might do this came from the Chief Constable, but I was the one who volunteered for the job. Secondly, I didn't do it impetuously: I've thought out the odds. If your man was killing with a knife or a pistol, I wouldn't be offering you my services. But he's a strangler; possibly a rapist too, but even that now seems uncertain. I've got a brown belt for judo, and I hope to take the black before too long. I'd back myself against the Strangler.' She allowed herself a tight little smile at her bravado, almost apologizing that she should put forward her virtues so immodestly. That was the attitude expected in this man's world.

Lambert muttered, 'I'm still not happy about it.'

Harding said, 'Would you allow a man to take a calculated risk to try to catch this man?'

Lambert smiled. 'Yes, I suppose I would. Are you saying I'm being sexist?'

'I'm saying my first thought was exactly the same as yours. That I had to convince myself that anyone, male or female, should take this kind of risk. But if we really think there are going to be more killings, we have to take a chance.'

Lambert said, 'All right. But let's discuss the details

166

before we finally commit ourselves.' He looked at the contrasting faces opposite him and said hastily, 'I'd want to do the same if it was a man I was putting in.'

Ruth David grinned. 'I'm glad to hear it. I wouldn't want to work for anyone who threw me in without calculating the odds. I thought about them carefully myself before offering my services.' She could not tell them how she thought in bed at night about these women being killed, and no woman involved in the hunt for this madman: that romantic nonsense was no more objective than old soldier Lambert's instinctive rejection of the idea that a woman should be involved. 'I'm already a member of the *Roosters*, because I happen to be a football fan. They've got a good team, despite Charlie Kemp. But I've never let on there that I'm in the police: it's not an occupation to win you friends among the regulars these days. And as I work in Bath, no one there has rumbled me.'

'But are you—' Lambert fumbled for words—'are you the kind of woman our man is going to go after?'

She grinned at him, enjoying his discomfort. 'Am I a Tom, you mean? No, not even on a part-time basis. Though Cambridge gave me the chance to build up a lucrative future clientele, if I'd been inclined. But with a new wardrobe and a bit of assistance with the right make-up, I can give a very good impression of a tart. Anyway, as I understand it, the Strangler might go for any unprotected woman. The first girl was raped and murdered, but she wasn't on the game, was she?'

'No. But there is a possibility that there might have been some kind of previous relationship with her killer. It's a lead we're working hard to follow up at the moment.'

The Chief Constable said, 'Sergeant David has done a lot of acting in the past, John.'

'But with due respect, amateur dramatics are hardly the preparation for playing games like this, sir.' Lambert noticed how he brought out the 'sirs' only when he was uneasy. He knew now that he was going to accept this ploy, but he still wasn't happy about it. He couldn't see how he was going to protect this girl. She reminded him too much in her bright confidence of his own younger daughter, Jacqueline. 'What exactly is it that you plan to do?'

Sergeant David looked at the Chief Constable and was given a brief nod of acquiescence. 'Paul Williams of the drugs squad will be in the club at the same time as me. He won't act unless there is an emergency, because it's vital for his own investigation that his cover is preserved. I don't think there will be any crisis at the *Roosters*. When our man strikes—and we aren't even certain that he frequents the club—it will be when he has a girl on her own in some isolated situation, judging by the previous killings.'

Lambert nodded a reluctant agreement. 'Williams could listen to the talk when you weren't there. If they were suspicious of your new persona, he would be likely to pick up the talk.' He realized as he voiced that thought that he had now acquiesced in the scheme.

'Yes. He could report the reactions of the people in the club when I wasn't there. They might be of considerable interest.'

'He would also be the best test of whether your impersonation had been rumbled.' Lambert turned to his Chief Constable. 'I think we should try it. The only stipulation I would make is that I insist on withdrawing Sergeant David immediately if there is even a suggestion that her cover has been blown. There's no guarantee that the Strangler would stick to his methods if he felt we were getting near to him.'

Harding nodded. 'That is a rider I should have added myself. I think we should now put the scheme into action as quickly as possible.'

Lambert looked at the girl opposite him. Now that the scheme had finally been sanctioned, she was striving to conceal her excitement. For the first time since the idea had been broached, Ruth David felt nervous. But there was no trace of that in her voice as she said, 'I'm ready to move into the *Roosters* tonight, sir.'

CHAPTER 17

Darren Pickering was at once bored and uneasy. The *Roosters* was quiet for a Saturday night, and those that had made the effort to come out were not doing much dancing.

Perhaps the Strangler and all the talk about him was having a dampening effect upon the club. No one had said officially that these murders centred upon the place, but the regulars, unconsciously in some cases, had divined it for themselves. There were fewer girls in than usual. People watched each other more closely, were quicker to take offence. The laughter, when it came, rang loud and self-conscious across the big room with its expanse of shining dance floor.

Darren lounged back between the wooden arms of his chair and surveyed his third pint of beer. He could not raise a lot of enthusiasm even for drinking tonight; he kept thinking of the way the police had questioned him about the death of Amy Coleford. Despite his professed contempt for them, he wished he could provide himself with an alibi for the time of that killing. But he knew very well that no one was going to come forward to say that they had seen him on his motorbike that night.

Beside him, Ben Dexter sipped his beer and studied his companion. He wondered how long it would be before Pickering relinquished his earring. He would tell him in a week or two that it would be a point of weakness in any street fighting when the new season got under way. All the signs were that there would be bigger crowds around, as Oldford made their bid to get into the league. The Strangler would give the team a certain abattoir glamour: he wondered if they could build him into some of their chants. There might be more murders before the season began: Ben Dexter smiled his secret, mirthless smile at the thought.

'Useful bit of crumpet on the next table,' he said to the

doleful Pickering. 'Might give her one myself, if she's a good girl.'

Pickering wondered how much success Ben Dexter really had with women. He had not seen much public evidence to support his companion's suggestions of his sexual successes. 'She's been in before, but she looks different tonight,' said Darren. 'More—more available.'

'Big word for a young lad like you,' said Dexter. He looked across at the long expanse of black nylon, stretching out to where the ankles crossed above red heels; Ruth David had decided that fishnet tights would be too abrupt a change from her previous hose. 'If you mean she's flashing her fanny and asking for it, you're right.' He stared appreciatively at the point where the black leather skirt creased over the transition from thigh to stomach.

'Time you were putting it about again yourself, young Darren. Lack of oats is making you moody. You're not the same man now that you're not able to poke young Julie.' He knew he was on dangerous ground, but as always he enjoyed the excitement of being close to danger. And he got a perverse satisfaction out of speech and attitudes much coarser than those of his lumpish companion.

'I've told you before. Leave Julie out of your conversation!' Pickering leaned across the table, and for a moment Dexter thought he was going to feel those large hands on his immaculate white shirt.

'Steady on, old lad.' He backed off quickly; then, when he saw Pickering relax, resumed his thesis in more general terms. 'All I'm saying is, if the tarts are putting it about a bit, let's have our share. Grab a handful of—'

'Julie wasn't a tart!' Pickering's eyes blazed with a righteous indignation that Dexter found wholly amusing.

'I didn't say she was, Darren. But it was you who told me she'd been playing away from home with an older man.' His face was full of his appeal to reason, his mind full of malice.

'Just shut up, can't you? Leave Julie out.' Darren was shouting now, full of the indignation of the inarticulate man who knows he is right but cannot find the words to justify himself. People on other tables around them were looking across to see what the disturbance was about.

Ben Dexter said, 'Cool it, Darren. All I'm saying is, don't waste opportunity when there's skirt like this about.' He gestured with his head towards the delights available on the adjacent table.

Ruth David, who was aware of his scrutiny but ostensibly concentrating upon her companions and her gin and tonic, uncrossed her ankles, studied the red toes of her shoes for a moment, and crossed her legs again at the knees. The Footlights had hardly prepared her for this. All acting was supposed to proceed from movement, she knew, but she found this role difficult without a script. She had never entertained any illusions that she could make a professional career on the stage, though a succession of moonstruck intellectuals at her ancient seat of learning had assured her breathily that she had the looks for it.

Calf-love, no more. She surveyed those two most desirable of her features and worked assiduously at the body-language which was the only script this part seemed to afford. Leaning back to make the most of breasts she had always considered small but beautifully rounded, she widened her green eyes interrogatively at Paul Williams.

The drug squad sergeant had had months to get inside his part. He stroked his stubble reflectively, then jerked his head wordlessly towards the dance floor. It was the kind of invitation which would have brought a sharp rebuke from her normally. Now she ignored its presumption and rose with a grateful eagerness, tossing her halo of ash-blonde hair, parting eagerly the lips to which she had assiduously applied too much bright red lipstick in the cloakroom. Her acting was improving.

The dance floor was sparsely populated, but that suited her purpose. Williams danced with the glazed eyes of a man well dosed with pot, moving in time with the rhythm, but with the air of one cocooned in a dream-world of his own. He was watching the people he wanted to observe, the men who waited for their summons to the room of

171

Charlie Kemp, but no one would have known it from his actions.

Opposite him but divorced from him, Ruth David did not indulge in violent movements. She swayed gently, with a reptilian sinuousness, as though the bones which supported her slim frame had become temporarily plastic. Her arms moved first one way and then the other in unison, the longest finger of her right hand touching the back of her left. Her head was thrown back, so that her hair dangled behind her, lit occasionally by the coloured overhead lights so that it looked like hair in some undersea grotto. The large green eyes were almost closed within their patches of eye-shadow, witchlike but infinitely desirable. The garish lips were slightly parted, the nostrils dilated as though she were aiming at a slow, infinitely prolonged orgasm.

She quite enjoyed the part, to the extent that she had to remind herself of the dangers it was deliberately courting. She wondered if she was overdoing things, but the faces around the dance floor told her that she was not. Men were credulous creatures at the best of times, so that fact might as well be used to advantage in this, the worst of times for women. They said that there was a touch of harlot in the make-up of every woman; well, she was allowing hers full rein tonight.

And the men in their naïvety was taken in. By the time the acned youth who led the group on the dais at the end of the room strummed his last frenzied chords and flung his guitar dramatically to one side to signal the end of the number, there was no man who was unaware of Ruth David. She looked at the faces, pale and dark, which were dotted in an uneven line around the dance floor. The women were trying to look indifferent; perhaps a few of them were. But she felt the male eyes upon her, roving like hands up and down her body, as she forced herself to move unhurriedly back to her seat.

Not many of them dwelt long on her face: she felt them upon her flanks, roving unashamedly, assessing up them to the depression of her crotch and the round curve of her buttocks, and thought for a moment that she could not

172

carry this through. But wasn't this the effect she had desired, had worked hard to contrive? It was of her making, not theirs. She had taken what these simple creatures scarcely understood about themselves and laboured to exploit it. It was the old Mae West thing: 'Is that a revolver in your pocket, or are you just pleased to see me?' The difference was that here she couldn't laugh at sex to remove its danger.

Women on the catwalk had this attention to contend with all the time. But it was the clothes people came to see on those lean figures. The eyes which watched her were taking her clothes off, dwelling with lascivious conjecture on what lay beneath the leather of her skirt and the thin silk of her blouse. Well then, Sergeant David, the act was a good one, the plan was working. Don't let it go wrong now.

She went back to her chair without touching Paul Williams, distancing herself from him as both of them knew she must if the scene was to progress further. She blew out warm air between lips that were almost closed, watching it move the strands of hair that had fallen over her face in the dance. She lay back in her chair, simulating exhaustion, stretching the long legs straight and a little apart away from her. She could almost hear the collective intake of breath around her when she made that movement. What easy creatures men were to manipulate!

Vic Knowles, the new Oldford FC manager, to whom she had been introduced twenty minutes earlier, raised his glass to her from fifteen yards away and gave her an out-rageous wink. No doubt he would be over to ask her to dance at the first opportunity; he was fingering his watch as though it were some sort of talisman. He was not a bad-looking man, though his teeth were a little too promi-nent and his clothes were too young for him.

With his lined, lived-in face, he looked older than his years. She could just remember him playing, passing the ball skilfully in midfield, when she had begun to watch football, a determined small girl alongside her scornful elder brothers.

Darren Pickering had folded his arms across the legend

173

on his T-shirt which proclaimed that 'Bikers do it on full throttle' as if he wished to conceal that unsophisticated propaganda. He broad face carried a strangely abstracted grin; he was looking at her appreciatively and pulling at his left earlobe; she wondered if this was some masonic signal of his intentions of which she was as yet in merciful ignorance.

She did not turn her head as she felt a body sliding into the vacant chair on her left. She could hear him breathing, waiting for her to turn. She did so unhurriedly, half-closing her eyes, forcing herself into the bored look that men considered sultry. She found herself looking into blue eyes that glittered without a trace of humour beneath carefully cut yellow hair. When the words came, they were in cut-glass tones, with each syllable clearly enunciated.

'You and I could have a lot of fun together,' said Ben Dexter.

CHAPTER 18

Darren Pickering did not spend much more of that Saturday night at the *Roosters*. For some reason he could not quite explain, the sight of the rest of the men in the room ogling Ruth David irritated him. And Ben Dexter's monologue about her charms annoyed him even more.

He tried to analyse his feelings in the car park, walking gloomily between the lines of gleaming status symbols. Ben should not have spoken like that about Julie. If the flash bugger did it just once more, he'd smash him up. What had been between him and Julie was theirs, a place not to be trespassed upon by others who knew nothing of how they'd been with each other. That other, older man had been nothing. A passing phase, which had been over when she died. Julie had told him that, and he'd believed it. They'd have been together again now, if only . . .

He wished he had come to the club on his motorbike. Then he would have been able to get right away out of the town, shutting out all the things about Oldford which puzzled and dismayed him as he put on his helmet. He loved to feel the wind racing past his face as he opened up the 500 and controlled the smooth power pulsing beneath him. Sometimes he felt the only moments when he could really be himself now were on the bike.

It was dark now, with the last vestiges of natural light banished by the harsh orange neon of the street lighting. He wondered if he should wait for Ben to come out of the club, so that he could have it out with him here and now. Without an audience. If it came to a fight and the use of his hands, he could handle Ben Dexter. But the idea shocked him as he thought of it. They were friends, weren't they? No use falling out, even over Julie. He'd tell him to keep off that subject, though.

He wondered if Ben was getting off with that Ruth inside the club. For all his talk, he didn't seem to be particularly successful with the girls there. That disloyal thought gave Darren a little satisfaction. Anyway, if he did come out with her on his arm, he wouldn't want a mate around. He paused for a moment beside Ben's blue metallic Porsche, then turned abruptly away from the *Roosters* and walked along the side of the football ground.

Two pairs of eyes watched him go. One of them belonged to the detective-constable who was posted to watch the exits from the social club. He had observed Pickering curiously ever since he had emerged, thinking at first that he was planning to steal a car. He was quite disappointed when the big man paused by the Porsche and then moved away: it would have done him no harm to arrest a murder suspect, even on a minor charge.

His instinct was to follow Pickering when he moved away into the shadows thrown by the high brick wall of the soccer ground. But his orders were to wait here until Ruth David emerged. There were plenty of other officers patrolling the streets of the area, which the Strangler's crimes had ensured would be well-nigh deserted until the pubs began to debouch their customers.

The other man who took a brief glimpse over the car

park as Pickering delayed his departure was Charlie Kemp. Earlier, he had looked down with interest on Ruth David's dancing inside the club. When he had more time, he would give that young lady his full attention.

Now, poised at the top of the fire escape which led down from the hospitality suite, he breathed deeply for a few moments, then went back into the meeting to complete the briefing of the men who were to retail the drugs he had purchased earlier in the day.

Pickering did not have any clear idea of where he was going. His only instinct was to get well away from Ben Dexter. He found himself going not towards his home but through the streets where he had once walked with Julie Salmon. He wondered if there was something morbid in the choice his brain had made for him before he was aware of it, but he did not turn aside from the route.

He was surprised when he saw the girl, for there were few males moving alone on this moonless night, let alone females. She was standing at a bus stop, her dark shape silhouetted against the light of the lamp behind her. He could see her outline from a hundred yards away; it meant he had plenty of time to deliberate what to do as he approached.

The girl was as conscious of her isolation, of the darkness in the starless skies above her, as he was. She was wishing that her adolescent petulance had not made her defy her mother so dramatically. She had stormed out of the house three hours ago, refusing to reveal where she was going. She had been nowhere more sinister than to her friend's house; perhaps it was the very innocence of that destination which had made her reluctant to reveal it.

She was only just seventeen, only just learning that one could behave foolishly when one was in pursuit of what one fancied was a principle. She had secretly hoped that her friend's father would have run her home in his car, but the girl's parents had been out for the night. Now she felt the bravado with which she had left her friend's house seeping away through the soles of her trainers, as she looked in vain for the comforting headlights of the bus in the distance.

Darren Pickering said, 'I don't think you're going to get a bus here, m'dear. Not at this time of night.'

'I—I was told there should be one at any time.' She tried an older woman's haughtiness, staring past him into the night towards the bus which would not come. But she was still developing the techniques for attracting boys, not rejecting them; the dignified brush-off of an unwanted approach was beyond her present range.

Pickering's confidence grew with her uncertainty. 'No chance, m'dear. Last one went hours ago.' He thought he was probably right about the buses, but he had no certainty: it was a long time since he had used one. 'We could probably stop a taxi, if we wait a bit.'

He watched her, realizing now that he was alongside her that she was much younger than he had thought at first. He saw her dismay when he mentioned the taxi, and was near enough to her in age to know immediately what was wrong. She had no money, or very little. He said, 'Where do you live, miss?' He spoke dispassionately, imitating the tones of the police who had stopped him so often in the days when he was a kid on a moped. They had spoken politely like that to girls, though they had reserved a more brusque and aggressive tone for him.

'Brunswick Avenue. Number 31.' She answered automatically, a schoolgirl trained to do so, and then wondered whether she should have given up the information so easily.

He knew the place. It was a quiet, respectable road of 'thirties semis, parallel to the one where Julie had lived and within two hundred yards of it. 'It's not very far, is it? I'll walk with you, if you like.'

He had turned with the words, was a yard in front of her in the direction she had to go. He seemed to bar the way to her home, and she felt that it might be more dangerous to refuse than to accept his offer. And in truth, his large and powerful physical presence was a reassurance, when added to his friendliness. The earring and the burly forearms which thrust from the T-shirt on the summer night did not seem repulsive to her, as no doubt they would have done to her mother. It would be nice to arrive home escorted by

177

a diligent older man: that would be one in the eye for her mother. Darren was only twenty-one, but he seemed to her immensely mature.

They walked a hundred yards without speaking. Then she took the arm which he had held awkwardly stiff at his side as an invitation since they began the journey.

He told her that he had been at the dance at the *Roosters*, but had found it boring and come away early. That seemed to her to argue an immense sophistication. She told him that she was still at school, not because she wanted to be but because she found no ready means of evasion. To her surprise, he understood about A levels and applying for universities, even told her with an air of immense experience that she should make the most of her chances, that perhaps her mum and dad had a point when they worried about her going out at nights.

As he talked to her on these lines, like a rather serious uncle, the Strangler was in both their minds. But neither of them thought it a good idea to mention him.

He shortened his stride to match hers. Once they were in step, she put her other hand across to his forearm, watched it lying there for a moment, marvellously small against the brawn of that limb, and then linked it with her other hand as it emerged from beneath his elbow. They walked for a while then without words, feeling their way towards the degree of intimacy that was appropriate to a meeting which had begun so uncertainly.

She had trainers of the same make as his, worn blue jeans, and a light green anorak. It was like the one that Julie used to wear, but a different colour: he was glad of that. He wondered how to tell her about his bike, but he didn't want to sound boastful: he knew that his enthusiasm for it might come out like that. Besides, he had been telling her to listen to what her mother said, and mothers always hated motorbikes.

She made him think that Ben Dexter had been right about one thing, after all. He couldn't cut himself off from normal relationships with girls for ever; he had to accept that Julie was gone, and get on with the rest of his life. He was enjoying having this edgy, slightly vulnerable presence at his side; enjoying the role of protector which he had allocated to himself.

They took a route which meant that they did not walk past the end of Julie's road. He was glad at the time that she accepted the slightly longer walk without questioning it. But the question it raised in her mind, the tiny embryo of puzzlement which grew first into uncertainty and then into fear, was at the root of everything which followed.

He detached her hands from his arm and slid it gently around her, feeling for her slim waist beneath the anorak and nestling his fingers gently into the warmth. He felt the slight stiffening, the tiny shiver which ran through her whole body. But he was not after all very experienced— Ruth David back at the *Roosters* understood far more about men than Darren did about women—and he did not think her reaction signalled fear. When no further movement followed, he thought it had probably been a little thrill of pleasure or excitement. Young men, as Ruth could have told him, tend to be absurdly optimistic about these things.

They had turned into Brunswick Avenue now. In a few minutes they would be at her house. He had better do what he wanted to do now, or never. He stopped and turned her towards him, sliding both hands lightly up her back, feeling her shoulder-blades, sharp and slender even beneath the layers of clothing. She pushed her face into his chest, so that he could not see her eyes.

That was a pity, for he might have seen a warning in them and desisted, while there was still time. Instead, he moved his hands to turn her chin gently up towards him. He would kiss her gently, doing no more than pressing his lips lightly upon hers. He feared rejection too much to do more than that now. In truth, there would not be much pleasure in it, but it was a necessary move in this game in which he was only pretending to understand the rules. Pleasure might come later.

It was the moment when his questing fingers touched her throat that was fatal. The image of the Strangler had been thrust to the back of her mind, but not expelled. With that touch from those strong fingers, it came leaping back like a recurring nightmare. She clawed at his arms, felt the bare flesh on the back of his hands, scratched at it fiercely with the nails she had striven so hard to grow long.

And as he gasped with the pain and the shock, she screamed. A long, scarcely human, screech which tore aside the dark night and made both of them thrill with horror. He stepped back, saw too late the terror in her eyes, fought to produce words which would still her fear and explain what he had wanted.

Speech came only fitfully, but it would not have mattered if he had been far more articulate than he was. For she went on screaming, building to a long, eldritch howl which shut out all words, all argument, all reason. It had that effect on both of them, for now he panicked in turn. He knew that she was hysterical, that he should give her face a sharp slap, restore communication between them.

Instead, he turned and ran.

The girl was soon restored. The lights went on in the quiet road, and people looked out. But it was her mother who was there first, the mother whom she had rejected with contempt a mere three hours earlier. Her mother did not think of that. She wrapped her arms about her daughter; held her tight for a moment; muttering soothing, age-old sounds of comfort; half-carried her into the house with her arms still around her; sat her in the big chair by the open fire; brought her a little brandy and a lot of tea; persuaded herself and her daughter that there was after all little damage done.

Darren Pickering was less fortunate. He did not heed where he was going. He ran with only one idea: to put as much space as possible between himself and the frightened girl who had first encouraged and then rejected him.

He was at the end of the road where Julie Salmon had lived when he ran into the arms of the policemen.

CHAPTER 19

The atmosphere in the Murder Room was tense as the hours dragged past on that Saturday night.

It was one of those occasions when John Lambert wished he still smoked. There was nothing to do except wait, and waiting was a frustrating process when things were happening in the town outside and the rest of the team were most of them involved in the action.

Because of the suggestion that a police officer might possibly be the Strangler, not many of the eighty officers now involved in the hunt knew about the way in which Ruth David was being used, though of course the news of it would trickle round among them if the identity of the Strangler was not swiftly discovered.

Sergeant Johnson was the duty officer, but there was little more he could do at the moment other than to note the radio messages coming in from men and women patrolling different parts of the town. Most of them were negative, recording that there had been no sightings of males acting suspiciously or following women. No news was good news, in a sense, but everyone sensed that until there was more action from this killer no one would be able to rest easy. If he was to be arrested, the probability now was that he would have to reveal himself by another murderous move. The team would have both to frustrate that attempt and to ensure that he was captured in the process of it.

It had been a long day at the end of a long week, but Lambert did not feel tired. He knew from previous experience that when this case was over he would sleep the clock round and feel the effects of several sixteen-hour days. But for the moment, the adrenalin derived from heading this inquiry stimulated his long frame.

He was glad, though, that he did not have to deal with Chris Rushton's bureaucratic fussiness as they waited for news. The inspector would have disapproved of the deployment of Sergeant Ruth David at the *Roosters*, for sure, and reiterated his disquiet about it at every opportunity. Lambert was glad that for the moment Rushton knew nothing of it. He had looked so white and drawn after the media conference in the morning that Lambert had insisted he take the rest of the weekend off.

He wondered now whether Rushton had gone in pursuit of the wife who had left him or whether he was sitting in white-faced misery at home. He could not see that very serious young man—people of thirty were definitely young to him now—drowning his troubles in drink, or finding any other sort of escapism effective for very long.

Lambert went moodily across to his room in the CID section and tried to catch up on some of the paperwork connected with lesser cases which had been piling up on his desk during the week. His concentration was not good, and he was glad when he heard the voice of Don Haworth, who had come in to do a blood test on a drunken driver. The man's passenger would be charged in due course with being drunk and disorderly; they could still hear his noisy protests echoing up from the distant cells.

'Any news of the Strangler?' said Haworth. The police surgeon was slotting his equipment carefully back into its box; perhaps he only asked for form's sake, knowing how the case was dominating the thinking of the station. It was good to have someone around who had other concerns than the Strangler. Lambert was grateful anew for the lively interest shown in the case by a doctor who must have a busy practice to attend to during the day. For a moment, he almost told him about Ruth David, then checked himself. Many of his senior officers had been kept in ignorance: he must not tell someone who in strict terms was outside the team.

'We've nothing new as yet. Perhaps the officers who are out there tonight will come up with something. Sooner or later, someone close to our man will say something significant, whether wittingly or not.' He put forward the thought without much confidence. It had happened with serial killers in the past, but he had no great confidence that it

182

was about to happen this time. He was uncomfortably aware that there had sometimes been seven or eight killings before some chance remark set in train the kind of successful pursuit he had just mentioned.

'It must be difficult for your men, listening to the talk in pubs and so on. Trying to sift the one per cent that might be useful from the ninety-nine per cent which is dross.'

Lambert grinned. 'That's the argument for police procedures. If you go through the same routine each time, you build up a kind of expertise, I suppose.' He said it without a lot of conviction. John Lambert had never been a great one for routine procedures. Yet sometimes, following instinct, he was more thorough than even the book suggested. He had Bert Hook out now, going round the relations of the dead victims, tactfully covering ground that had already been covered, trying to unearth the one significant fact which might have been overlooked until now.

Don Haworth said, 'I find it fascinating, you know, all the details of police work: you've probably noticed. Perhaps I'm still a schoolboy at heart.' He laughed, and Lambert wondered whether someone had accused him of that recently. 'Well, I must get on my way. I shall be glad to get to bed tonight, and I expect you will too. I hope you have good news soon.'

He went breezily out to his car and left Lambert to take up again the nervous business of waiting to see if the Strangler would attempt anything that night. The Superintendent turned to go back to the Murder Room, though he was aware that if anything dramatic had turned up Johnson would have let him know immediately.

As he went across the station yard, a white patrol car swung in between the big gates. He looked automatically at the back seat, where any arrested man would be held. A white, square, face stared back at him apprehensively in the split second when the light which illuminated the yard fell upon the window. By the time the patrol men had extricated their prize from the car, Lambert was waiting beside it.

Standing with his arms thrusting from the T-shirt that

was a little too tight, with the handcuffs at his wrist gleaming in the shadows of the car, Darren Pickering looked a pathetic rather than a menacing figure. His head hung down, and his shoulders were hunched, as though he was ashamed of his height and bulk. The truculence he had tried to maintain when he was interviewed in the preceding days had dropped away. There was not even a pretence now at aggression in his bearing. The reaction of the girl to his advances had seen to that. He was still in shock from her screaming.

The driver of the police car answered Lambert's unspoken query. 'He was running away from a girl when we stopped him, sir. He's told us that already. Doesn't know her name, he says. But obviously his attentions were not welcome.' The constable, who was even younger than Pickering and full of the excitement of this arrest, held up his hand to the light, lifting Pickering's with it where it was handcuffed at the wrist. The blood from the scratches on the back of the hand was still drying. Four crimson ribbons showed where the panic-stricken girl's nails had dug deep.

'And how did you come by those?' said Lambert.

Pickering's face was set sullen as a child's who knows he has done wrong but will not admit it. He said, 'I've nothing to say to you. I want a lawyer.'

Lambert looked down to where blood ran from the other hand as Pickering tried to conceal it. 'You may need more than a lawyer,' he said. He turned to the patrol car officers. 'Put him safe in a cell for the moment,' he said. 'I'll be down to see you presently, Mr Pickering. In the meantime, I advise you to consider your position.'

He turned abruptly and walked away. He would get nothing out of Pickering immediately; it would do him no harm to sweat in a cell for a little while he checked on what was happening elsewhere. He was still more worried than he dared to reveal about the way they were using Ruth David.

Back in the Murder Room, he looked round to check they were not overheard before he said to Jack Johnson, 'Any news yet?'

The Sergeant knew the source of his anxiety immediately. 'She's left the *Roosters*. A few minutes ago. She'll be on the route we agreed by now. The first man's just radioed in to say she's left his patch. Nothing abnormal to report.'

'Let's hope they know what they're doing.' That was just a symptom of Lambert's nervousness. The men who were stationed along the streets of Oldford were trained, experienced officers who knew their jobs.

But they could not radio in until she was well away from them, with no sign of assault or pursuit, so as not to give away any sign that this was a trap to their adversary. That gave a delayed, unreal feeling to her progress to those in the Murder Room. Lambert, following the route they had agreed on a street map at the end of the room, felt like a general who has sent out his troops to do battle and remained well behind the lines himself.

For Sergeant Ruth David, policewoman-turned-harlot at the front of the action, it was a strange journey. She knew that she was being watched by friends, but she saw none of them, as their expertise in this macabre game dictated that she should not. But their invisibility meant that she had to assert her reason at the expense of her senses, for those senses told her that she was alone in a dangerous world.

She could see no human presence in the lights which shone and reflected on the wet tarmac. But the shadows thrown by the lamps, advancing and retreating as she moved past each standard, would have suggested to a receptive mind that there were creatures abroad in the dark recesses of the buildings. Her steps echoed with unnatural loudness in the prevailing silence. Lambert and she had chosen a route with little traffic, and the noise of the occasional car in adjacent streets seemed as it ebbed away only to leave the stillness here more profound and threatening.

She swung her shoulder-bag and sauntered forward resolutely on her high heels, trying not to think of that one pair of baleful eyes which might be following, waiting, preparing to strike. She had to force herself to move like a streetwalker, when she wanted to hurry. Prostitutes would never tout for trade in this deserted place, but she must keep up the part if she was to preserve the deception. It was important, she knew, that she did that, for the psychopathic mind does not take kindly to the idea of being duped.

She thought back to her boisterous, attention-grabbing departure from the *Roosters*, and wished that she was surrounded again by all those people and all that light and noise. She had been a popular figure by the end of the evening, though she had needed to work hard in the few breathless phrases she had permitted herself to keep up her tarty image. In those last few minutes at the club, she had refused several offers from would-be escorts to see her home.

Now, on her lonely journey along the deserted streets of the agreed route, she had to remind herself for the fourth time that she had volunteered herself for this, that she had in fact leapt at the chance of a central role in the hunt for the Strangler.

If it was successful, it would further her career. But she knew that it had been the excitement, the wish to be involved at the centre of this hunt, that had really motivated her. That grizzled old bugger Lambert had understood that, had told her he knew it when he had delivered her final briefing, after they had agreed the route. His last words for her, perhaps in compensation for the way he had opposed the scheme earlier, had been that her lust for the hunt made her a better copper. She fancied that that might be his highest professional compliment.

It seemed to take her a long time to make the lonely journey. Once a drunk lurched up to her, offering maudling, beer-soaked compliments to her beauty, trying to put a clumsy arm round her shoulders. It took all her self-control to avoid doing him serious injury: her first instinct was to strike before a man who might be the Strangler got near her throat. Instead, she moved smartly aside, recoiling from the warm stink of stale beer which wafted across her face.

The man, surprised by the sudden absence of the support he had relied on, stumbled and fell, rolling with one arm in the gutter and a sudden obscenity on the lips which had been mumbling about her attractions. She turned back when she was twenty yards on and saw him, rubber-limbed with drink, struggling on all fours and chuckling at the difficulty he was having in regaining equilibrium.

She smiled to herself at the alarm she had felt, but she was surprised how her fingers trembled; she had to grip the strap of her shoulder bag firmly to stop them. She forced herself to saunter rather than hurry past the deserted house where Julie Salmon, the first of the murdered girls, had been discovered, reminding herself that she was overseen by invisible, friendly eyes. She could see the raw new boarding across the door of the house through the darkness, as she tried not to think of the body which had lain undiscovered within the place for two days.

Another man approached her on the last section of her journey. He seemed to advance for minutes on end down the long, straight road where they met. But when he was thirty yards from her, he crossed the street and passed her safely on the other side, his head turned ostentatiously away. Probably he had not wished to alarm her; perhaps, she thought with a grim smile, he had feared that he would be accosted by a prostitute looking for trade. She wiggled her hips with jaunty determination.

Nevertheless, she was glad to arrive at the house they had specified, where she was to sleep for the night: if the Strangler was observing her, it would give the game away immediately if she went back to the station. She looked up and down the street behind her before going up the two steps to the door; this moment could be the one of maximum vulnerability for a woman surprised. But there was certainly no one within thirty yards of her. She had a nightmare moment when she could not turn her key in the lock, but then it worked and the door opened.

Inside, there were warmth, and friendly faces, and a hot drink and congratulations. She realized a few minutes later that the policewoman who had received her felt a sense of anticlimax, which she tried hard to share. Instead, she felt only relief.

187

She went into her bedroom, looked at the face of the exhausted whore in the mirror, and could scarcely believe that it was her own. She rubbed away that strumpet face with cold cream and tissues and flushed it down the lavatory. Then she removed the clothes she had adopted for the evening, put on a dressing-gown, and went down to the telephone in the hall to ring Lambert.

He was low-key, professional, reassuring. He made no reference to her ordeal, and for that she was curiously grateful. It put it in context, made it seem once again a part of a job, not a decadent charade. The men along the streets had reported in as agreed once she had cleared their sections of the route. None of them had seen anyone following her who seemed likely to prove their man. They were checking out the men who had tried to walk her home from the *Roosters*; Paul Williams had been able to give them the names.

Darren Pickering, one of their leading suspects, had apparently assaulted a girl in another part of the town. He was safely in the cells; Lambert was about to interview him with Bert Hook, who had just returned to the Murder Room after talking to the parents of the first murdered girl, Julie Salmon.

This account of the search for the Strangler which was going on everywhere without her was strangely reassuring to Ruth David, the woman who had planned to trap him by her own daring ploy.

As Lambert went through the door of Pickering's cell, she was falling into an exhausted sleep, with the Superintendent's last words ringing in her brain, 'If we haven't made an arrest, you go again tomorrow night.'

CHAPTER 20

On that Sunday morning Lambert did not get to sleep until almost three. At six, he was suddenly awake again, with an idea in his mind that was there even as he woke.

He revolved it, pulled at it, tried everything he could think of to dispose of it. It was an appalling idea, but it would not go away. Each argument he marshalled against it turned upon him like a spiteful cat in a corner, spitting malevolently where he had hoped for reassurances. He told himself repeatedly that the idea was the product of a fevered, overworked brain. And each time some small new fact emerged from his recollection to support rather than destroy the outrageous notion.

He lay beside the sleeping Christine, staring at the ceiling with dry, unblinking eyes. There was no proof. Even the circumstantial items which kept suggesting themselves in support of his astounding hypothesis were sparse. But cumulatively they were growing more convincing with each harrowing minute of speculation.

'What time did you get in?' said Christine. She had not taken long to divine that he was awake and thinking, as she always seemed to do. Before seven, she had made coffee for herself and tea for him in the small, neat kitchen.

'I don't know. It was almost three, I think.' He and Bert Hook had spent an hour with Darren Pickering. It was Hook, by an intuitive mixture of bullying, common sense and cajoling, who had eventually got the man to talk. It was Hook who had been convinced when they had finished that Pickering had meant no harm to the girl, that he had been clumsy rather than dangerous. In view of Pickering's proximity to the other killings, that took a lot of believing. Rushton had not been around last night, or there might well have been a real dust-up between Inspector and Sergeant.

Lambert decided that he should make sure that Hook was present when the girl was interviewed today. That should settle the matter, one way or the other, with luck. He tried to speculate about Pickering, but he was aware that he was merely diverting himself from the notion which held sway in his mind and was not going to be denied.

Christine cooked him the bacon and egg she now denied him on all but special occasions. Perhaps she too was trying to turn him aside from the thought which gnawed so persistently at him. She observed him surreptitiously from the door of the kitchen, concentrated, intense, abstracted from his surroundings. She had seen him often enough like this over the years; indeed, his single-mindedness had almost destroyed their marriage twenty years and more ago. There was one new element now in his appearance as he sat slightly hunched at the table, toying with the cutlery and staring at the wall on the other side of the breakfast-room. He was ageing now, more rapidly than she cared to admit to herself.

She divined just how involved he was in this case and its climax when she found that he had gone out and left a rasher of bacon and a tomato untouched.

The Chief Constable lived in a large house in a splendid garden, one of the last in the area to be built in genuine Cotswold stone. It had a stone wall at the end of its front garden, only four feet high, but soaring at the entrance into high pillars which supported wrought-iron gates.

George Harding enjoyed his garden. It was his haven from the multifarious cares of his office. He was out there even before breakfast on a Sunday, examining a summer-flowering clematis which had a promising profusion of buds and trying to forget all about the Strangler for a few hours. His initial reaction when he saw Lambert's old Vauxhall crunching cautiously over the gravel between his gates was one of irritation.

Professionalism took over immediately. Lambert was not the man to arrive like this without reason. As the Superintendent levered his long frame rather stiffly from the driver's seat, that opinion was confirmed by his grey-faced concern.

They went inside to a small, comfortable study, lined with books and decorated with the well-polished scale replicas of the cups Harding had won in long-dead tennis triumphs. In that small, private room, where the two men were securely insulated from the world they had to deal with, Lambert told his Chief Constable of the notion that had burned in his brain from his first moment of consciousness on that Sunday morning.

Harding found it at first as preposterous as he had. Then, slowly, reluctantly, as Lambert drip-fed him with a series of tiny supporting facts, he came round to the view that there might after all be something in it. He was not committed to agreement: caution had been too deeply built in as he rose up the slippery pole of office for that. But he agreed that the notion must be tested. Meantime, the idea must be kept strictly to the two of them.

Ruth David only spoke to Lambert on the phone, so that she did not notice that he was even more uneasy on the Sunday night than he had been on the Saturday. She listened patiently while he repeated the instructions she had heard several times before. He was like a nervous mother telling her child to be wary of a busy road, she thought.

It annoyed her: did the man not realize she was jumpy enough, without the old-hen anxieties of her superiors? Sooner or later, the Strangler was bound to strike, if they went on with this deception. That was a thought that had excited her when she was persuading the top brass to use her in the scheme. Now that it was in progress, she felt fearful rather than excited.

Last night it had felt like amateur dramatics when she had put on the black tights and the garish make-up, as though there would be two hours of make-believe and giggling congratulations at the end of the evening. But tonight did not feel like a second night of the same play.

She had a new rose-pink silk blouse which exactly matched her make-up; she tried to give herself a smile by wondering how she might enter the details of it on her expenses claim. With the tight black skirt and the red shoes, it seemed to give the right impression of availability and brassy sex. She studied herself in the mirror, shook her ash-blonde hair free, and murmured 'Come on, Raunchy Ruth!' at the reflection she saw. The smile she so wanted to see would not come. Perhaps it would be all right when she was on stage: it always had been in the past.

And it was, in the sense that the part seemed to take her over. The *Roosters* was busier that night, even though there was no live music. She managed to sit at a table in the centre of the floor, where she could create her effects without having to strain too hard. Without being upstaged by anyone, she thought grimly.

She noticed that there was a bigger cross-section of society in the place tonight, a better representation of the various groups of supporters a football club attracts. Don Haworth, the club doctor and police surgeon, was sitting with a couple of members of the board at a table at the end of the room furthest from the bar. They looked at her curiously; perhaps they had seen her in here before, but not in this persona. And of course they would not know that she was in the police, since she had never worked in Oldford before. Haworth smiled at her, then turned to speak to a woman who was the theatre sister at Oldford Hospital. Ruth preferred not to contemplate what tonight's impersonation might be doing to her reputation.

Ben Dexter came and sat on her table. He did not speak to her directly, but began to include her in the talk of his group, as if in due course he hoped to strike up a more personal conversation. She was glad to see Paul Williams keeping a surreptitious eye on developments from the next table. There was no sign of Darren Pickering. She had found herself hoping that Lambert would say that they had charged him when he rang, so that she need not attempt again to spring the trap on their anonymous psychopath.

She was studying her surroundings and displaying her legs when a waiter in his maroon trousers and white shirt appeared at her side and put a large gin and tonic on the table at her elbow. Someone had done his research: that was the drink she had sipped last night, though she had made sure that most of it was tonic. When she looked her puzzlement, the waiter said impassively, 'With the Chairman's compliments, miss.' It was impossible to tell from his expression whether this was a service he had performed many times before.

Ruth picked the glass up, eyed it curiously, rolled it in her hands for a moment, and then sipped it. That was the reaction her part seemed to demand, though she wished

192

she had been prepared for this bit of stage business. There was much more gin than tonic in this glass. She turned her head slowly, wondering if it was really the football club Chairman had favoured her with this early salvo at her dubious virtue.

She had to raise her eyes before she saw the source of it. From the small landing outside the hospitality suite he used as his own, Charlie Kemp watched until she noticed him, then slowly raised his own glass in salutation and smiled. In his dark suit, he looked curiously like a figure from a vintage Hollywood movie she had seen at the university cinema club. She could almost hear him saying, 'Here's looking at you, doll!'

She would have been amazed to learn that Kemp had taken the gesture from exactly such a film, as he took most of what he thought of as his social poise. He gave her his Edward G. Robinson smile and went back into the panelled room behind him.

Sergeant Ruth David did not have time to ponder on what he might be planning there. Vic Knowles, busy acknowledging the greetings appropriate to the new manager of Oldford FC, detached himself from a group of admirers and came across to talk to her. He was dressed informally but well, if a little too flashily for her taste. The red and white of his expensive sweatshirt might be in the team colours, but the silver bracelet on his left wrist was a little over the top. For the first time that evening, she managed a little inward smile, at her own expense. She was hardly the one to be criticizing anyone for dressing to attract attention.

She looked round the animated scene, and decided that she was attracting plenty of interest; perhaps the news of her conduct in here last night had spread. In truth, she underestimated her looks in that judgement. She was a striking woman, with strong features and the ash-blonde hair that made men's heads turn easily enough. Her willowy, athletic figure had brought plenty of excitement to the young bloods of the *Roosters* even before she had decided to accentuate her obvious charms. The difference now was

193

that she was declaring herself more available. Perhaps even generally available, to those who could afford it.

When someone offered her the opportunity with a comment about money, she laughed loudly and said, 'Well, a girl's got to make a living somehow. And believe me, it ain't easy in these hard times.' The giggle with which she topped this off was itself a come-on. She sounded to herself like a parody of the real thing, a send-up of a vapid good-time girl, but that would hardly matter in this assembly. The important thing was to be noticed.

She looked around at the animated array of male faces around her, steeling herself to ignore the resentful looks from the females. She wondered for a moment whether any of those myriad eyes which were intermittently upon her belonged to the Strangler.

Then she banished such conjecture; in the circumstances in which she was operating, which demanded all her concentration, it was a dangerous indulgence. In any case, the Strangler might not be here at all. There appeared to be a connection with the *Roosters*, but that might be no more than that the murderer had waited for his victims outside the club, following them from there until he found a suitable place to strike them down.

Back in the Murder Room at Oldford CID, Lambert experienced the familiar helplessness of waiting and wondering. He was glad that DI Rushton was still not present, for he had already caught himself snapping irritably at Johnson when the Sergeant had made an innocent query. Rushton's punctilious attention to detail, his need to occupy himself with paperwork as the crisis approached, would have needled him tonight.

The situation was made worse by the fact that only he and the Chief Constable were aware of the suggestion Lambert had made that morning about the identity of their killer. The concealment of information from the rest of his team was unique as far as John Lambert was concerned, and it made him uneasy with himself as well as the situation.

At ten o'clock, George Harding came into the room himself. There was a hasty fastening of buttons among the uniformed men, a tightening of ties pulled slack by the plain-clothes officers who wore them. He took Lambert outside for a moment, leaving a rustle of excitement and speculation in the room behind him. The Chief Constable in at ten o'clock on a Sunday night? Things must be moving! Each man and woman nervously checked the parts assigned to them in the night's business. It would never do to make a mistake with the Chief Constable breathing down your neck.

It was purely a conditioned police reflex to the sudden presence of top brass. With a serial killer about and three girls already dead, attention was not going to wander. Most of the men in the Murder Room that Sunday night now knew that one of their own number, Ruth David, was at the centre of the night's efforts. Certainly not one of them was going to give less than a hundred per cent to the job.

George Harding found himself actually enjoying the excitement of an investigation. Contrary to popular police mythology, some chief and deputy chief constables did miss direct involvement with the arrest of criminals. Harding was copper enough still to scent the successful conclusion of a serious crime investigation.

He envied Lambert the air of excited anticipation which hung about the station, understood tonight why the Superintendent clung to his direct involvement in the investigations he headed. He understood also why Lambert now fretted at the enforced inaction, why he found waiting for things to happen the most difficult task of all.

Harding said impulsively to Lambert, 'Go out on the route she's to take yourself, if you like, John. Choose your own point, but don't upset the system.' It was the first time he had used his Superintendent's first name. Perhaps it was a sign of the trust he now accorded him.

He tried to thrust aside the idea that if Lambert's preposterous idea should turn out to be just that, it would do no harm if it was the Superintendent who was close to it when it was exposed, while his Chief Constable was safely distanced. He could not be sure of course, but he did not think that that had been his first consideration.

When it was time to leave the *Roosters*, Ruth David found it difficult to do so on her own. Both Ben Dexter and Vic Knowles had made bids to accompany her during the last hour at the club, and there were other offers as the glasses were collected and the disco player was disconnected.

She took advantage of some noisy exchanges in the gents' cloakroom to pass quickly from the brightly lit foyer of the club into the summer darkness outside, slipping quietly through the door before her departure could be noted, or her own resolution weaken.

It was dry tonight, with only a light breeze, but the sliver of moon was too low in the sky yet to offer much illumination, especially as the early part of her route was between narrow streets of tall houses. She walked casually, with one arm resting on her shoulder-bag and the other swinging lightly at her side. The sounds of noisy departures from the *Roosters* gradually receded into the darkness behind her.

When there were gaps in the houses on her left, she could see an orange glow on the horizon, the aura of the lights from some larger town: Cheltenham, she fancied, but her geography had always been patchy, and her sense of direction not that which might reasonably be expected of a police officer. Telling herself this, she realized that she was trying to divert herself from the business in hand.

That was not a good idea. The Strangler merited her most intense concentration.

They had varied the route a little from last night, making it even more lonely, taking her through a redevelopment area, where terraces of empty houses were presently to be demolished. The same team of unseen officers was overseeing her progress, losing a second night of their weekend to the demands of the scheme. Normally the team would have been changed, but Lambert, mindful of the thought that the killer could possibly be a policeman, had wanted to keep the knowledge of this attempt to as few people as possible.

What Ruth David had not appreciated was that in this area there was virtually no street lighting. There must have been two hundred yards between the single lamp which shone outside the small pub which still functioned after the loss of its clientele and the brighter, newer lamp which blazed where the muted orange behind the curtains showed that the houses were occupied.

This, if anywhere, was surely Strangler territory. It was not as dangerous as it looked: Ruth knew that there were officers sited in at least two of the empty houses as she passed between them. The sound of her footsteps echoed eerily back to her from the dark brick walls as her high heels rang over the old flagstones. She tried to whistle as she sauntered jauntily past the house where she thought there were friends, but could produce no sound from her dry lips.

It looked as if tonight's journey was going to be even quieter than Saturday's. The only person who had been anywhere near her was an elderly man walking a small dog on a lead, and he had turned away at her approach and moved down a street which ran at right-angles to hers. There was no sign of even an approach such as that fumbling, amiable drunk had made last night. She would welcome that harmless presence now.

She was acting on behalf of all women. If this plan succeeded and the Strangler was caught, the women of Old-ford, of the whole region, would be safer as they walked the streets of the places where they lived. That grandiose purpose did not seem to raise her spirits on these dark streets as it had when she had first enthused about the scheme.

She reached the end of the area that was earmarked for redevelopment, began to move again among houses which had lights. Behind those upstairs windows, people were going peacefully to bed. Perhaps a few of them were making love. Legitimately. She glanced up as she went along, counting the lights on each block as she passed, ticking off the doors as once she had ticked off the days to a family holiday at the seaside.

There was one patch of darkness on her left, a dark cave on another road that had been included now on her slightly extended route. As she came up with it, she saw the agent's board advertising the development of luxury flats, and realized with a little frisson of apprehension that this must be the place where Hetty Brown, the second of the victims, had been killed.

It was perhaps because she was looking to her left that the man got close to her before she saw him. He came from the right, out of the shadows of the trees at the ends of the long front gardens there. There were lights behind him, but they only made his features more obscure, confining his visibility to no more than a silhouette against the distant amber light from the bay window of a detached house. He held up his right hand as he came, in a gesture that was meant to be reassuring, and he called a greeting in a voice which she recognized.

It was an educated voice. The confident voice of a professional man, who was used to dealing with the public and having their unquestioning respect. A voice which threw her off her guard, for the split second which could have been fatal.

He did not stop talking as he came right up to her. It was only when he raised both hands at once that she saw that he was wearing some sort of mask over the lower part of his face. And the hands which came at her throat glistened with plastic. Transparent plastic.

She knew the rules of combat. She should not have allowed the hands to get to her throat, but once they were there, you did not try to drag them away: that would be a contest of strengths, and a man would be stronger. Especially a madman, as she knew now this must surely be.

She tried to thrust her right foot round behind his left heel, so that she might throw him backwards, might crash his head on the flagstone, might smash it until there was no life there. She was reduced in the moment when those cold plastic hands fell upon her throat to a vicious fighting animal, wanting not merely to survive but to kill her adversary.

Her ploy did not work. She had always feared these high heels, but they had been a necessary part of her costume for the role. Now, as they scratched ineffectively to get a grip on the stone, they were going to kill her.

The Strangler, as they had all said, was swift and efficient. She felt his thumbs pressing into her throat like a tightening vice. Vagal inhibition, they called it: it was quick, and the pain was short. With all her remaining strength, she drove her knee up into the man's groin, trying to make it even sharper as she felt it drive accurately into his genitals.

She heard him gasp, felt him jack-knife almost double with the pain. But he kept his grip upon her throat, bearing her backward into the hedge, moving her towards the spot where he had laid out Hetty Brown like a mediæval effigy, beginning to shake her like a rag doll. He was glad it was a Sunday night, as he watched the dying eyes. He would lay her out, he decided in this her last moment, exactly as he had laid out that other girl who offered her favours too easily. In exactly the same spot. The symmetry of it pleased him.

He never even heard the running feet. As the blood pounded in his ears and the blood-lust in his brain, he heard neither the shouts nor the whistles. He saw Ruth David rising gingerly from the hedge, heard her reassuring her colleagues that she was all right, without understanding the deception that had been practised upon him.

His arms were pinioned firmly behind him as Lambert uttered the words of the caution, so that it had to be police fingers which undid the straps and removed the green cotton which covered his face below the blazing eyes. They put him in the back of the patrol car with the thin plastic of the surgical gloves still upon his hands.

Dr Donald Haworth would be the first police surgeon to be convicted of multiple murder.

CHAPTER 21

Rushton looked better when he came in on Monday morning. He had still not got his wife back home, but he had rested and looked more like his normal efficient self. But he was resentful that the case should have reached its climax without him.

He stared dully at his computer. He was glad the Strangler had been caught. Of course he was. But it was almost a personal affront that they should have caught the man without his presence. Without even the assistance of the complex system of cross-referencing of which he had been so proud. He had not even made a file on Don Haworth, though he had carefully recorded much of the medical information the doctor had fed them so cunningly.

Detective-Inspector Christopher Rushton looked sourly at the modern technology he had used so proudly and decided that on this occasion it had been a dead loss.

When he said as much, Lambert said generously, 'Not entirely, Chris. It helped to eliminate a lot of people from the search, and it concentrated our minds on the common factors in the killings.' In truth, he felt a little guilty that he had insisted on Rushton's absence over the weekend; he was so much a natural hunter of criminals himself that he understood the feelings of the younger man perfectly. He said by way of apology, 'You did look pretty seedy at our meeting on Saturday morning, you know.'

Rushton gave a faint, acknowledging smile. 'I was, sir. I haven't had much sleep lately.' It was as much weakness as he would admit to, for they were not alone. The two sergeants, Bert Hook and 'Jack' Johnson, were in the Murder Room with them, deciding which items among the multitude of evidence they had accumulated would have to be kept for the court case and which could now be discarded.

Rushton said dolefully, 'I'll be able to get rid of all the

stuff on what we thought were our leading suspects.' It was beautifully organized—and now, it seemed, totally wasted.

Lambert shook his head. 'Keep everything on Charlie Kemp. He was arrested early this morning,' he said with satisfaction. It would raise morale in the CID to have the man who had cocked a snook at them for years behind bars at last. 'Paul Williams was right when he said the drugs squad was waiting its moment to move. They arrested two of the international suppliers at Heathrow yesterday: a Greek and a Lebanese whom Interpol have been pursuing for months. Kemp had just bought a large consignment of heroin from them; Williams and the drug squad had pinned down both Kemp and his circle of retailers. Kemp was meeting some of them in his suite at the *Roosters* at the time when Hetty Brown was murdered. He pretended he'd been on his own because he couldn't tell us that, but it left him without an alibi for her killing.'

The Superintendent grinned at Rushton. 'Oldford FC will be needing a new Chairman, if you fancy the hassle.'

'And a new official doctor for their medical certificates,' said Rushton grimly.

'What about Darren Pickering and Ben Dexter?' said Bert Hook.

Lambert grinned. 'You'll be happy to hear that you were right about Pickering. The girl who scratched him on Saturday night has confirmed that she simply got scared and screamed the place down at the thought that he might be the Strangler. She's quite apologetic about it today, and feeling suitably foolish. And the lad seems to have no involvement in the drugs case; he isn't even a user.'

'Unlike Dexter,' said Hook sourly.

'Dexter will be done for possession, certainly. Coke and crack, not just pot. Williams thinks he was toying with the idea of becoming a pusher, but I suspect it will be difficult to make that stick: he seems to have been biding his time on the edge of things, as usual. But at least he'll have a record: maybe that will bring him to his senses.'

Lambert smiled wryly at his team. 'We'll still need a lot of the Scene of Crime findings for the court case. It's just that we may have to re-align our sights a little to see the relevant evidence. Haworth was very clever at feeding us the information he wanted to plant, especially when we discussed the other suspects.'

'The CC said you realized yesterday morning that it was Haworth,' said Johnson.

Generous of him not to claim the idea for himself, thought Lambert. He decided that he approved of the new Chief Constable. 'I put the idea to him then, yes. Fortunately, Haworth knew nothing of the plan to use Ruth David. We put a tail on him when he left the *Roosters* last night. But there was no case against him until then that would have stood up in court; we had to catch him in the act to clinch it.'

Bert Hook looked round at the four men clutching mugs of steaming coffee, relaxed now with success where there had been only tension forty-eight hours earlier. 'I suppose I'm the goon who's supposed to say, "What put you on to him, sir?"'

'You're a much appreciated straight man, I'm sure,' said his chief. 'You produced one of the pointers yourself, Bert, when you went round to talk to Julie Salmon's parents yesterday. Haworth had been Julie's GP; we already knew that—indeed, he mentioned it to us himself at our conference—but it hadn't seem important. But when you put it together with this mysterious older man she'd had a relationship with, he became a candidate we should have checked out much earlier. It must be a sign of my age, but I thought of older men being about forty. Julie Salmon was nineteen: to someone of her age, anyone around thirty must have been very definitely a much older man.'

'He could have been struck off for it,' said Rushton. The enormity of Haworth's professional transgression seemed for a moment as shocking to him as murder.

'Undoubtedly he would have been, if Julie Salmon had revealed a sexual relationship with him. I think it was her knowledge of that and her loyalty to him which ensured that she would never reveal his name. We've found her missing handbag in his flat. I suppose he removed it in case it contained anything which might connect him with her, but it probably didn't. No one else knew the name of the man she had associated with; that's why we were left looking for this mysterious "older man", who was so vague that some of us began to wonder if he even existed, outside an adolescent girl's imagination. But it was her ending of the relationship with Haworth which sealed her death warrant. He couldn't take that. He said as much this morning—he's confessed to all three murders, incidentally.'

Hook said, as if reluctantly conceding credit where it was due, 'The forensic psychologist said the rape of Julie Salmon and not the two subsequent girls suggested that there had been a relationship there.'

'It was a power thing, as Stanley Warboys said. Haworth couldn't take his rejection, especially in favour of someone like Darren Pickering. But there were other clues as well—small things, but cumulatively they added up to something significant. You remember how with the second murder, that of Hetty Brown, he put the time of death at between twelve and one a.m., and reminded us two or three times of it. The official time from the post-mortem gave a wider margin, of course, and she was in fact killed earlier. The twelve to one time gave him a perfect alibi, if he'd needed it. He'd planted the idea himself, but because we thought him above suspicion we accepted it for a long time. I remember being grateful to him for trying to be so precise.'

Rushton said, 'He even reminded us several times that the twelve to one time was only an opinion, which wouldn't stand up as medical evidence in court. That must have been to cover him if he was ever challenged by the autopsy findings.'

'And the shoeprint we found at the scene of that murder —a city shoe. Was that his?' asked Johnson.

'I think we shall almost certainly find it was. He attended to certify the death in bright white training shoes, if you remember. He'd changed, of course, between the murder and his official arrival at the scene of death. The print of the city shoe became something which would have exonerated him rather than incriminated him in our minds.'

203

'If we'd ever considered him seriously in the first place. The English class system is an insidious thing. I never even thought of him as a candidate,' said Bert Hook bitterly. For a boy brought up in a Barnardo's home, the idea that he had been blinded by middle class polish was a bitter thought.

'It wasn't just that,' said Rushton defensively. 'When a person's job is to save life, you somehow don't think of him as a killer. And he'd almost made himself part of our team.'

'At least it wasn't a policeman,' said Johnson. For him, that would have been the worst thing of all. He would never need to admit now that he had even entertained the wild thought that the Strangler might be DI Rushton, when he had looked at him after the conference on Saturday, white, distraught, deprived of his wife, and cursing all women.

Lambert went home early for once that Monday afternoon. He made himself a mug of tea and sat in the armchair which had seen so little of him in the last week. There he waited for his wife to come home from school, wondering how to tell her the news of Don Haworth's arrest.

He need not have worried. The news was round the staff room by lunch-time; most of them presumed that Christine would already know all the gory details, and left her feeling that her ignorance was a failure on her part.

She made quite a noise coming in, but she did not disturb John Lambert. The batsmen in the test match flickered to and fro on the television screen unwitnessed. The mug of tea was full and cold at his elbow. A curling strand of grey hair had fallen across his forehead, as if taking advantage of the opportunity to break ranks.

The Superintendent slumbered deep and untroubled in his chair.